After Strange Texts

After

Peirce · Althusser · de Saussure · Bloom · Foucault · Lukács · Todorov · Marx · Said · Burke · Levi-Strauss · Benjamin · Derrida · Kristeva · Lacan · Freud · Barthes · Jakobson · Heidegger · Nietzsche · ?

Strange Texts

The Role of Theory in the Study of Literature

EDITED BY

Gregory S. Jay AND *David L. Miller*

The University of Alabama Press

"Tea and Totality: The Demand of Theory on Critical Style" by Geoffrey H. Hartman, Copyright © 1984 by Geoffrey H. Hartman

"Shakespeare and the Exorcists" by Stephen Greenblatt, Copyright © 1984 by Stephen Greenblatt

Library of Congress Cataloging in Publication Data

Main entry under title:

After strange texts

  Papers from the University of Alabama's Ninth Annual
Symposium in English and American Literature, 1982.
  Bibliography: p.
  Includes index.
  Contents: Tea and totality / Geoffrey H. Hartman—From the piazza to
the enchanted isles: Melville's textual rovings / Edgar A. Dryden—
Hawthorne's genres / Peggy Kamuf—[etc.]
  1. Criticism—Addresses, essays, lectures. I. Jay, Gregory S., 1952– . II. Miller,
David L., 1951– . III. Alabama Symposium in English and American Literature
(9th : 1982 : University of Alabama)
PN85.A34 1985   801'.95   84-160
ISBN 0-8173-0223-9
ISBN 0-8173-0224-7 (pbk.)

*To our colleagues in
the Department of English*

Contents

Acknowledgments ix

The Role of Theory in the Study of Literature?
  GREGORY S. JAY AND DAVID L. MILLER 1

Tea and Totality: The Demand of Theory on Critical Style
  GEOFFREY H. HARTMAN 29

From the Piazza to the Enchanted Isles: Melville's Textual Rovings
  EDGAR A. DRYDEN 46

Hawthorne's Genres: The Letter of the Law *Appliquée*
  PEGGY KAMUF 69

Sexual Politics and Critical Judgment
  ELIZABETH A. MEESE 85

Shakespeare and the Exorcists
  STEPHEN GREENBLATT 101

Auerbach's *Mimesis*: Figural Structure and Historical Narrative
  TIMOTHY BAHTI 124

Between Dialectics and Deconstruction: Derrida and the
Reading of Marx
  ANDREW PARKER 146

Notes 169

Suggestions for Further Reading 188

Contributors 190

Index 192

Acknowledgments

The idea for this book grew out of The University of Alabama's Ninth Annual Symposium in English and American Literature, where some of the essays collected below were first presented. The symposium was in large part made possible through the assistance of a research grant from the National Endowment for the Humanities. Closer to home, we deeply appreciate the encouragement, enthusiasm, and financial support given that event and this book by the Department of English, the College of Arts and Sciences, the Continuing Education Center, and the University President's Office. We want particularly to thank a number of administrators who gave at the office: Joab Thomas, Roger Sayers, William Macmillan, William Bryan, Claudia Johnson, and especially Douglas Jones, who as Dean of the College did so much to make the symposium series a vital part of the University's intellectual life.

The department's graduate students cheerfully aided us in running the symposium. The students in our critical theory seminar deserve special thanks for their patience, energy, and spirited interest. Our editorial labors were lightened by the good-natured efficiency of those who processed our words: Angela Duncan, Donnie Wier, Karen Nelson, and Amelia Mitchell. At The University of Alabama Press we have benefitted from the courtesy and guidance of Director Malcolm MacDonald and from the care of our editor, Hilde L. Robinson.

As our dedication indicates, we feel a tribute is due to our colleagues in the English Department. They have backed this project from the start with their confidence and good counsel. Their intelligence and friendship have sustained us through many critical passages.

The successful completion of a volume like this one depends on many people, but of course editors are most notoriously at the mercy of their contributors. In this case such dependence was a pleasure, as each of them was prompt and cooperative at every stage of the manuscript's development and revision. Finally, the editors find themselves with the awkward but happy task of thanking each other. Over the last three years we have organized, taught, written, and edited together until the individual authorship of particular ideas and phrases disappeared in the play of mutual inspiration and affectionate forbearance. We may never quite be ourselves again, but will probably both be better for having been so often and so thoroughly confused.

After Strange Texts

The Role of Theory
in the Study of Literature?

GREGORY S. JAY AND DAVID L. MILLER

Framing, as the nature of modern technology, derives from the Greek way of experiencing letting-lie-forth, *logos*, from the Greek *poiesis* and *thesis*. In setting up the frame, the framework—which now means in commandeering everything into assured availability—there sounds the claim of the *ratio reddenda*, i.e., of the *logon didonai*, but in such a way that today this claim that is made in framing takes control of the absolute, and the process of representation—of *Vor-stellen* or putting forth—takes form, on the basis of the Greek perception, as making secure, fixing in place.
> —Heidegger, "The Origin of the Work of Art"

That which produces and manipulates the frame sets everything in motion to efface its effect, most often by naturalizing it to infinity, in God's keeping. . . . Deconstruction must neither reframe nor fantasize the pure and simple absence of the frame.
> —Derrida, "The Parergon"

While this introduction will provide a framework for the essays to follow, we will not attempt a comprehensive survey of recent theoretical approaches to the study of literature. The last few years have brought an abundance of explanatory books and articles on such topics as structuralism and poststructuralism, deconstruction, Marxism, feminism, semiotics, hermeneutics, psychoanalysis, and rhetoric.[1] Every reader will have a different familiarity with one or more of these movements and a different set of opinions about them. Rather than offer a hasty sketch of the entire field (repeating helpful but already available generalizations), we have chosen to outline a problem common to all these schools for interpretive scandal: How does the choice of a particular theoretical perspective alter the practice of reading, and, reciprocally, how do altered practices of reading open new theoretical perspectives?

With two exceptions, the essays in this volume were presented at a symposium entitled "The Role of Theory in the Study of Literature."

Some readers may conclude that an equally apt title might have been "The Role of Literature in the Study of Theory." This sliding of the topic between seemingly opposed standpoints is only to be expected, since practice always implies its own theory, while theory exists only as a form of practice. Instead of a well-marked passageway from generally accepted rules to their effective application, we enter a peculiarly atopical "space" of transformation, revaluation, and exchange, in which we are neither here nor there but always en route.* Disciplin-

---

*For the reader who cannot function except when securely anchored, the unsettling effects of theory present special problems. A case in point is Wayne Booth's genial befuddlement with the title and logo of the present volume. We quote at length from the opening paragraph of "Rhetorical Critics Old and New: the Case of Gérard Genette," in *Reconstructing Literature*, ed. Laurence Lerner (Oxford: Basil Blackwell, 1983):

> The Ninth Alabama Symposium on English and American Literature is advertised under the title, "After Strange Gods: the Role of Theory in the Study of Literature." [Note that Booth here misquotes our title—eds.] The brochure includes an epigraph from Genesis—"We have dreamed a dream, and there is no interpreter of it"—and a spiral of critics' names, in handsome large italics, running from outer rim to centre, in this order:
>
> *ALTHUSSER · PEIRCE · BENJAMIN · DERRIDA · KRISTEVA · LACAN · FOUCAULT · BLOOM · DE SAUSSURE · LÉVI-STRAUSS · BURKE · SAID · MARX · LUKACS · BARTHES · FREUD · NIETZSCHE · TODOROV · JAKOBSON · HEIDEGGER · ?*
>
> It is a curious list, no matter where you stand as you try to become the "interpreter of it," especially when you consider that no name on it occurs either among the speakers or their titles. What do the stars have in common? Is it that we can count on some among us to be in some general way *for* them all and some others among us to be vaguely *against* all or most of them? Probably the cons would be more clearly united than the pros.   (p. 123)

The message between the lines, of course, is that at least one old pro won't be conned. A page later, he concludes:

> The conference list, viewed as a group to be admired or abhorred because they are all somehow connected with some sort of *nouvelle critique* or structuralism or post-structuralism, is simply a meaningless heap.   (p. 124)

Any reader who looks at the cover (or title page) of the present volume can track Booth to his lair. There lurks a distinguished critic (and past president of the Modern Language Association) who has not read the "text" he criticizes. The word is on the page, but where we write "text" Booth reads "god." The reader may also observe that the spiral we have designed does not simply run "from outer rim to centre, in this order," etc., but runs, and may be read, in *either* direction and sequence—from the periphery in, or outward from the central question mark. Booth "quotes" the logo in a linear form that silently erases every reading but his own. Yet it is only when we reverse

ary boundaries are dislocated too, so that readers of current criticism find themselves stranded between poetry and psychology, novels and political economy, drama and anthropology, or literary criticism and philosophy. This errancy has been variously castigated and celebrated, depending on how one takes the double genetive in "lack of discipline": as the loss of a true framework or as the blind spot intrinsic to every point of view.

The metaphor of framing may in fact prove a useful way of setting forth the question of what critical theory is and how it is linked to the study of literature. Theory is a way of delimiting what qualifies as a poem or novel or play, of describing how it is built, what and how it signifies, and where it connects to what gets defined as "outside" the text (its author, tradition, and historical milieu). In this sense theory is always at work, however inadvertently, in the provision of such backgrounds as biography, genre, and socioeconomic matrix. Even aesthetic, formalist, and rhetorical criticism require a concept of art, an idea of the difference between form and matter, and a distinction between trope and reference before their practices can go forward. There really is no way to read a text in and for itself. Only a repetition of every word in its "original" sequence could represent the work in its purity, and even then, as Borges's Pierre Menard learned, the act of writing and its local circumstances alter what the text signifies. Every critical reading, then, necessarily casts the work within another nar-

---

the arbitrary course of this reading that the title "After Strange Texts" actually does come *after* the strange text of the logo, unravelling its outward spiral into a conventional line of type.

To the extent, then, that our spiral logo does reflect certain designs upon the reader, it is precisely *not* an invitation to take up by reflex a position pro or con, thereby reducing its careful design "to a meaningless heap." Rather it offers a visual analogue to that dislocation of reading "positions" which theory aims to produce. This is a loaded gesture, to be sure—especially from the perspective of those who already enjoy "positions" with which they are understandably satisfied. "What do the stars have in common?" asks Booth, and we offer two replies. First, the names we used have in common a certain metonymic function: any one name in the spiral might be replaced by several others—"Bloom" by "De Man," for instance, or by "Fish"; or "Kristeva" by "Irigaray," "Serres," or "Deleuze." But this is not the only sense in which the names work metonymically: the second thing they have in common is their various associations with discourse that tends to unsettle complacent habits of reading. So while any one "star" in the constellation might be replaced by various others, it is true that none could be replaced by the name "Booth."

rative: in a story of moral values, psychologies, societies, religious and philosophical truths, editorial procedures, political conflicts, or aesthetic techniques. Many have pointed out that the very quality of "literariness," that essence we need in order to say what is or is not literature, depends on a framework of presuppositions that cannot (without going in circles) be construed as simply literary.

We can neither make theory a literary discipline, therefore, nor use literature to discipline theory, for their interdependence violates rules of order based on the demarcation of inside and outside, structure and content, or speculation and application. Each of the essays below employs one or more of the most recent, and controversial, frames for analysis, and so crosses over into the troublesome margin of contemporary criticism. As a group they represent no single school or technology of thought, but rather explore what is at stake in the determinations that create such institutions and instruments of analysis. In this they join a growing number of critical studies whose character resists any certain definition. Often these works take the undoing of traditional limits as their primary goal; in extreme cases we find critics like the late Paul de Man rigorously demonstrating the impossibility of interpretive decisions and thus condemning the reader to a perpetual state of "suspended ignorance."[2] This array of books and articles, imported and domestic, drawing on a long list of "nonliterary" thinkers, was at first mistaken for an offering of new "methods." In many studies the result was (and still is) the attempted transformation of theoretical discourse into an instrument for exegetical knowledge. Ideas, terms, and readings borrowed from outside the normal canon were to be internalized, "disciplined," and made to serve the accepted purposes of professional academic literary study. Even in the preface to a recent anthology of poststructuralist essays we are "reminded" that theory "is most useful insofar as it serves the criticism of specific works."[3]

But surely it is erroneous to begin by distinguishing theoretical work from textual analysis, especially without asking about the value placed on such loaded terms as "service" and "use." We do not even know what a "specific work" is, at least not in any way that provides Archimedean leverage on questions of theory and practice. A recourse to common-sense notions of the object or of perception would only preempt investigation into how we make "sense" of the signs around us. Recognizing an object is an act of reading, an interpretation whose claims are not themselves objective but theoretical. Better to start by asking how we perform such readings, or what procedures we follow in constituting signs as things we deem useful.

Theory after all is not a device, like a compass or divining rod, that can be cast aside when the treasure is found. Sometimes, as John Barth remarks, the key to the treasure is the treasure. "If works were indeed autonomous artifacts," writes Jonathan Culler, "there might be nothing to do but to interpret each of them, but since they participate in a variety of systems—the conventions of literary genres, the logic of story and the teleologies of emplotment, the condensations and displacements of desire, the various discourses of knowledge that are found in a culture—critics can move through texts towards an understanding of the systems and semiotic processes which make them possible."[4] One can move farther, however, as Culler himself has in arguing more recently that critical theory constitutes a "heterogeneous genre" whose practice ought to be recognized in its own right.[5] The radical distinction between theory and the various types of practical criticism can then be productively dislocated by a consideration of the framing operations that inform all approaches to cultural works.

The work or object in question, be it poem, painting, historical event, social structure, or individual psychology, comes *into* being for us only in the application of a technology, a way for it to appear significantly, truthfully, against a determining background and within the determinate outlines of its own identity. "The etymological link," notes Christopher Norris, "between 'theory' and 'seeing' (Greek *thea* = spectacle) becomes a forgotten or sublimated metaphor underlying the certitudes of science."[6] Theory enables the critic to "see" Hamlet's indecisiveness, the sexual politics in *Jane Eyre*, Faulkner's sense of history, or the textual variants distinguishing the several versions of *The Prelude*. Such perceptive techniques are not merely implements used to manipulate already-given objects; as our epigraphs suggest, they are part of a general method for bringing things before us according to a principle of gathering and expression (*techne* + *logos*). Heidegger attempts to distinguish between a coercive modern technology that falsely fixes things in place and an ancient Greek mode of letting truth (*aletheia*) disclose itself. Derrida's distinction between logocentrism and dissemination follows Heidegger's lead, but it also denies that presence could come forth without the technologies of representation, writing, and "textuality."

Considered as framing, then, theory is *the operation that allows for representation*, for the appearance of what practice is and what it understands. Yet in order for theory to work it must be repeatable or remarkable, capable not only of authorizing practice but of being represented itself. Now the operation that enables representation can of course be represented. But can it both ground representation and under-stand its own grounds *in the same motion*? Can the frame frame itself? No—unless it does so in that dizzying spectacle of reduplication epitomized by the pictorial device of the *mise en abŷme*. To make such a speculation into a science of "metatheory" would simply reify an infinite regression; one might as well call theory "metapractice." The bankruptcy of metatheory takes place at the same limit as those of metalanguage or metacommentary, neither of which can close the hermeneutic circle to provide itself with an original basis. What we call theory and practice borrow from each other in an economy neither can comprehend.

Critical theories and interpretive frameworks are necessary but unpresentable ghosts of authority—prerequisites to presence that are themselves incapable of appearing except within the shadow of their own effects. This riddle has of course been the chief preoccupation of what has lately come to be called deconstruction. Whatever else it may be, deconstruction proceeds as a kind of endless worrying over what happens when you try to articulate the theory of theory. This is not a new question, nor is deconstruction the first discourse to pose it forcefully; rather it is one more instance of a dilemma intrinsic to our culture and its significant productions. The directions it takes today are avowedly overdetermined by its historical setting (witness the word "deconstruction," itself calculated to interrupt a specific history whose major points of reference are Heideggerean "destruction" and French "structuralism"). If we take deconstruction as a way to reopen the relation between theory and practice in literary study, it is not in the misguided belief that its modern appearance will put an end to the history of metaphysics or of literature; we cite deconstruction here as an index to the dilemma of representation, not a dogma for its resolution. As a name for the effort to reinscribe the effaced operations that produce our apparent theories and practices, deconstruction suggests the kind of critical work that turns the frame of representation into an unhinged opening. Thus while not the explicit subject of most of the essays below, and not itself a method for literary study, deconstruction can serve as a frame or "marginal justification" for our own examination of the role of theory in the discourses of feminists, Marxists, historicists, rhetoricians, and literary historians.

At this point the skeptical reader might ask: "Isn't deconstruction just another frame-up? Aren't such subversive critiques, outlining the truth about our illusions, always reducible either to nihilistic relativism or to a perverse return of absolutism?" The answer, naturally, is yes *and* no, with a resolute care to entertain the possibilities of that "and" between mutually exclusive positions. "When I try to decipher a text," responds Derrida, "I do not constantly ask myself if I will finish answering *yes* or *no*, as happens in France at determined periods of history, and generally on Sunday."[7] This kind of deciphering must of course devise a frame and produce through practice a set of meaningful results. Yet it disassembles this framework in the very act of applying it, and so displaces the results of its reading into another, perhaps finally ungovernable, series of reframing perspectives. What should be emphasized here is that this maneuver does not simply negate the knowledge produced by a conceptual technology any more than it tries to synthesize contradictory conclusions within some total vision. Instead, both the theoretical framework and its practical application are strategically re-marked in affiliation with unforeseen networks of metaphors, cultural attitudes, and social institutions—just as words or other symbols gain new signifying determinations from the constellation of relations that traverse them when they are placed in different texts.

Deconstructive framing cannot, therefore, be offered as a representation of the truth about framing, since in practice it defers the question of its own essence. This is instructive for critical theory because it points toward the uncanny way that interpretive devices allow for truth and presence only in the moment of their own disappearance. In response to this dilemma, critical texts have increasingly become two-handed engines. A theory is proposed whose use in practice is either implied or demonstrated; at the same time, the theory of the theory is itself so scrutinized that its claims are unsettled and a different field of practice created. Such duplicity tends to disturb the either/or choices sanctioned by the canonical terms and methods of a given discipline, leading into the (supposedly) neutral borders, margins, and betweens that foreground conventional objects of study. In deconstruction, for example, a hierarchical opposition (speech/writing, presence/absence) is discerned and up-ended. Then, in order to avoid simply affirming or negating the structure of the classical dualism, the text disseminates a third term (*différance*, supplement, hymen, *pharmakon*, et al.) that cannot be synthesized or governed by the old conceptual scheme.[8]

Derrida's reading of Kant, Hegel, and Heidegger, for example, follows the interlaced strands of aesthetics and metaphysics until they lead to just such a third term for the economy between art and philosophy: *parergon*. Kant introduces this archaic Greek term in order to discuss "ornamentation (*parerga*), i.e. what is only an adjunct, and not an intrinsic constituent in the complete representation of an object." "A *parergon*," Derrida comments, "is against, beside, and above and beyond the *ergon*, the work accomplished, the accomplishment of the work." Analysis detects here an entire series of oppositions crucial to both art and philosophy: form/matter, inside/outside, essence/ accident, unity/incoherence. Derrida's reading will once more demonstrate that what is translated as an "ornament," "hors d'oeuvre," "remainder," or "supplement" participates nonetheless in the very origin and production of the work itself. The *parergon*'s seeming detachment (aesthetic or otherwise) is never complete. Its interest in the work produced is both peripheral and essential; its operations, like those of theory, are apparent, yet difficult to discern:

> The *parergon* is distinguished from both the *ergon* (the work) and the milieu; it is distinguished as a figure against a ground. But it is not distinguished in the same way as the work, which is also distinguished from a ground. The parergonal frame is distinguished from two grounds, but in relation to each of these, it disappears into the other. In relation to the work, which may function as its ground, it disappears into the wall and then, by degrees, into the general context. In relation to the general context, it disappears into the work. Always a form on a ground, the *parergon* is nevertheless a form which has traditionally been determined not by distinguishing itself, but by disappearing, sinking in, obliterating itself, dissolving just as it expends its greatest energy.[9]

This indeterminacy of theoretical grounds serves, on the other hand, as a split perspective from which to view the acts of understanding taking place between art and metaphysics: "If the *parergon*, this supplementary hors d'oeuvre, has something like the status of a philosophical concept" in Kant's text, "then it must designate a general formal predicative structure which may be carried over, either *intact* or *consistently* deformed, reformed, to other fields, where new contents may be submitted to it."[10] In Derrida's hands, the *parergon* gets carried away. His reading shows that Kant's text must elevate the "ornamental" and "secondary" term to the primary status of a "general formal predicative structure." The argument that was supposed to delimit the thing-in-itself instead designates the priority of a para-thing. The universality Kant sought for philosophical concepts becomes, in the illustrative case of the *parergon*, the interminable displacement of fixed forms and contents.

Derrida calls this mode of analysis "double writing," one stylus marking down the truth and the other tracing an opening at the very point of conclusion.[11] Double writing both participates in the frame-up and squeals on the perpetrators. Punning on this illogic of textual (re)folding—the "pli" that articulates the either-and-both structure of these strange third terms—one might say that framing always turns itself in. Of course not all critical theorists have adopted the specific procedures of deconstruction. But increasingly they follow a double itinerary that both inhabits a given framework and transgresses its limits. Each writer emerges from some recognizable discipline or discourse with the understanding that there can be no simple methodological step ("pas de méthode") beyond it. All the tools and regulations of the system are required, since it is in their very applications, histories, and institutions that criticism finds what is lacking, and hence what requires its supplementary comments. However ironically, the theorist must repeat the flaws of the old school; repeat them not as an observer but as a participant, in the very work done to exhibit the flaw. The distinction between such a theorist and the largely mythical "ordinary practitioner" does not concern levels of awareness as regards their repetition of a particular flaw; it involves what steps are taken, and how effectively, to preclude one's results from becoming yet another illusory closing of the gap.

By following the dictates of a given interpretive practice to its limits, then, criticism reactivates the contradictions whose presumed resolution constituted the theoretical bases for that practice. Fidelity to the canonical procedures themselves leads to a break, a *coup*, at a

fundamental juncture in the theoretical apparatus. An effort to rethink the theory of the theory is precipitated by this break and goes to
work altering the boundaries of subsequent analytic practice. In dis-
cussing the deconstructive approach to literary criticism, Derrida sets
off the strategy of double reading and writing from the tradition of
"doubling commentary," the latter being defined as an effort (always
necessary) to marshall textuality into understandable concepts. The
double reader or writer seeks to exhibit the "signifying structure" informing such concepts, to display the unapparent "writing" that
frames the book, the author, and the truth about them:

> To produce this signifying structure obviously cannot consist of re-
> producing, by the effaced and respectful doubling of commentary, the
> conscious, voluntary, intentional relationship that the writer institutes
> in his exchanges with the history to which he belongs thanks to the ele-
> ment of language. This moment of doubling commentary should no
> doubt have its place in a critical reading. To recognize and respect all its
> classical exigencies is not easy and requires all the instruments of tradi-
> tional criticism. Without this recognition and this respect, critical pro-
> duction would risk developing in any direction at all and authorize it-
> self to say almost anything. But this indispensable guardrail has always
> only *protected*, it has never *opened*, a reading.[12]

Writing with two hands at the same time, one balanced on the guard-
rail of tradition and one wielding the instruments that cut through
foundations, the critical theorist becomes a marginal character in an
awkward position. Inside philosophy, feminism, politics, history, or
literary criticism, the theorist turns out to be the outsider who takes
seriously the job of never knowing for sure what he or she is doing.
Nonetheless such work is literally essential, since it always pertains to
the definition of what the object of study is and what the true representation of its identity and history will be.

While deconstruction has lately become notorious for challenging
the borders of critical thought, its advent and contribution remain inseparable from a variety of movements that have been equally active
in shattering the received frameworks of interpretation, disenchant-
ing previously captive readers, and provoking wonder at the star-

tlingly different intellectual landscapes they reveal. What goes by the name of critical theory may be reductively traced as a genealogy of these transgressions, or as a family romance concerned with how we (re)produce our objects of knowledge through the positions we assume in order to make them appear. Phenomenological criticism narrated the reading experience as an intersubjective communion, based on a seductive mythology of authorial consciousness, *oeuvre*, and hermeneutic rapport. Reading was produced within a theater of philosophical psychology and dramatized the return of consciousness to itself through the agency of an other. Structuralism demystified the leading roles granted to author, *oeuvre*, and consciousness, substituting its own linguistic metaphors in order to translate critical discourse into the formalized spectacle of impersonal signifying processes. Yet both these interpretive schools disputed the classical constraints used to define the literary object, its mode of production, and the reader's function in the advent of significance; if they relied, finally, on premises that once more foreclosed the "play" (*jeu* = game, risk, move, gamble, uncontrolled shift) of the text, it was only after they had broken previously unquestioned habits of literary study. More importantly, the debates they prompted underscored the degree to which the accepted objectivity of the book, the writer, the reader, and the meaning had been undermined. No matter which side critics took, from E. D. Hirsch to Joseph Riddel, it became clear that an argument was underway that extended into the margins of literary criticism and scholarship and there met issues touching upon a number of previously discrete disciplines.

Any critical genealogy focussing on modes of production must acknowledge, whether as founding father or bastard son, the contributions of Marx. The current return to and rereading of Marx has challenged our ways of thinking about the generative ties linking text and context.[13] Marxist analysis undercuts the transcendental position accorded to cultural ideals, writing them back into a story of money and power. Moreover, a tantalizing correspondence seems to join the Marxist discourse on materialism, dialectics, economy, contradiction, and ideology with contemporary textual reinscriptions of the superstructure called "Western metaphysics." For example, in a way too complex to investigate here, Derrida grafts Saussure's antiessentialist linguistics and Heidegger's destruction of metaphysics onto the Marxist critique of ideology, which is thereby transformed into the de-construction of "Western metaphysics" as a whole. Ideology in the restricted sense turns out to be only a local instance of a master plot to make the products of culture and history appear to be natural or even divine truths. To the literally economic and political origins of ideo-logical thought designated by Marx, Derrida adds his concern with the representational technology that brings identity and structure out of the differential Being of the world. His departure from Heidegger occurs at the moment when *Dasein* becomes Da-sign, when the disclo-sure of truth (un)folds in representation and theory fails to account for itself fully. In turn, Heidegger's critique of Western ontology serves Derrida's rereading of such key Marxist terms as dialectics, ma-terialism, value, exchange, circulation, production, and above all *economy*.[14]

Lengthy qualification would be required before an accommodation of Derrida's thought with that of Marxism could be negotiated. In "Di-alectics and Deconstruction," Andrew Parker surveys the latest round of negotiations, only to find them constrained by a familiar meta-phorics of insides, outsides, boundaries, and mastery.[15] Marxism and deconstruction, as Parker reads them, repeat within their respective operations the lacuna that seems to divide them. The breakdown of Marxist efforts to reconcile the relative autonomy of cultural forms with the determinism of an economic base appears inevitable from this perspective, recapitulating as it does the endless incommen-surability of signifier and signified. Parker sees the turn to semiotics common to much recent Marxist theory as yet another dead end, since one can scarcely hope to "cure" the very condition of significa-tion by constructing or importing a science of signs. Instead, he sug-gests, it will be necessary to reread Marx in a certain way—not to de-construct his texts but to trace the rhetorical operations that traverse them. Such an approach would have little to do with a literary appre-ciation of Marx; rather it would seek to recover rhetoric as the es-tranged other to economic theory, constituting tropology as a textual system of exchange. It is within such a context that Parker anticipates the difficult rethinking of such grounding concepts as contradiction, dialectic, and the material. In the meantime, and despite their com-mon thematics, the two discourses remain incongruous with respect to the spiral of theory and practice. Marxist critics may approach this longstanding puzzle by recognizing its supplementary economy, but Marxism in any recognizable sense must remain committed to an agenda of action or choice. Deconstruction, as we have already noted, frustrates the desire to decide. Derrida's hint of an alliance with "open Marxism" does nothing to close this irreducible gap, which bedevils all attempts to employ deconstruction as a method in the service of particular ends.

As part of a movement with deep investments in the need for theory to alter political and cultural economies, feminist criticism has likewise found much to resist, as well as appropriate, in recent critical theory. Emphasis on the way ideologies structure fields of difference into binary patterns quickly appeared amenable to a critique of sexism and all its products, textual or otherwise. "What is often most fundamentally disagreed upon," argues Barbara Johnson, "is whether a disagreement arises out of the complexities of fact or out of the impulses of power. . . . The differences *between* entities (prose and poetry, man and woman, literature and theory, guilt and innocence) are shown to be based on a repression of differences *within* entities, ways in which an entity differs from itself."[16] Johnson's diction points out how the interests of feminism, its frame and point of view, edge deconstruction toward an explicit analysis of power and repression.

In pursuing these issues at the level of theory, feminism finds itself compelled to undertake its own revisionary return to Freud, since psychoanalysis (along with Heideggerean ontology) is the modern discourse posing the most radical difficulties to any investigation of the boundary between nature and culture. Derrida's inclusion of "phallogocentrism" within the general deconstruction of Western modes of thought both pleased and disconcerted many feminists. The "dissemination" of phallogocentrism acknowledged the call to overthrow male privileges, but to many it seemed to perpetuate the phallus as a negative center and so to continue the tradition of castration philosophy. Tangible matters of property and power appeared lost in an arcane philosophical inquiry remote from the sociopolitical institutions that re-present and enforce sexist ideologies. Derrida's response has been at once to elaborate the metaphorics of "hymen" and "invagination" and to insist that phallogocentrism was never essentially male in reference. Male castration anxiety has the penis as referent, to be sure, but what Derrida calls "phallogocentrism" is the framing operation that precedes and enables such reference.[17] Deconstruction "reinscribes" the referent by demonstrating how such operations of framing, or inscription, actually produce the objects that seem to precede writing as its origin or referent. The referent is thus an *effect* of theory, not its source or cause. Neither can theory be the source or cause of the referent, strictly speaking, since it cannot be determined as an identity and remain what it is. "Theory" so determined would simply become another referent. Here, as with Marxism, a conflict arises between a theoretical practice with designs toward material effects and a theory that disables the simple production of the effect we call "the material."

Yet feminism is not in fact *a* theoretical practice. A wide array of contemporary feminist projects challenge the received truths of our cultural traditions.[18] Such resource and agility may be attributed to the history of the women's movement, which got underway in the margins as an errant and skeptical questioning of foreclosed possibilities. It may be, then, that the current debate over whether feminism can or should "rise to the level of theory" poses the wrong challenge. For if culture is a field of relations without positive terms, it could well be regressive to seek a nature and identity for "the feminine": such determinations risk redomesticating their referents. Sexual identity (like theory) is not an essence or truth, but a difference that emerges in the work people do. Such work, like the work of art, never appears in any simple way as an empirical starting-point for analysis; it must be "commandeered into availability" by the interested work of theory. So for example in "Hawthorne's Genres: The Letter of the Law *Appliquée*," Peggy Kamuf begins with a calculated effort to cross-stitch the empirically distinct categories of gender and genre. Hawthorne's insistence on the narrative category "romance" illustrates the intersection between sexual and textual laws-of-kind that Kamuf locates as her beginning: the subtitle *A Romance*, she observes, "was meant to be read as *Not a Novel* and *The Scarlet Letter*, therefore, as not a scribbling of feminine design."

Kamuf's design, however, is no simple chiasmus: antithetical terms can exchange places easily without disturbing the hierarchy that grounds their operation, as her remarks on the Norton "authoritative" edition make abundantly clear. Her essay traces another path, oddly yet not inappropriately imaged by the "tendency to speculation"

Hawthorne attributes to his heroine in "Another View of Hester." Unlike the narcissistically closed circle of interpretation within which both Dimmesdale and the Puritan state read the world's traces as reflections of their own destinies, this other trajectory "does not close a circle but opens the possibility to thought of a woman who is essentially not a woman." Needless to say, this itinerary and the vistas it opens onto are the effects of certain classically Derridean moves, but they are by no means arbitrary; the movement that unsettles the symmetry of law and guilty subject retraces the threadwork of Hawthorne's text assiduously, unravelling the "application" of Puritan law to Hester by following out the pattern of her own fantastic embroidery, from the surface of the notorious A to the scarves and ruffs of the magistrates who condemn her, where it resurfaces according to a logic not of law but of "policy."

Kamuf's strategic choice of "the feminine" as a point of departure marks her alliance with feminism. Yet her reluctance to close the interpretive circle reflects a commitment with which many feminist critics remain uneasy, as Elizabeth Meese's remarks on the notion of "difference," in "Sexual Politics and Critical Judgment," attest. Kamuf dislocates figures of authority (the dour custodians of Puritan theocracy, the "authoritative" text and its modern custodians) by attending to them *textually*, and having once textualized the questions of sexual identity and transgression in this way she is careful not to essentialize them all over again by redefining "woman." Meese, by contrast, while conceding the danger of "role-reversal" and the need for a new language, argues that feminist criticism must now accept the burden of self-definition.[19] To do less, she suggests, is to blunt the power of critical discourse to "transform the structures of authority."

And yet if Meese's essay reflects a dissatisfaction with poststructural criticism, the reason is not that such work undermines the ideology of "objective" knowledge. On the contrary, she feels that American academics have failed to carry this critique far enough: "Poststructuralists," she says, "have made only a beginning in their attack on the historically rooted traditions of criticism." Meese's essay urges that to be effective, this attack must focus very clearly on the nexus joining politics and epistemology, the "power-configuration" that structures the critical community. Her analysis of Stanley Fish's *Is There a Text in This Class?* calls attention to the self-imposed limits of an epistemologically sophisticated theory that evades crucial political questions. Fish opens the categories of "criticism" and "literature" with an epistemological relativism that is in principle unbounded—but only in principle. What Fish gives with one hand he takes back with the other, locating constraints on interpretive knowledge not in the objective properties of texts but in the consensual judgments of "interpretive communities." Such communities operate, he explains, on the basis of shared assumptions, conflicts at the level of what is assumed being mediated by all the resources of persuasive rhetoric: "If you want to persuade someone else that he is wrong you must first persuade him to the assumptions within which what you say will be convincing."

But this hypothetical community of equals, mediating internal disputes rhetorically, appears ideologically complacent from the perspective of the disenfranchised. Meese argues that feminist criticism has failed to achieve an impact in the profession commensurate with its intellectual production, and she attributes this failure to the "patriarchal substructure" of mutually indifferent (or even antagonistic) communities within the discipline of literary criticism. In communities organized hierarchically and riven by differences in assumptions too fundamental to be negotiated by persuasion, there is really nothing that compels the privileged to acknowledge the force of competing practices. Meese's argument implies that a purely "theoretical" openness and relativity of judgment is quite compatible, in practice, with the operation of unacknowledged forces of exclusion. Ironically, it is precisely those "excluded from the terms of truth" who are able to see the inadequacy of a reigning paradigm and—most important—who "experience the sense of urgency required to address it."

Meese's and Kamuf's essays reflect the special pressures faced by feminist critics: to be at once explicit in theory and efficacious in practice, to operate both in the openness of speculation and in the restricted domain of choice. An ethical imperative shadows the feminist project, asking its readings to serve as well as explore, to illustrate as well as negate, to offer truth as well as demystify illusion. This imperative makes itself felt in practical demands all too well known to women who must choose and act daily in their social and professional lives. It is an imperative they share with Marxist critics in particular, and both groups pose it as a troublesome question to the rest of the theoretical community, which is now turning in many ways toward the "extratextual" dimensions of discourse, those intangible as well as material institutions that house or imprison what can be known and done. This imperative has been felt by Derrida himself, often put on the defensive by Marxists and feminists who question the effects of his work. His rejoinder has included efforts on behalf of philosophical education in France and its role in the critique of ideology, and has resulted in formulations such as the one that appears early in *La Verité en peinture*, where for "deconstruction" one may substitute "critical theory" in the sense we have been elaborating here, including feminism:

> According to the consequences of its own logic, [deconstruction] attacks not only the internal constitution, at once semantic and formal, of edifying philosophemes, but also what it would be a mistake to call their external housing, or the assigned and merely extrinsic requirements of their practice. These working conditions include the historic forms of their instruction and the social, economic, and political structures of their pedagogical institutions. Because it concerns solid structures and affects "material" institutions, touching upon more than discourses or signifying representations, deconstruction always differentiates itself and marks its distinction from analysis or "criticism."[20]

Analyses of institutions, their social forms and structures, necessarily entail the concept of the "historical" and all the dilemmas pertaining to its definition and deployment. An ethical tone has also lately pervaded calls for a return to the framework of history, a plaint sometimes implying that critical theorists concerned with "textuality" are mere nominalists out to smash the productive machinery of historical knowledge in the name of aesthetic hedonism. More seriously, it has become clear that many recent theoretical discourses face a common problem, variously posed as the issue of the relation of consciousness to time, of the signified to the signifier, of culture to nature, of superstructure to base, or of sexuality to gender. In each instance we find a synchronic pattern proposed as a reading of diachronic events—in other words, an attempt to systematize and govern the correspondences between meaning and history. "History" functions variously, sometimes oppositely, in such discussions as an index pointing to a narrative of revealed significance, a chronology of factual events, a code word for sociopolitical and economic forces, a seriality without paradigm, or the domain of empiricity (natural and cultural) in which the human concept of time is not strictly even a factor. History is a powerful trope, invoking as it does the promise of a return to the real, and to effective responsibility for it. When criticism intervenes purposively at the juncture of the sensible and the intelligible, subverting this dichotomy and the schemes of significance it produces, then history as the intelligible narrative of sensible events falters in theory and in practice. And metahistory may prove no more successful in mastering the economy of matter and form than were metalanguage, metacommentary, or metatheory.[21]

It is hardly new or controversial to assert that history appears as a reading which unites (or coerces) the sensible and the intelligible into a coherent pattern. This formula, however, does stress the complicity of the idea of history with a certain philosophical tradition that stabilizes such an opposition and allows for its reconciliation in the form of meaning. History is a product of what Derrida calls the "general text": not writing in the colloquial sense, but the process (never value-neutral) of organizing differences into identities, facts, and truths. History and the history of meaning are inseparable. Nothing would be more fallacious than to think of history and textuality as a binary opposition, as if one could take a position for or against one or the other. Histories in the conventional sense take place in the same way as all productions of meaning: they foreclose the general economy of the sensible and the intelligible into an order that does work. Looked at in this perspective, history is preeminently textual, and vice versa.

The data of history, then, cannot serve simply as the foundation for theory, since they are themselves the effects of a historical activity primordially theoretical in nature. History re-presents itself and retrospectively invests its concepts and institutions with an aura of inevitability, naturalness, or even divine sanction. This ploy of self-authorization is what both Marx and Derrida find epitomized by Hegel's teleological philosophy of history, in which the losses and negations of time are recovered profitably in the sublime present of absolute knowledge at the end of history. Hegelian or otherwise, metahistory authors its historical origins in a circular phenomenology that evades the question of its own framing. To reinscribe history in the general text is to ask about the interests, concepts, and powers served by "useful" views of history.

Obviously this does not entail a denial of the role played by politics and society in the history of meaning. Their role must be insisted upon, but must also be conceived in terms of the general textual production of meaning out of which languages, works of art, and cultural institutions all interdependently emerge. The double writing of history would require both the repetition of a foreclosing interpretation and a displacement of that interpretation's conclusive claims. Specifically, literary analysis could shift its attention to the structures of figural language at work in texts proclaiming their allegiance to the banner of the historical. This is Timothy Bahti's procedure in "Auerbach's *Mimesis:* Figural Structure and Historical Narrative." Taking the crisis of historiography in contemporary theory as a point of departure, Bahti frames his reading of Auerbach with deliberate self-contradiction, sketching a thumbnail *history* of this crisis. He finds it doubled: the Anglo-American controversy within which he reads Auerbach may itself be read, according to Bahti, as the aftershock of a "so-called 'crisis' or 'loss of faith' in historiography, and in literary history in particular," that "played itself out earlier and more decisively [in Germany] than elsewhere in the West." Without for a moment questioning their validity as generalizations, we may call attention to the strategic value these statements have for Bahti's argument: his own text, it appears, intervenes in this history at a moment both equivalent to Auerbach's and distinct from it, and does so in order to engage a parallel set of problems. Moreover, it engages these problems precisely by "reflecting" on Auerbach's response to them, retracing the path of *his* intervention. All this occurs in the mode Derrida calls "the effaced and respectful doubling of commentary," and yet leads to the classic deconstructive move of displacement from within. "Inhabiting" *Mimesis* through painstaking analysis of both its argumentative structure and its rhetorical texture, Bahti undoes the resolution of history into Hegelian allegory. In this way his "speculation" or mirroring of Auerbach breaks its own frame, for what he stages is not after all *Mimesis*'s repetition but its internal difference. Starting with certain specific historical conclusions, Bahti reopens the play of figurative language in Auerbach's literary history in a way that indefinitely suspends the framing of thematic, psychological, ethical, or historical conclusions. Within such a perspective history, whether literary or social, can make its appearance only as a forgetting of the differences that metaphors bridge over.[22]

Meeting this suspension of history from the other direction would be an analysis of the general text informing social and cultural interests that demand foreclosures in their favor. Power and knowledge, as Michel Foucault has repeatedly shown, belong to the same discursive scheme:

> There are manifold relations of power which permeate, characterise and constitute the social body, and these relations of power cannot themselves be established, consolidated nor implemented without the production, accumulation, circulation and functioning of a discourse. There can be no possible exercise of power without a certain economy of discourses of truth which operates through and on the basis of this association. We are subjected to the production of truth through power and we cannot exercise power except through the production of truth.[23]

Institutions and traditions, whether tangible or intangible, are inextricably a part of this "economy of discourses," within which the foreclosure of what something means is neither aimless nor universal but directed toward, and enabled by, the specific exercise of power. It is to establish and further a certain history of meaning and its distribution, then, that interpretations enforce conclusions. The arrangement of differences into hierarchies of value, and their functioning in narratives of what is true and proper, produce material effects that impinge upon us daily. For those concepts or people ruled out of bounds by such conclusions, the results can literally be fatal.

One may illustrate this process in the sphere of literary study by reducing its simultaneity to a series of levels. The written marks on the page are construed as a language. The figurative play of language is subsumed under an interpretation of the text's meaning (the moral dilemma of *Antigone*, the crisis of English history in *Middlemarch*, the search for faith in *The Waste Land*). These meanings are themselves grafted from supplementary histories (of human nature, political rights, religious truth) which are interesting texts as well. The meanings produced by reading participate in decisive framing imperatives that cut through the reader, the text, and the society from which they spring. Literary works, cultural interpretation, and sociopolitical institutions (including "higher education") cooperate to manufacture cultural objects and their values. Critical readings are part of this heterogeneous production, and may "double write" against it from within by refusing to stop with the work itself or the institution alone;

they may read into the margin of a more general text to discern what establishes the privileged sets of meanings and authorities found in both regions. To double write history would then require both the demonstration of a social text and a deferral of any temptation to reconstitute it as historical ground in an objective or cause-and-effect way; it would also require a calculated displacement of the analyst's own pretension to represent the repressed of history.[24]

Stephen Greenblatt offers just such a divided return to the historical under the rubric of "cultural poetics." Remembering that values exist only within economies—that value is always exchange value and always in circulation—Greenblatt drops the piety with which we so often reify the literary masterpiece, as if works of art were immanent with some ineffable humanist charisma. Adopting in its place a thoroughly structural model of culture and society, he asks what transactions produce the value of a work like *King Lear*. What he resists is the tendency to elevate Derridean undecidability or de Manian *aporia* into universal principles. Criticism, he writes, "must not discount the specific institutional interests served both by local episodes of undecidability and contradiction and by the powerful if conceptually imperfect differentiation between the literary and the nonliterary. . . . I would argue that in actual literary practice the perplexities into which one is led are not moments of pure, untrammeled *aporia* but localized strategies in particular historical encounters."[25] In "Shakespeare and the Exorcists" Greenblatt investigates an episode in the encounter between the Elizabethan theater and the Church of England: Shakespeare's borrowings in *King Lear* from Samuel Harsnett's *A Declaration of Egregious Popish Impostures*.

One consequence of accepting a structural model for historiography is what Greenblatt terms a "loss of epistemological innocence." It should therefore come as no surprise that the writers he finds most useful in framing his readings are not conventional historians but figures like anthropologist Clifford Geertz or (on the present occasion) sociologist Edward Shils. The readings of past cultures and societies produced by such writers are essentially speculative rather than positivistic, as the example of Shils's "central zone in the structure of society" should make clear. Far from serving as an objective ground for his reading of *King Lear*, then, "history" in Greenblatt's essay reappears as a provocative *theory* of ecclesiastical politics in Renaissance England.

This theory is designed to situate Harsnett's jihad against exorcism within a dynamics of institutional power: he exposes popish impostures in order to prompt a return to Anglican truth. His exposure of exorcism takes the form of an extended effort to read it as unconfessed theater, staged and scripted by priests and acted by highly suggestible chambermaids. Thus "when Shakespeare borrows from Harsnett," Greenblatt asks, "who knows if Harsnett has not already, in a deep sense, borrowed from Shakespeare's theater what Shakespeare borrows back?" What Harsnett borrows, of course, is the sense of theater as brazen imposture; his polemic, as Greenblatt notes, "virtually depends upon the existence of an officially designated commercial theater, marked off openly from all other forms and ceremonies of public life precisely by virtue of its freely acknowledged fictionality." But when Shakespeare reiterates the official position in the context of a theatrical performance, he produces a different set of effects: not "an intensified adherence to the central system of official values" but "a deeper uncertainty, a loss of moorings, in the face of evil."

This "emptying out," as Greenblatt calls it, of the official position serves no interest but that of the theater, which "empties out everything it represents" and in the process "makes for itself the hollow round space within which it survives." The theatrical institution, in other words, houses an officially marked-out space of pure representation, where any and every official truth may be at once confirmed and dislocated, or where *mise en scène* has always been *mise en abŷme*. Greenblatt's argument necessarily concludes in a tentative way. Short of readmitting the abyss as a transhistorical essence, he can only suggest that the play's career from Harsnett's time to our own has been a discontinuous succession of such transactions and investments, authorized by cultural ideologies that continue to sanction its "limited autonomy" in return for the homage it ostensibly pays to existing institutions.

"Cultural poetics" of this kind owes a broad and freely acknowledged debt to the way recent theories of textuality have disabled the inside/outside and cause/effect paradigms that once dominated accounts of literature's relation to social history. At the same time, these theories have also generated a more literal approach that frames literary history as a species of intertextuality. Reading turns its attention from the isolate meaning of the literary object to the affiliations and displacements among various texts in the traditional canon. The individual literary work appears against the background of the language, conventions, and stylistic devices it appropriates and rearranges. In a certain way every work rewrites literary history, selecting a canon of pretexts to enable its own authority. The new work spins itself into a texture already interwoven, changing the pattern of the threads. Its meanings lie in the work of differentiation it initiates between itself and the literary history that is both its origin and product. This latter paradox should suggest that the "creative" work of art, like the critical act, is also a framing; it stands upon the ground of a tradition whose genealogy can be traced or constituted only through a reading of the text itself.

Tradition, observed T. S. Eliot, "cannot be inherited, and if you want it you must obtain it by great labour."[26] The great labor of the literary work entails the exclusion, theft, and revision of the already-written. Like history, literary tradition ceases to be seen as an objective verity and becomes a variable economy whose shape is determined by each effort at cutting a new pathway within it. Thus in "From the Piazza to the Enchanted Isles: Melville's Textual Rovings," Edgar Dryden tracks Melville's style through the labyrinth of the already-written, down passageways that lead into "Hawthorne's prefaces, in particular the preface to *Mosses from an Old Manse* . . . Melville's earlier enthusiastic review of that volume . . . Shakespeare's plays . . . *The Faerie Queene* . . . Tennyson's poetry . . . Melville's own novels . . . the Bible . . . [and] *The Pilgrim's Progress*." There is something of the Gothic in all this, "haunting presences" and bodiless voices that steal into Melville's prose, where (to quote one of Dryden's epigraphs) "they invoke in us a sense of leprous insubstantiality, of a contagion that might spread over language as a whole." Strictly speaking, of course, the intertextual labyrinth is no labyrinth at all. Even the most tortuous maze has a stable architecture, whereas here the turnings are echoes and allusions that trope the language of Spenser or Hawthorne into the texture of Melville's prose even as they start its designs unravelling. No wonder Dryden finds in these texts an anxious thematics of "imposture and belatedness." The critic entering such treacherous passages had better have his wits about him, and Dryden steals his way in with quiet duplicity. On the one hand he takes his bearings in all the expected ways, employing familiar points of reference: Melville's development as a writer and his relationship to Hawthorne, the nineteenth-century problematic of the imagination, the genre of romance narrative, and the canon of English literature. On the other hand he begins an essay on Melville's allusive style with a series of quotations affirming the dislocative effects of quotation. From this divided beginning he enters the doubled space of Melville's piazza, demonstrating with patient exactitude the way all the scenes and voices we encounter are haunted like the language itself by ghostly presences. This Gothic motif of invaded selfhood appears as the dark other to the romance theme of enchantment, breaking the wishful spells woven by a Romantic imagination.[27]

Dryden joins literary historians like Geoffrey Hartman (and Harold Bloom) who have supplemented Eliot's meditations on tradition and the individual talent with psychological and rhetorical finesse, giving a new twist to the old adage that every writer tries to leave his mark. Frivolously aesthetic as it may at first appear, the history of style turns out to be the style of history itself, a genealogy of interruptions and recollections artfully contrived into meaning. The application of style—that which cuts, wounds, spaces, limits, distinguishes, empowers, forbids, identifies—allows us to read a history of which the "literary" is only a single, if ostentatious, instance. As a *practice* of writing, style is decisive action in an overdetermined context; which means that like other forms of action it is multiple and uncertain in motive and effect, a play of values that we stabilize within categories like intention and decorum. Stability of this sort is an effect of all those framing techniques we impart to our students under the rubric "composition," as its pictorial meaning may suggest. Communication theory and traditional persona poetics are similar strategies, as Hartman observes in the introduction to *Saving the Text*:

> We tend to suppose that every act of speech, spoken or written, has a specifiable frame of reference. Speech is *signed* by or *assigned* to a particular person (a "speaker" or "persona") and *addressed* to a particular person or assemblage. Yet when we look more closely at this frame of reference, we become aware how much is presupposed. The frame of reference is often a frame-up. It allows us to economize words or their resonances: to synthesize or disambiguate them. Should the frame be lost, so that speaker or addressee become indeterminate, then the

meaning also becomes less settled. . . . Referential meaning is tied to
this matter of framing: where we draw the line becomes as important as
what is delimited. To "forget" writing, then, is to mistake or underestimate the question of framing: yet only writing itself can reverse the forgetfulness we show to writing. Where writing is, something without
properties appears.[28]

No doubt it would be going too far to substitute the name "Hartman"
for "writing" in this last epigram; and yet the difficult, playful, elusive
quality of so much that he writes may be understood at least partly as
a sustained reversal of "the forgetfulness we show to writing." In this
context it should be clear that when Hartman defends his own practice by arguing that "we don't always know what we mean," he means
something difficult and precise. The most defensive misunderstand-
ings of his recent work show a common failure to appreciate the complexity of such a deceptively simple remark.

To see Hartman's style as merely self-indulgent or narcissistic is especially ironic in light of the themes elaborated in *Saving the Text*.
Drawing on (or playing off) Derrida and Lacan, Hartman suggests
that precisely our impulse to mastery over the signifying force of language may be a secondary narcissism, a sort of "mirror stage" of
style. "For so retentive of themselves are men," says Stevens (who
also labors under the occasional imputation of dandyism),

> That music is intensest which proclaims
> The near, the clear, and vaunts the clearest bloom,
> And of all vigils musing the obscure,
> That apprehends the most which sees and names,
> As in your name, an image that is sure,
> Among the arrant spices of the sun.
>   ("To the One of Fictive Music")

In much the same key, Hartman writes that "the search for the absolute word, or minimally for the *mot juste*, is like that for the good
name." Style is the undoing of this search, as for instance in Stevens's
word "arrant"—which comes into its latter-day sense of "downright"
or "absolute" only by way of an etymological wandering that begins
with the root-word "errant." This is why, for Hartman, "the appropriate hermeneutic . . . is like the interminable work of mourning, like
an endless affectional detachment from the identity theme as such."[29]

The ways and means of such a hermeneutic are many, but important among them are the puns and echoes that sound in Hartman's fictive music and often provide his subject matter, which has lately resembled a distorted reflection of Saussure's anagrammatology in Derrida's looking-*Glas*. Proper names house identity-feeling; they answer to "the expectation that a self can be defined or constituted by words, if they are direct enough." Echolalia shatters the illusion of an absolute word that could give us back the image of an equally absolute self: "The less ego the more echo seems to be the rule." Perhaps when Lacan's work has been more thoroughly assimilated in this country we will be less inclined to hear critical egotism in Hartman's mock-manifesto, "Where the word was, the pun shall be."[30] Hartman's meditations on the value of extravagant language harken back to a theme familiar from Wordsworth: the dislocative force of hearing, its power to chasten "the dominion of the eye," or the dominion of visual experience as a metaphor of thought. That predominance is lucidly illustrated by Derrida in "White Mythology: Metaphor in the Text of Philosophy," where we see clearly the eclipsed metaphoricity of "natural" centers of perspective like the sun. Hartman uses Derrida's own *Glas*, however, to support his counterstatement of the blessings a wounded style may bring.[31]

Hartman's spirited essays in defense of the "*extraordinary language movement within modern criticism*" amount to an amiable polemic against the mirror stage of style as a critical norm. His intermittent reflections on the history of critical discourse shatter the composed image of a self-possessed expression, and gesture toward a horizon of antithetical values: "The process of incorporating what continues to violate one's identity—I mean on the level of cultural conflict or exchange—may lie beyond the range of values associated with such words as *pleasure, taste, civility, irony, accommodation*. This beyond may also become the domain of the literary essay, the more urgent and severe its aim."[32] The text presented here, "Tea and Totality: The Demand of Theory on Critical Style," continues this transgressive history by focussing now on the period from 1920 to 1950 and on the "friendship" or conversational norm that so effectively dominated Anglo-American critical prose. Hartman breaks the frame of this style by calling attention to the social and linguistic myths that install colloquial ease and referential directness as the *nature* of critical discourse.

His own language for the occasion is a kind of extended troping on the style he calls into question. He takes us through a conversational turn-style that prevents our re-turning to the premises we have departed. In this way he reminds us again what plain-dealing rhetoric forgets: that "style is what cannot stand still."

The diversity of styles to be found among recent critical theorists bears out Hartman's observation. The various movements in criticism exhibit no common characteristic more readily identifiable than this invention of different voices. What future can we anticipate for such an undisciplined conversation? While debates over critical theory will always be a matter of frameworks assumed, discarded, broken, or repaired, the dispute between formal and historical modes of interpretation seems likely to be the major point of disagreement for some time to come. The essays to follow have been arranged according to this perspective. Seen as a series, they move from a specific focus on the styles of criticism and literature to more general concerns about the relations of writing to social institutions and cultural histories. Taken simultaneously, all contain within themselves the dialogue between linguistic and historical explanations. Thus we begin with Hartman's reflections on what the Anglo-American critical essay has been, and what it may become: Hartman argues that the choice of a critical style is intricately, at times ironically, tied to the assumption of a theoretical position, and that both are shaped by the history of literary discourse. The approaches to criticism offered by our other contributors may be seen as responses to the dilemmas Hartman describes, or as alternatives to his way of describing them. Edgar Dryden's essay on Melville's style conducts an aural archaeology inspired partly by Hartman's previous work on the echoing voices and wounded ears in the tradition of Romantic poetry. The play of quotation and allusion overheard by Dryden in Melville's prose spells out an intertextual "history" that unsettles the writer's authority over his language. Dryden's own authority is self-consciously muted in much the same way, with citations and allusions that keep other texts "before" us as we read. Peggy Kamuf then shifts our attention to the inscription of legal as well as literary authority in *The Scarlet Letter*. Here literary and social history merge, as Kamuf demonstrates how the conventions that govern Hawthorne's choice of genre appear indistinguishable from the cultural determination of gender and the legal determination of guilt. Elizabeth Meese shares with Kamuf a feminist perspective on the way traditions and institutions treat feminine characters. But while Kamuf takes Hawthorne's exploration of law, guilt, and sexuality as an occasion for rethinking feminine identity and its devices, Meese turns to look directly upon modern criticism as itself a kind of *polis* or community that devises emblems of authority. Taking issue with some recent accounts of how interpretive communities function, "Sexual Politics and Critical Judgment" questions the dynamics that invest certain readers and ways of reading with canonical status.

Meese's concern with the often unacknowledged role that social and political attitudes play in constituting "aesthetic" objects and interpretive practices also has affinities with Stephen Greenblatt's approach to Shakespearean theater as a cultural institution. "Shakespeare and the Exorcists" insists that the understanding of dramatic art requires a historically informed interpretation of the artful practices at work in the particular culture that surrounds the play. Greenblatt sees the Elizabethan playhouse as an equivocal institution, a sort of cultural reservation where the subversive force of theatricality could be at once released and contained, and so provisionally sanctioned by the social order it tended to destabilize from within. Against Greenblatt's desire for a theoretical *history* of cultural representation as an economy of power, we set Timothy Bahti's reiteration of the problems raised by the play of representation *within* historiography, witnessed here in the exemplary case of Auerbach's staging of literary history in *Mimesis*. Bahti's work is to Greenblatt's roughly as Kamuf's is to Meese's: all four chart the opening between rhetorical analysis and historicism that so much contemporary criticism struggles to cross or to close, Bahti and Kamuf from the side of rhetoric, Greenblatt and Meese from that of politics and history. Andrew Parker's "Dialectics and Deconstruction," with which we close the volume, focusses on recent efforts to negotiate this disjunction by combining Marxism with semiotics. He proposes an extended revaluation of Marx's rhetoric as the way to begin reconceiving the commerce between history, society, politics, economics, and those specialized modes of production that bear the ancient name of culture.

Tea and Totality:
The Demand of Theory on Critical Style

Geoffrey H. Hartman

In almost every order of discourse there has been a call at one time or another for a higher seriousness. We are asked to pursue "some graver subject" or a more exacting style. The call may come, as in Milton or Keats, from within the poet's sense of a vocation spurred on by exemplary forebears: the reputed career of Vergil, for example, who left the oaten pipe of pastoral and playful song for the pursuit of didactic verse in his farmer's manual *The Georgics*, which is climaxed in turn by the trumpets stern of his epic *Aeneid* that deals with a warrior become culture-bearer. This call for a higher style or a graver subject has also burdened philosophy. However diverse their mode, in Husserl, Heidegger, and Wittgenstein the ideal of rigor besets what with a phrase from Spenser's proem to the *Faerie Queene* we may term their "afflicted style."

It is not otherwise in literary criticism. Grave it certainly is, and didactic, so that the formalist or playful thinker who does not justify his enterprise by appealing to theory or science is not considered worthwhile. The real terror we have experienced, and are still experiencing, produces a pressure on our purposes that is itself not unterroristic. "A theory of culture," George Steiner writes in *Bluebeard's Castle* (1971), "an analysis of our present circumstances, which do not have at their pivot a consideration of the modes of terror that brought on the death, through war, starvation, and deliberate massacre, of some seventy million human beings in Europe and Russia, between the start of the first World War and the end of the second, seems to me irresponsible."

But as we read this appeal, from a book that asks with anguish why European high culture could not stem Nazi barbarism, we wonder how far even a relevant "theory" would take us. It would remain an interpretation; it would raise the further question of how interpretations acquire the force to change anything. The sincere thinker, moreover, need not be the effective one: men and women of conscience

29

may unwittingly trivialize a subject by becoming obsessed about it. At a time when the air is as full of strident sounds as it was once of fairy folk, the question of what kind of seriousness our discipline may claim, or what sort of style might best convey it, is more troublesome than ever. The purpose of literary commentary cannot be simply its amplifying the cliches of our predicament.

Some question of style has always existed. Literature, we are told, should please or move as well as teach. Rhetoric has forensic and religious roots, however cognitively developed. Our culture depends on formalized arts of verbal exchange, which have their rules and limits, as in an adversarial court system and a parliamentary mode of debate; and they determine what is evidence rather than what is truth. They may even put obstacles in the way of those who think they know the truth, for we don't live with each other in an unmediated relation but in a strongly rhetoricized world where verbal and stylistic choices must constantly be made.

Yet just as logic tries to escape or purify rhetoric, so literary criticism too has tried to control words or else recall them to their directest, most referential function. It may seem strange to admit that the literary critic is often no friendlier to imaginative literature than the logician. In this self-deputized censor, the critic, there is love-hate rather than friendship; and recently this passionate engagement has tended to sort itself out in a schizoid way. The drift toward the extreme in modern art is so strong that it is not, on the whole, resisted. The resistance comes, rather, when a critic breaches the ramparts of decorum and modifies the language of literary criticism itself.

For that language has remained as unpretentious as possible. Critics, after all, should be critical, and fend off inflated rhetoric, faked authority, and indigest foreignness. Suspicious of their love for literature, they are even more suspicious of the literary element in themselves. They are sober people who shield themselves from contamination by the hygiene of their practice. Their tone is nicely aggressive and their nasty conservatism is great fun, after the fact—however pernicious and parochial it may have been in its own time.

How many know of Stuart Sherman's attack on Mencken in a book called *Americans*? His essay is entitled "Mr. Mencken, the *Jeune Fille* and the New Spirit in Letters"; and the *jeune fille* clearly plays the same role for Sherman as the young corruptible student does for

Denis Donoghue, who worries about creative critics inciting their disciples to dithyrambs instead of dissertations. Here is one of Sherman's sallies:

> The *jeune fille* . . . feels within herself . . . an exhilarating chaos, a fluent welter. . . . She revels in the English paradoxes and mountebanks, the Scandinavian misanthropes, the German egomaniacs, and, above all, in the later Russian novelists, crazy with war, taxes, anarchy, vodka, and German philosophy. . . . Lured by a primitive instinct to the sound of animals roving, she ventures a curious foot in the fringes of the Dreiserian wilderness vast and drear; and barbaric impulses in her blood answer the wail of the forest. . . . Imagine a thousand *jeunes filles* thus wistful, and you have the conditions ready for the advent of a new critic. At this point enters at a hard gallop, spattered with mud, H. L. Mencken high in oath. . . . He leaps from the saddle with sabre flashing, stables his horse in the church, shoots the priest, hangs the professors, exiles the Academy, burns the library and the university, and, amid the smoking ashes, erects a new school of criticism on modern German principles.[1]

Sherman has some reason to be apprehensive of the Germanizing spirit in literary studies: unfortunately even his name sounded as if a German were pronouncing "German." He wanted to save America from the Saxon in Anglo-Saxon.[2] What a paradox that the *jeune fille* would not prefer the delicacy of the French tradition which has named her type to the Carlylese coarseness of Mencken. Sherman intends the *jeune fille* to read Sainte-Beuve rather than Nietzsche, though he concludes that Mencken's style, "hard, pointed, forcible, cocksure" might substitute for a stiff freshman course in rhetoric and remove the softer forms of "slush" and "pishposh" from her mind.

It is, clearly, not only Mencken's macho manners (Sherman's are nothing to boast of) which cause the offense. As today, there is a struggle going on to define the American spirit in its true independence. There is, further, a struggle over what democracy means in education. Finally, there is a near-physical disgust at German philosophizing as an idiom that could infect our entire verbal constitution. How would Sherman react, now that even philosophers in the Romance languages have succumbed to the Germanizing style? Sartre, Lévi-Strauss, Lacan, Foucault, Derrida, Kristeva, Althusser—where may delicacy and true aesthetic feeling be found?

You will notice that I have been dealing with prejudices about style rather than with particular philosophical issues. Critics in the Anglo-American tradition are arbiters of taste, not developers of ideas. Their type of judiciousness, moreover, is almost always linked to a strong sense for the vernacular: more precisely, to the idealization of the vernacular as an organic medium, a language of nature that communicates ideas without the noise or elaboration of extraverted theory. In fact, to argue too much about what is deeply English or American means one has to acknowledge the outside; and being inside—an insider—is what counts. Perhaps this assumption of inwardness can be laid to every nationalism. Acculturated, one secretes one's culture. Yet unselfconsciousness or antiselfconsciousness, however attractive it may be, is surely a limitation rather than expansion of the critical spirit. In the Anglophile tradition, the critical spirit, as it approaches Mencken's gallop, is suspected of being a modern form of enthusiasm as dangerous as the dogmatic spirit it displaced.

This suspicion of the critical spirit reaches an English high in the most influential of modern arbiters: T. S. Eliot. Such pronouncements, especially, as "From Poe to Valéry" and *Notes towards the Definition of Culture* are urbane exercises to limit criticism in the name of culture. It is symptomatic that the epigraph on the title page of *Notes* is taken from the *OED* and reads: "DEFINITION: 1. The setting of bounds; limitation (rare)—1483." Back to 1483, then? This finicky scrutiny of words, which communicates itself even to strong epigones like Trilling (just as Heidegger's etymological virtuosity turns up in Derrida) causes Eliot to say that rescuing the word *culture* is "the extreme of my ambition."

Let me now come to the extreme of *my* ambition. It is to understand what happened to English criticism in the period of roughly 1920 to 1950, when a "teatotalling" style developed in academic circles despite so many marvelous and often idiosyncratic talents, from Eliot himself to Richards, Empson, Leavis, and (in America) Trilling.

Now what happened is, in a sense, that nothing happened. An order of discourse strove hard to remain a discourse of order. The happening was all on the side of art and literature; and the courage of the critic lay in acknowledging the newness or forwardness of modernist experiments. Compared to his own *Waste Land*, Eliot's essays are prissy. Compared to the novels of Lawrence, Leavis's revaluations are cultic gestures, precise elliptical movements charged with significance for the one who has truly read. Criticism is asked to exhibit an ideal decorum, to show that despite the stress of class antagonism, national disunity, and fragmentation, concepts of order are still possible.

In adopting this demeanor English commentators followed an ingrained tradition. They took no solace from the notion of a science or a theory of literature: that was the Continental way, leading from Dilthey to Lukács, and then increasingly to reflections inspired by Marxism and structuralism. The English classical writer, even when the stakes were high, wished to please rather than teach, and to remind rather than instruct. This critical tradition, keeping its distance from sacred but also from learned commentary, sought to purify the reader's taste and the national language, and so addressed itself to peers or friends—in short, to a class of equally cultured people.

Indeed, the highest recommendation of such criticism was the artfulness of its accommodation. Richards's *The Philosophy of Rhetoric* is as careful of its audience as Ruskin's *Sesame and Lilies*. It is not philosophy as Lukács, Adorno, Heidegger, or Benjamin practiced it, who can leave ordinary language behind or beat it into surprising shapes. I emphasize these writers in German not because they had no choice but precisely because they did have a choice: namely, German classical prose as it culminated in Goethe, and still provided Freud with a style that made his science accessible.

The "friendship style" (as I tend to name this accommodated and classical prose) has political as well as sentimental ramifications. Writers in the later eighteenth century can talk of a "republic of letters," and Keats of a "freemasonry of spirits." Indeed, in Matthew Arnold the idea of culture moves to oppose the idea of class: culture, he said, exists to do away with classes. Even if the audience addressed in the friendship style may be as provisional and uncertain as Addison's and Steele's was when they published *The Spectator*, the guiding fiction is that all the members of this society correspond on equal footing. They are "lettered"; and in terms of style there is an attempt to erase from their demeanor the "patronage style," that is, a vacillation between exaggerated modesty and extreme gravity, between presenting oneself as "all too mean" and all too manic. The friendship style cancels the disparity between the social class of the writer and his transcendent subject-matter or ambition.[3]

Criticism, then, treads lightly: its prose can be savage, but only when affronted by pedantry or the self-inflated nonsense of other writers. From the time of the neoclassical movement in seventeenth-century France, it was a form of good conversation, a discourse among equals. This speak-easy quality still joins *The Spectator* to *The New York Review of Books*, which is notorious for using Anglos. Only in Germany, and then after Hegel—when an attempt is made to separate the *Geisteswissenschaften* ("moral" or "human" sciences) from the natural sciences—is literary criticism burdened by ideas of *Bildung* and *Aufbau*, as if it had at once to anticipate and survive "absolute spirit." (So Dilthey's Berlin Academy lectures of 1905–1910, coinciding with Lukács's literary prentice years, were entitled "Der Aufbau der geschichtlichen Welt in den Geisteswissenschaften" [The construction of the historical world in the human sciences].) Yet even after the First World War, when Lukács published his *Theory of the Novel* (1920), then *History and Class Consciousness* (1923)—works whose emphasis on "totality" may be said to have inaugurated the philosophical type of criticism that was to dominate France as well as Germany—even in that postwar decade the radical editor A. R. Orage (*The New Age*) would caution Herbert Read in words that reflect the decorum of Anglo-French criticism, whose pattern-book was Sainte-Beuve's *Causeries*. "Not articles," Orage advises Read, "but causeries." "Beware of the valueless business that insists on *essay* in place of causerie. 'Everything divine runs on light feet.'"[4]

If we take the position, itself a literary one, that how we say it is as important as what we say, then the contrast that developed between English and Continental types of discourse should not be disregarded. There is no need, of course, to insist that one style must be used for every situation; and there may well be a mingling of tones, sometimes uneasy, in the best critics. But the contrast between "tea" and "totality" is too striking to be evaded by mere habits of tolerance.

Let me recapitulate my argument so far. The great virtue of the English, Basil de Selincourt said in the 1920s, is their unconsciousness; and Goethe remarked of Byron: "All Englishmen are as such devoid of inwardness [*eigentliche Reflexion*]; distraction and party spirit do not allow them to achieve a quiet development. But they are imposing as a practical people."[5] I do not quote these statements to malign a critical tradition but to point out a paradox in it that should make us wary of its practical emphasis. So deliberate an unconsciousness tends to quiet the real unconscious. It does so, Goethe suggests, by diverting the mind from spiritual to practical matters. And when we think of the contemporary situation in America, who will cast the first stone? Talent is taking refuge in business schools, law schools, and computer science; and *eigentliche Reflexion*, even when it appears, as in certain types of philosophic criticism, is denounced as navel-gazing or mandarinism.

The dominance of review essay and expository article reflects in a general way the self-delimitation of practical criticism in America and England. Though these forms of commentary serve primary texts, they now claim to teach rather than preach. And to teach as unselfconsciously as possible. "Culture is the one thing that we cannot deliberately aim at," Eliot remarks in his *Notes* on culture. The intrusion of large questions involving religion or philosophy puts the exegete at risk; not because such questions are unimportant but because they are so very important. The practical is defined as the teachable rather than as "lived religion" (Eliot) or the *Umwelt* of "birth-death-existence-decision-communication with others." Paul Ricoeur, author of this rather Germanic sentence, associates "preaching" with such a "totality" as it informs every effort to articulate what we know. Preaching, he emphasizes, invades all good teaching; and teaching that claims to be method rather than discourse—that claims to be a purely objective mode of questioning or communication—has not understood anything about theory, or the domain of preunderstanding.[6]

My own purpose is more modest than to rethink the relation of teaching and preaching, although it seems obvious enough that great preaching did not reject ordinary language, but through the mode of parable, for example, or Swift's "attacking play" (C. J. Rawson) produced a strange intersection of ordinary and extraordinary conversation. My purpose is to reconstruct historically the provenance and character of the classical style in criticism, which has now become the teatotalling style. With a book like Denis Donoghue's *Ferocious Alphabets* we are, in terms of argument, not far from Maugham's summing up of the tradition he embodies. "To like good prose is an affair of good manners. It is, unlike verse, a civil art." To understand why alternate and challenging styles have developed in the last thirty years one must first value an older prose that was, at once, classic and journalistic.

I begin by stating the obvious: a battle of styles as well as books broke out in the seventeenth century, from which there came the clarified expository and journalistic medium we relish today. The Royal Society in England as well as the French Academy played an important role in the spread of this purified style; in America too it gradually took hold against the "fantastic school" represented by such forceful theological writers as Cotton Mather. Mather intended to humble the understanding, to make it aware of its "imbecility" by a contagious parody of impotent speculative maneuvers adorned with puns and quibbles. In Mather it is sometimes hard to tell whether his display of learning and parascientific knowledge is a genuine attempt to "solve the phenomena" by elevating the mind toward the wonders and riddles of the universe (that "totality" which mere tea-drinkers can never taste) or whether it is not a subversive manifestation of fallible wit in even the most splendid of bookworms. Whatever the truth, Mather knew his style was questionable, and in his handbook for the ministry, the *Manuductio* published in 1726, he defends himself as follows:

> There has been a great deal of ado about a STYLE; So much that I must offer you my Sentiments upon it. There is a *Way of Writing* wherein the author endeavours, that the Reader may have *something to the Purpose* in every Paragraph. There is not only a *Vigour* sensible in every *Sentence* but the Paragraph is embellished with *Profitable References,* even to something beyond what is *directly spoken.* . . . The Writer pretends not unto *Reading,* yet he could not have writ as he does if he had not *Read* very much in his Time; and his Composures are not only a *Cloth of Gold,* but also stuck with as many *Jewels,* as the Gown of a Russian Embassador. This *Way of Writing* has been decried by many, and is at this Day more than ever so. . . . But, however *Fashion* and *Humour* may prevail, they must not think that the Club at their *Coffee-House* is, *All the World.* . . . After all, Every Man will have his own Style, which will distinguish him as much as his *Gate* [gait].

It was indeed the coffeehouses mentioned by Mather that played a certain role in producing the new, chastened prose; and except for the exigencies of alliteration, I might have entitled the present essay "Coffee and Totality." In the sober yet convivial atmosphere of the coffeehouses news and gossip were exchanged, and the *literati* conversed on equal footing. As Socrates brought philosophy down from the heavens into the marketplace, so Addison and Steele insinuated it into these bourgeois places of leisure, less exclusive than clubs yet probably as effective in transacting business in a casual setting. I am no sociologist, however, and do not want to ascribe too much to either tea or coffee. Yet in the pleasant spirit of generalization, adapted from the English sphere, one might say it was in these sociable places that "theories" were tested, that the conversational habit became the opium of the intellectual, and a lucid, unpedantic form of prose developed. It is in this era, too, that the English tradition modifies both the scientific and the French demand for a univocal and universal language by appealing to the mingled force of a middle or epistolary style. More exactly, by appealing to the symbiosis, rather than clash, of learned and vernacular traditions, a symbiosis that had previously characterized English poetry, even if the results were as different as Spenser and Shakespeare. The mingled style develops into the ideal of unaffected conversation, in which something is held in reserve and solicits reader or listener. It intends to provoke a reply rather than to dazzle, and it subordinates ingeniousness to the *ingenium* of natural wit. Such an ideal naturalizes rather than banishes Latinity, or seeks an equivalent in English to the philosophic ease of Plato's Greek. "It is straight from Plato's lips, as if in natural conversation," Pater will write, "that the language came in which the mind has ever since been discoursing with itself, in that inward dialogue which is the 'active principle' of the dialectic method" (*Plato and Platonism*, 1896).[7]

The triumph of modern English, though not quite yet of modern American, is anticipated by this ideal of criticism as an extended conversation, civilizing difficult ideas without falling back into gossip or opinionation. That criticism as a causerie may have had its origin in French circles of the seventeenth century, that it was formalized and even patented by Sainte-Beuve (so much so that Proust, closer to Pater, wrote an *Against Sainte-Beuve*), does not make it less attractive to the British. It is true that many intermediary developments should be taken into account, such as the nervy style of Hazlitt; and that even in recent times the grip of the causerie has not gone unchallenged.

Many writers between 1920 and 1950 try to make criticism more professional. They feel its dandyish or donnish character, and they signal a return to the vernacularist movement in Puritan England, which intended to "ratifie and settle" English as the national language. "It is more facil," George Snell wrote in 1649, "by the eie of reason, to see through the *Medium,* and light of the English tongue; then by the more obscure light of anie forreign language . . . to learn unknown arts and terms" (quoted in R. F. Jones, *The Triumph of the English Language*).[8] Yet both in journalism and in the university the following basic features of genteel criticism kept their hold.

It should be neither utilitarian as in business, nor abstract as in pure science, nor highly specialized as in scholarship. These types of discourse are allowed in only when dressed down, reduced to a witty gentility first attributed to the "honest man" (*honnête homme*) in seventeenth-century French culture—a person, that is, whose rank or profession could not be discerned when he talked in polite society. "Honest" here means *not* relying on privilege, *not* imposing on a potential peer group because of rank or social standing or expertise. When a cultured person writes or converses, you cannot tell his profession or background because, as La Rochefoucauld said, "il ne se pique de rien." Or, to quote from the definition of the *honnête homme* given by the *Dictionary* of the French Academy: "un galant homme, homme de bonne conversation, de bonne compagnie," that is, "a courteous man, a good conversationalist and interesting to be with."

Certainly an appealing ideal, for today we are even less able to talk in a nonspecialized manner. The art of conversation has not improved. But if it has not, perhaps the older ideal was the wrong way of democratizing discourse or limiting pedantry and snobbery. Without the conversational style (still practiced in Oxbridge tutorials) our situation might be worse; yet it must be said that those who presently uphold the art of criticism as conversation too often stifle intellectual exchange. The conversational decorum has become a defensive mystique for which "dialectic" and even "dialogue" (in Plato's or Gadamer's or Bakhtin's strong sense) are threatening words.

In Pater the conversational ideal is the last refuge of a neoclassical decorum striving to maintain the mask of a unified sensibility. Yet it is merely a mask. Pater holds onto the beautiful soul, the *schöne Seele.* It is time to try something else.

What might that be? It is hardly surprising that English studies should resist the influx of a French *discours* heavily indebted to post-Hegelian German philosophy. Tea and totality don't mix. Something should eventually grow from within the English tradition, even if the pressure comes from without. Richards and Empson certainly made a beginning; and criticism did become more principled, more aware of the complex structure of assigning meaning and making a literary judgment. But the problem of style remained, that is, of communicating in colloquial form the theory or methodology developed. Today George Steiner and Frank Kermode are the only successful translators of technical or speculative ideas into an idiom familiar to the university don brought up "before the flood." Yet it might be said that they are superb reviewers rather than originative thinkers: their vocation is the Arnoldian diffusion of ideas and not a radical revision or extension of knowledge.

We seem to have reached an impasse. What alternatives are there to the conversational style if we grant its necessity as a pedagogical rather than social matter? Yet this shift of perspective, however slight, indicates that such a style is useful rather than ideal, and no more "natural" than other kinds. We know, moreover, that pedagogical tools can become merely tools: "instrumental reason," as the Frankfurt School calls it, may affect language by homogenizing it. The critic who uses the conversational style because of its propriety may actually be doing a disservice to language. However difficult Blackmur, Burke, Heidegger, or Derrida may be, there is less entropy in them than in those who translate, with the best intentions, hazardous ideas or expressions into ordinary speech. Kermode's translative skill is great; one admires how rebarbative concepts from German hermeneutics or French semiotics steal into the English idiom, but something has leaked away.

We have accepted difficulty in art, but in criticism there is still a wish to "solve the phenomena." The irony and intricacy of art were fully described, not resolved, by the New Criticism; nevertheless, a sort of pedagogical illusion arose that codified the language of explication and exempted it from the very analysis it so carefully applied to art. It is not surprising, therefore, to find that Paul de Man's *Blindness and Insight* (1971) is subtitled "Essays in the Rhetoric of Contemporary Criticism." In the aggressively modern thinkers he takes up, de Man was concerned to show traces of a "Hellenic" ideal of embodiment which continued to privilege categories of presence and plenitude.[9] What was passed over, according to de Man, was the "temporal laby-rinth of interpretation" with its purely negative kind of totality (Sartre had coined the phrase *totalité détotalisé*). But now, some ten to twenty years later—de Man's essays were all written in the sixties—the situa-tion has changed. It is no longer a pseudoclassical notion of *paidea* that needs scrutiny but a para-Marxist and utopian notion of pedagogy.

I mean by that a "dream of communication" that looks not only to-ward the transparence of the text or the undistorted transmission of messages from sender (writer) to receiver (reader) but also toward a social system that is supposed to create that language-possibility in-stead of merely enforcing it. Yet everything we have learned from politics or pragmatics has put the dream of communication in doubt. It is an ever-receding horizon like Hegel's end-state, where subject and substance, real and rational, concrete and universal coincide. That end-state remains a *topos noetos*, a heaven in the form of a hori-zon, a glimpse of totality that converts every end into a means and so proves to be the moving principle it sought to arrest. Every style (stile) is also a Gate, to pun with Mather; but a style is at once open and closed.

Developments in criticism since about 1920 show that language can be analyzed more closely than was deemed possible, but not purified by prescriptions arising from the analysis. The intimate alliance of writing with "difference" we find in Derrida, and such typical asser-tions that "language is the *rupture* with totality itself . . . primarily the caesura makes meaning emerge," are symptomatic of a cautious atti-tude toward both theory and the dream of communication. "The the-ory of the Text," Barthes has said, "can coincide only with a practise of writing." We are now as aware of our language condition as of the condition of our language.

Derrida is important also because he exposes the privilege accorded to voice in the form of the conversational style as it aspires to Pater's "inward dialogue." Derrida's deconstruction, of course, does not aim at a historical style but at the dream of communication which that style, as the proprium of all styles, underwrites. The columns of *Glas* are cut by the arbitrary "justification" of the margins and the edginess of pages that interrupt, like a caesura, the words. *Glas* becomes a stylish reprisal against style—that word whose *y grecque* was hellenized into it during the Renaissance. Derrida rescues style from its confusion with Greek *stulos*, column, and so recovers its link both with stiletto, a pointed weapon, and *stiglus* or *stigma* that emphasize cutting, pointing, branding. Style is, in fact, short for *vertere stilum*, or turning the incising stylus to its blunt side, which was used to erase the impression made on waxed tablets; writing stylishly is thus to erase what is written and write over it.[10] The term "verse" takes up the other half of that phrase, as in Wordsworth's "the turnings intricate of verse"—although the metaphor accrues overtones of the turning earth, the turning of the plough, and so forth. Style is what cannot stand still.

୬

I want to conclude with a few remarks on a philosopher's recent attempt to introduce the conversational style once more. This attempt is a valiant throwback to the Age of Hume, when the conversationalists had won out, at least in prose. Yet philosophy remained under the imperative of not entirely forsaking the quest for a universal and immutable discourse. It honored the conversational mode for its virtues of social accommodation. It was philosophy for the salon. But subversively so, if we recall that it led to such strange conversation as *La Philosophie dans le Boudoir*, which put nature out of countenance. The contemporary post-Wittgensteinian attempt to revive the conversational ethos and to use it as a critique of fundamentalist perspectives in philosophy is of course that of Richard Rorty.

Rorty's *Philosophy and the Mirror of Nature* examines three modern thinkers who have had an immense influence on both professional and nonprofessional philosophers. The careers of Wittgenstein, Heidegger, and Dewey are taken to be exemplary: each began with a project to make philosophy "foundational," that is, to discover a basis for distinguishing truth from falsity, science from speculation, and verifiable representation from mere appearance. Each of the three breaks free of this project (labelled "epistemological" and "Kantian") so that their work becomes therapeutic rather than constructive, or as Rorty also likes to say "edifying" (in the secular sense of the adjective, that conveys the German idea of *Bildung*) rather than systematic.

Indeed they warn us against the very temptations acceded to in their earlier, scientific phase.

Rorty ends with a section entitled "Philosophy in the Conversation of Mankind," alluding to Michael Oakeshott's well-known "The Voice of Poetry in the Conversation of Mankind," published in *Rationalism and Politics* (1975). He latches onto the idea of "conversation," which suggests an alternative to the rigorous terminology and analytic pretensions of epistemological inquiry. Contemporary issues in philosophy, he writes, are "events in a certain stage of conversation—a conversation which once knew nothing of these issues and may know nothing of them again." And he distinguishes between treating philosophy as a "voice in a conversation" on the one hand, and treating it "as a subject, a *Fach*, a field of professional inquiry," on the other. This denial of a special field to philosophers has an attractive Emersonian ring, and of course brings Plato back as our most edifying thinker. Yet Rorty stops short of exalting even Plato, mainly because "the conversation Plato began has been enlarged by more voices than Plato would have dreamed possible."

This conclusion is surprisingly close to what recent literary critics have wished for. They take back from philosophy what is their own; they are tired of being treated as camp followers of this or that movement in philosophy. When the privilege accorded to science spills over into philosophy, literary culture is considered a dilution of ideas originated by stronger heads, a crude and subjective application of those ideas. Literary critics are then deemed parasitic not only vis-à-vis creative poem or novel but also vis-à-vis exact philosophy. Their very attempt to think independently, intensely, theoretically, is denounced—often by other literary critics. They are said to be big with the "arrogance of theory" and accused of emulating a discipline that should be kept out of the fair fields of literary study. "Whereas a generation ago," we read in a recent issue of *Novel*, "fine American literary journals would devote complete issues to a Hardy, Yeats, Faulkner, or G. M. Hopkins, current journals devote whole issues to French professors"; and the complainant goes on to charge that it was Northrop Frye's insistence on criticism as a systematic subject that allowed the "pod-people, so many of them dropouts from technical philosophy, or linguistics, or the half-science of sociology, into the fair fields of Anglo-American literary study."

However comforting it is to have a philosopher like Rorty on one's side, and to have him appreciate the recognitive as well as cognitive function of words, a hard question must be put. Can Rorty's position do more than redress the balance between philosophy and literary studies by demystifying the scientistic streak in modern thought? Can it disclose also something substantive in literary study itself, as the distance between philosophical discourse and literary commentary is lessened by viewing both as "conversation"?

The term "conversation" is a metaphor. It slides over the question of style. Should we really name something "conversation" when it is written? There is "dialogue," of course; but Rorty's concept does not wish to be dependent on a formal or stylized exchange between persons. Perhaps he would say that all writing is internalized conversation, a select polyphony of voices. The problem is not adequately treated from a literary point of view; nor entirely from a philosophical point of view. Is Rorty arguing that thinking is possible in idiomatic language without special terms or neologisms? Or is he saying that noncolloquial language also, even when it seems harsh and abstract, as so often in Kant and Husserl—in all such Teuton-Titans—is figurative or inventive despite itself? Does he not, in fact, challenge *two* assumptions: (1) that technical terms (which diverge from so-called ordinary language) are necessary for rigorous thinking, but also (2) that ordinary language—vernacular, conversational—is more inventive or figurative than the language of abstruse, systematic thought?

To these challenges there may not be a resolution. What is important is the recognition aroused in us by contemporary philosophers like Rorty and Stanley Cavell that no order of discourse or institutional way of writing has a monopoly either on rigor or invention. Philosophy remains a "conversation" with unexpected turns that cannot all be predicted, though they can later be integrated by subtle adjustments or shifts in the way we think.

At the very moment, then, that Rorty seeks to deliver philosophy from pretentiousness (both metaphysical and epistemological), literary study is seeking to deliver itself from the ideal he propagates: *conversation.*

In fact, the gentility of literary dons and the avoidance of theory are on the increase, because science has invaded literary studies too, and the older ideal is becoming, in reaction, more defensive. Many otherwise intelligent critics turn into bulldogs of understatement as they try and preserve an elegance, however mouldy, and a casualness, however fake. In Christopher Ricks, for example, a word-chopping, ordinary-language type of analysis is directed against all who attempt theory, as if the big words were naughty words we had to be shamed out of, and as if any inventive, elaborated schematism were a sin against the English sentence.

What is appealing about Rorty's position is how little difference there is between him and Pater in *Plato and Platonism* (1893). Pater did not wish to distinguish sharply between dialogue and dialectic; the same holds today for Hans-Georg Gadamer (an "edifying" rather than "systematic" philosopher, according to Rorty). Yet however attractive this Hellenic ideal may be, the results have often been dismaying. An Anglicized version of Greek *paidea* (tutorials pretending to be dialogue) has now become an unthinking attack on theory and is in danger of returning literary study to a supercilious kind of lexical inquisition that undoes everything we have learned from the large-hearted stylistics of a Leo Spitzer, an Erich Auerbach, and others.

Yet it is also clear that to take back from philosophy what is ours cannot mean a method that applies specific philosophical ideas to literature. What does Heidegger really tell us about William Carlos Williams or Paul Ricoeur about Yeats? Or Derrida about Melville? Such mixing it up may have its uses, of course. We write by assimilating what we read: we could therefore read philosophy as a sister-art; and philosophy, in turn, could consider literature as something better than time out for conversation. "Literature" here should be understood to include essays, and also larger scholarly structures in context: Spitzer in the context of German philology and the making of dictionaries; Auerbach in the context of Marxism and socioeconomic philosophies; Frye in that of anthropology and the ecumenical unifying of all fables; Empson in that of English, abdicating its political supremacy as a culture yet asserting itself as a "moral science" by constructing a new language-centered ethos.

As we pursue this institutional analysis the thorny issue of whether we need an abnormal or special terminology (a metalanguage) becomes moot. Either we shall give up the idea that there is *one* correct way of talking about literature (in a terminology that is "logical" rather than "literary"), or we shall realize that all commentary is as much metacommentary (Fredric Jameson's term) as metacommentary or theory remains context-bound commentary. The real issue that will come forward is how skeptical we should be about *cultural translation*. Can the affairs of one culture (so dependent on a different text-milieu and not only on a different language) be understood by thinkers situated in another culture, even when the latter is a relative? (It may be easier to understand a culture when the distance is great enough to prevent easy rapprochement, or what translators call "false friends.") A creative skepticism about the crossover from culture to culture seems to me the right attitude. We need a "negative capability" that does not deny speculative criticism but engages with the highly mediated status of cultural and verbal facts. The basic question then is about the nature of understanding, and what sort of responsive style might articulate this understanding. Is a conversation between cultures possible? Or is such a conversation, as between persons, always mixed with imposition? Though we talk about "dialogue" and "keeping lines of communication open," it is hard to think of a conversation that is not forcefully interspersed with moments of appropriation and expropriation. The ruses of language, the cunning of reasonableness, the sheer display of intellect or personality enter an unpredictable equation. The perfect English style, Orage said, will charm by its power; yet power and charm are precisely what the resistant thinker would like to keep separate.

From the Piazza to the Enchanted Isles: Melville's Textual Rovings

Edgar A. Dryden

Every book is a quotation; and every house is a quotation out of all forests and mines and stone-quarries; and every man is a quotation from all his ancestors.

The originals are not original. There is imitation, model and suggestion, to the very archangels, if we knew their history. The first book tyrannizes over the second. Read Tasso, and you think of Virgil; read Virgil, and you think of Homer; and Milton forces you to reflect how narrow are the limits of human invention. The Paradise Lost had never existed but for these precursors.

—Ralph Waldo Emerson

The world is forever babbling of originality; but there never yet was an original man, in the sense intended by the world; the first man himself—who according to the Rabbins was also the first author—not being an original; the only original author being God. Had Milton's been the lot of Caspar Hauser, Milton would have been as vacant as he.

—Herman Melville

Quotations in my works are like robbers by the roadside who make an armed attack and relieve an idler of his convictions.

—Walter Benjamin

Quotation is a constant reminder that writing is a form of displacement. For although quotation can take many forms, in every one the quoted passage symbolizes other writing as encroachment, as a disturbing force moving potentially to take over what is presently being written. . . . Even in the form of a passing allusion, it is a reminder that other writing serves to displace present writing, to a greater or lesser extent, from its absolute, central, proper place.

—Edward Said

The richer or more loaded language is by quotation and allusion, the more it can subvert meaning. Puns, in which this load becomes an overload, are a special case of this subversion: however witty and explosive, however energetic their yield of meaning, they invoke in us a sense of leprous insubstantiality, of a contagion that might spread over language as a whole.

—Geoffrey H. Hartman

Herman Melville fully understood what Hannah Arendt has called the "modern function of quotations," for, like Walter Benjamin, he recognized that its power is "not the strength to preserve but to cleanse, to tear out of context, to destroy."[1] This is particularly obvious in *Pierre* and the works that follow, for here Melville focuses directly on questions of authority and originality and the related problem of representation. In *Pierre*, for example, empty conventions from the domestic sentimental novel and the American/European Gothic tradition combine with citations from and allusions to the works of Dante, Shakespeare, Milton, and others to produce a book that undermines the validity of literature itself. Both writer and reader are portrayed as the victims of the "lurking insincerity of . . . written thoughts," the enchanted dupes of books whose leaves "like knavish cards" are "covertly packed."[2]

The works that follow *Pierre* are less hysterical but no less critical and subversive. *Israel Potter*, *The Piazza Tales*, and *The Confidence Man* continue the personal, social, and cultural critique initiated by Melville in *Pierre* but in a more indirect and cryptic way. Like the later sections of *Pierre* these works represent a revaluation by Melville of his personal and literary past, including the literary tradition, his own published works, and his ambivalent relation to Hawthorne. The form of his revaluation is suggested by *The Piazza Tales*, where the text is burdened by quotations and allusions and troubled by images of ocular delusions, mirages, and sinister enchantments. This is especially apparent in "The Piazza" and "The Encantadas," and I want to focus here on these two sketches.

⊗

Melville wrote "The Piazza" in 1856 to preface a collection of stories that had been separately published over a period of three years in *Putnam's Monthly Magazine*. However, the sketch situates itself not only in relation to the stories that it introduces but also in reference to Melville's literary career. And one result of this "autobiographical impulse" (to use Hawthorne's phrase) is the release of a Babel of voices from the past. The sketch is filled with echoes and allusions, haunting presences from Hawthorne's prefaces, in particular the preface to *Mosses from an Old Manse*,[3] from Melville's earlier enthusiastic review of that volume, "Hawthorne and His Mosses," from Shakespeare's plays, from *The Faerie Queene*, from Tennyson's poetry, from Melville's own novels, from the Bible, from *The Pilgrim's Progress*; and all these blend together to disturb the clarity and meaning of the narrative voice. For almost every statement is qualified, twisted, or redirected by the other voices that speak through it, with the result that the present seems troubled by a past that can only manifest itself as a disturbing ghostlike presence.

> But, even in December, this northern.piazza does not repel—nipping cold and gusty though it be, and the north wind, like any miller, bolting by the snow, in finest flour—for then, once more, with frosted beard, I pace the sleety deck, weathering Cape Horn.
> In summer, too, Canute-like, sitting here, one is often *reminded* of the sea. For not only do long ground-swells roll the slanting grain, and little wavelets of the grass ripple over upon the low piazza, as their beach, and the blown down of dandelions is wafted like the spray, and the purple of the mountains is just the purple of the billows, and a still August noon broods upon the deep meadows, as a calm upon the Line; but the vastness and the lonesomeness are so oceanic, and the silence and the sameness, too, that the first peep of a strange house, rising beyond the trees, is for all the world like spying, on the Barbary coast, an unknown sail.
> And this *recalls* my inland voyage to fairy-land. A true voyage; but, take it all in all, interesting as if invented.[4]

This curious passage (my italics) suggests one of the important movements of the sketch. At work here is a process of recall and substitution that results in a progressive movement or turning from literal toward figurative meaning. Initiating the movement is a desire to use the memories of an adventurous past to revitalize a "time of failing faith and feeble knees" (p. 2). But the effect of the turn is to emphasize the distance that separates that past from a wearisome present, for words here seem used in improper senses, to have wandered from their rightful places.[5] The beginning of the passage is governed by the substitution of ship for piazza, made possible by an analogy that emerges from the phrase "sleety deck" to bridge the gap between imagination and action. But that association is introduced by another composed of elements that are less compatible. The figure that associates the north wind with a miller Melville borrows, appropriately, from *The Winter's Tale*, where a lady's hand is described as "soft and white as the fann'd snow that's bolted / By the nothern blasts twice o'er" (4.4.373–75); but he changes Shakespeare's figure in a way that disturbs its logic and initiates a series of asymmetrical substitutions. In Melville's rearrangement the primary meaning of the word "bolting" seems to be that of moving suddenly or quickly, and the sense of bolting as sifting that controls the logic of Shakespeare's figure is present here as a secondary meaning only because of the proximity of the words "miller" and "flour." The image suggested is that of a figure covered with snow in the same way a miller is covered by the flour he sifts, and that figure in turn suggests the narrator with his "frosted beard." But this is a series of associations generated by a sort of sliding process rather than by poetic logic, and the result is to reduce the persuasive power of the figures. Hence the passage goes on to acknowledge that the seagoing past belongs exclusively to memory, and the attempt to reexperience and represent that past can only lead to disenchantment as the narrator's strained attempt to turn landscape into seascape is linked to King Canute's effort to stop the rising tide. The reference here is probably to Thackeray's satirical ballad on the subject in his parody of *Ivanhoe*, entitled *Rebecca and Rowena*, where the "sick and tired and weary" king, surrounded by flatterers, tormented by a troubled conscience and visions of his approaching death, sinks into his "great chair" and tests the power of his divine authority by commanding the ocean to retreat. The results are predictable:

> But the sullen ocean answered with a louder, deeper roar,
> And the rapid waves grew nearer, falling sounding on the shore;
> Back the Keeper and the Bishop, back the King and courtiers bore.
>
> And he sternly bade them never more to kneel to human clay,
> But alone to praise and worship That which earth and seas obey;
> And his golden crown of empire never wore he from that day.
> King Canute is dead and gone: Parasites exist alway.[6]

Many of the complexities surrounding the reference to Canute must await the consideration of a set of related allusions, but we can notice at this point that it contaminates the narrator's attempt poetically to transfigure the landscape by suggesting that his effort has its source not in the memory of a lived experience but in other texts. The emphasis in the passage falls on the relations among literary works (*The Winter's Tale*, Thackeray's satire, *Ivanhoe*, Melville's sketch) and on the power these entities possess to generate others that displace and represent them. And this is also a major issue in the account of the inland voyage that will be the subject of "The Piazza."

As the title of the collection suggests, the piazza is a figure for the creative source or origin of the tales, and the journey recounted in the introductory sketch is a metaphor for the experience of the writer during the act of creation. In this sense it clearly follows the example of Hawthorne in the "Custom-House" and "Old Manse" sketches, both of which focus on the complex and problematic motives behind the acts of writing and reading. But whereas Hawthorne's explanation of these issues is carried out in the "transparent obscurity" of a nostalgia for a lost Spenserian world of enchantment and for an "honored reader" who, having been "ushered into [the author's] study" graciously receives the "bouquet" of "tales and essays" which had "blossomed like flowers in the calm summer of [his] heart and mind,"[7] Melville's examination sweeps away the "mirage haze" created by that perspective and replaces it with an atmosphere that systematically disenchants.

The Hawthornian point of view is suggested by Melville's epigraph from *Cymbeline*, the introductory lines to a sentimental, elegiac speech:

> With fairest flowers,
> Whilst summer lasts and I live here, Fidele,
> I'll sweeten thy sad grave: thou shalt not lack
> The flower that's like thy face, pale primrose;
> The azur'd harebell, like thy veins; no, nor
> The leaf of eglantine, whom not to slander,
> Out-sweeten'd not thy breath: the ruddock would,
> With charitable bill,—O bill sore shaming
> Those rich-left heirs that let their fathers lie
> Without a monument.—bring thee all this;
> Yea, and furr'd moss besides, when flowers are none,
> To winter-ground thy corse.

(4.2.219–28)

These lines would seem to suggest that the sketch and the tales it introduces are like Hawthorne's "tales and essays," which remind him of "flowers pressed between the leaves of a book" (p. 34), reminiscences that commemorate the spirit of a place or person. However, the scene in *Cymbeline* to which Melville alludes is richly ironic, filled with delusions and misreadings. The speaker in the passage cited above is Arviragus, a king's son who believes himself a "rustic mountaineer" (4.2.100) and who mistakenly mourns the death of a man who is his sister in disguise and who is drugged but not dead. Even his words are equivocated in his brother's answer:

> Prithee, have done;
> And do not play in wench-like words with that
> Which is so serious. Let us bury him,
> And not protract with admiration what
> Is now due debt to the grave.
>
> (4.2.230–33)

The relation between these two speeches suggests the movement and theme of "The Piazza," for it points to the inauthenticity of literary language, and the sketch both invokes and subverts such a language. The artificial and conventional nature of its world is apparent in the description of the landscape as a "picture" that is in turn copied by the "sun-burnt painters painting there" (p. 1). And this sense of the cultivated picturesque is enhanced by the narrator's assertion that the piazza serves much as a bench in a picture gallery, "for what but picture-galleries are the marble halls of these same limestone hills?— galleries hung, month after month anew, with pictures ever fading into pictures ever fresh" (p. 2). The piazza in short is a structure that represents an artistic or literary point of view and suggests the sentimental possibility of a happy reciprocity between man and nature. It is a place that combines the "coziness of indoors with the freedom of out-doors," an "easy chair" that allows a leisurely and appreciative view of nature's "purple prospect." Seen from the piazza, land becomes landscape as the viewer seems in unison with grass, birds, flowers, and mountains. Nature here, to paraphrase Sartre, is social and literary myth, for natural objects easily become intentional ones by way of figurative language:

> Whoever built the house, he builded better than he knew; or else Orion in the zenith flashed down his Damocles' sword to him some starry night, and said, "Build there." For how, otherwise, could it have

entered the builder's mind that, upon the clearing being made, such a purple prospect would be his?—nothing less than Greylock, with all his hills about him, like Charlemagne among his peers. (p. 1)

This is, of course, a metaphorics familiar to the reader of *Pierre*, a novel dedicated to the "Most Excellent Purple Majesty of Greylock." In *Pierre* Melville contrasts the "sweet imposing purple promise" (p. 343) Greylock offers, when "viewed from the piazza of a soft haze-canopied summer's noon" (p. 342), with the reality of "dark-dripping rocks" and the "mysterious mouths of wolfish caves" (p. 343):

> Stark desolation; ruin, merciless and ceaseless; chills and gloom,—all here lived a hidden life, curtained by that cunning purpleness, which, from the piazza of the manor house, so beautifully invested the mountain. (p. 344)

A similar contrast controls the development of "The Piazza" sketch, but it is articulated in a more subtle, less direct way:

> During the first year of my residence, the more leisurely to witness the coronation of Charlemagne (weather permitting, they crown him every sunrise and sunset), I chose me, on the hill-side bank nearby, a royal lounge of turf—a green velvet lounge, with long, moss-padded back; while at the head, strangely enough, there grew (but, I suppose, for heraldry) three tufts of blue violets in a field-argent of wild strawberries; and a trellis, with honeysuckle, I set for canopy. Very majestical lounge, indeed. So much so, that here, as with the reclining majesty of Denmark in his orchard, a sly ear-ache invaded me. But, if damps abound at times in Westminster Abbey, because it is so old, why not within this monastery of mountains, which is older?
> A piazza must be had. (p. 2)

Worth noting here is the fact that the earlier fanciful association of Greylock with Charlemagne ("like Charlemagne among his peers") has solidified into a mode of vision that affects the narrator's view of himself no less than his view of the surrounding landscape. For he comes to associate himself and his authorship with the authority of emperors and kings who "had the casting vote, and voted for themselves" (p. 3). Like the "high aspiring, but most moody, disappointed bard" who in *Pierre* christens the mountain "Mount of the Titans," he imposes the "spell of [a] name the mountain never afterward escaped" (p. 342) and thereby indicates that "Nature is not so much her own ever-sweet interpreter, as the mere supplier of that cunning alphabet, whereby selecting and combining as he pleases, each man reads his own peculiar lesson according to his own peculiar mind and mood" (p. 342).

However, as the passage goes on to imply, the "spell of a name" that generates the elaborate images of royalty and heraldry and suggests an idyllic relation between man and nature is not sufficient to maintain the autonomy of the figurative perspective. The allusion to *Hamlet* introduces an association that sharply subverts the sense of stately dignity and authority:

> Sleeping within mine orchard,
> My custom always of the afternoon,
> Upon my secure hour thy uncle stole,
> With juice of cursed hebona in a vial,
> And in the porches of mine ears did pour
> The lep'rous distilment; whose effect
> Hold such an enmity with blood of man
> That swift as quicksilver it courses through
> The natural gates and alleys of the body,
> And with a sudden vigour it doth posset
> And curd, like eager droppings into milk,
> The thin and wholesome blood; so it did mine,
> And a most instant tetter bark'd about,
> Most lazar-like, with vile and loathsome crust,
> All my smooth body.
>
> (1.5.59–73)

This ghostly voice discloses others, for the orchard of the "reclining majesty of Denmark" at once suggests and contaminates Hawthorne's description of the one at the Old Manse, where the trees possess a "domestic character" and suggest an "infinite generosity and exhaustless bounty on the part of our Mother nature" (p. 12); as well as Melville's interpretation of that orchard in "Hawthorne and His Mosses" as the "visible type of the fine mind that described it." The "spell" operating in "The Piazza" differs markedly from the one Melville earlier had found working in Hawthorne's preface to *Mosses from an Old Manse*:

> Stretched on that new mown clover, the hill-side breeze blowing over me through the wide barn door, and soothed by the hum of bees in the meadows around, how magically stole over me this Mossy Man! And

how amply, how bountifully, did he redeem that delicious promise to
his guests in the Old Manse, of whom it is written—"Others could give
them pleasure, or amusement, or instruction—these could be picked
up anywhere—but it was for me to give them rest. Rest, in a life of
trouble! What better could be done for weary and world-worn spirits?
What better could be done for anybody, who came within our magic
circle, than to throw the spell of a magic spirit over him?" So all that
day, half-buried in the new clover, I watched this Hawthorne's "As-
syrian dawn, and Paphian sunset and moonrise, from the summit of
our Eastern Hill."[8]

The horrible transformation described in the *Hamlet* passage stands in
stark contrast to and undermines the romantic idyllic language of the
texts to which it is linked metaleptically. As we move from the body of
the leprous king to the guests at the Old Manse "stretched among the
shadows of the orchard" (p. 28), then to the reclining narrator of
"Hawthorne and His Mosses," and finally to the lounging figure in
"The Piazza," a ghostly presence moves with us, disordering stable
worlds of similitudes with the intrusion of horrifying and unnatural
differences. And this sense of sinister transformations is not relieved
by the possibility of establishing a mediating piazza perspective, for
in nineteenth-century America "porch" and "piazza" were used in-
terchangeably to refer to a verandah. In short, the figurative use of
"porch" in the *Hamlet* passage puts into question both the literal and
figurative aspects of the piazza in the sketch and suggests a contagion
spreading through language in the same way as the "lep'rous distil-
ment" courses through the body of the king. The piazza, it appears,
can offer neither the protection nor the perspective that the narrator
expects, for he finds himself, like the weary and troubled Canute in
his "great chair," weakened and disenchanted.

> At length, when pretty well again, and sitting out, in the September
> morning, upon the piazza, and thinking to myself, when, just after a
> little flock of sheep, the farmer's banded children passed, a-nutting,
> and said, "How sweet a day"—it was, after all, but what their fathers
> call a weather-breeder—and, indeed, was become so sensitive through
> my illness, as that I could not bear to look upon a Chinese creeper of my
> adoption, and which, to my delight, climbing a post of the piazza, had
> burst out in starry bloom, but now, if you removed the leaves a little,
> showed millions of strange, cankerous worms, which, feeding upon
> those blossoms, so shared their blessed hue, as to make it unblessed
> evermore—worms, whose germs had doubtless lurked in the very bulb

which, so hopefully, I had planted: in this ingrate peevishness of my weary convalescence, was I sitting there; when, suddenly looking off, I saw the golden mountain-window, dazzling like a deep-sea dolphin. Fairies there, thought I, once more; the queen of fairies at her fairy-window; at any rate, some glad mountain-girl; it will do me good, it will cure this weariness, to look on her. No more; I'll launch my yawl—ho, cheerly, heart! and push away for fairy-land, for rainbow's end, in fairy-land. (pp. 6–7)

Here is a world in which man is not at home, where rest and peace are impossible, for nature is experienced as a feeling of threatening change and contagion, brought on by the encounter with deception and difference. The phrase "weather-breeder" implies an analogy of proportion—fathers are to children as the sweet September day is to subsequent storms—but in a manner that ironizes and contaminates the linkage. And the example of the Chinese creeper subverts the possibility of a relation based on a positive acceptance of difference. As a parodic version of the adopted child whose tainted blood resists the hopes and efforts of the substitute parent, the plant undermines any idea of a cultivated decorative nature. Hence in an act of poetic defiance the narrator determines to begin an ascending movement toward another realm nearer to the sky, toward a mixed transitional landscape that is the product of the magical forces of the imagination. Promising relief from weariness is the golden glow of the "mountain window," a "fairy sign" that had first appeared like a Hawthornian birthmark as a "small, round, strawberry mole upon the wan cheek of northwestern hills" (p. 5) on an autumn afternoon when the air seemed "sick" and the "sky was ominous as Hecate's cauldron." As the sign of a "haunted ring where fairies dance" that promises a cure for weariness, the glow recalls Hawthorne's description of the "Enchanted Ground" of the Old Manse that offers rest to those "weary and world-worn spirits" who come "within [the] magic circle" (p. 29), and it recalls too Melville's citation of that description in "Hawthorne and His Mosses" (noted earlier).

But Melville does not recall the magic spell of Hawthorne's fairy land and its earlier effect on him in order to celebrate unambiguously the positive aspects of such enchantments, nor to suggest that the "witching conditions of light and shadow" (p. 4) he experiences on the piazza duplicate those of the Old Manse. Here recall takes the form of a new, more negative reading of Hawthorne's text, one that brings to the foreground details the earlier analysis had ignored. "In one respect," Hawthorne writes, "our precincts were like the Enchanted Ground, through which the pilgrim travelled on his way to the Celestial City. The guests . . . felt a slumberous influence upon them; they fell asleep in chairs, or took a more deliberate siesta on the sofa, or were seen stretched among the shadows of the orchard, looking up dreamily through the boughs" (p. 28). Hawthorne refers here to a place in *The Pilgrim's Progress* just before the Land of Beulah, "one of the last refuges that the enemy to the pilgrims has," for the "air there [tends] to make one drowsy . . . and if a man sleeps tis a question some say, whether ever he shall rise or wake again in this world."[9] It is this dark aspect of enchantment—suggested through Hawthorne's reference but never developed in his preface—that troubles the text of "The Piazza." The reference to Hecate's cauldron, for example, reminds us that she and the other witches in *Macbeth* "about the cauldron sing, / Like elves and fairies in a ring, / Enchanting all that you put in" (5.1.41–43), and hence suggests that enchanters have complicated, perhaps sinister, motives. And sleep, of course, does not always bring relief from weariness, as the example of Lady Macbeth makes clear; a point also suggested by the narrator's reference to *A Midsummer Night's Dream*, a play where fairies "following darkness like a dream" (5.1.393) "streak" the eyes of sleepers with enchanted juice and fill their minds "full of hateful fantasies" (2.1.257–58).

Quite clearly, the narrator's description of his interest in fairy land, his desire to seek out the "queen of fairies at her fairy window," is disturbed by a series of allusions suggesting some of the dismaying dangers such a pursuit involves. And these unsettling suggestions continue to accumulate as the narrator describes his search for "rainbow's end, in fairy-land." For unlike the voyages of Melville's earlier first-person narrators, the writer's journey here takes him "inland" (p. 4), and his search is rendered from the beginning in terms of strained metaphors that call attention to their figurative or merely fanciful nature and at the same time nostalgically invoke real adventures of the past. The "golden mountain window" dazzles "like a deep-sea dolphin"; his "yawl" is a "high-pommeled, leather one"; the guiding stars are present in the forms of a "wigged old Aries, long-visaged, and with a crumpled horn," a "milky way of white weed," and "Pleides and Hyades, of small forget-me-nots" (p. 7). But this is a pattern that cannot be long sustained. The "yawl" is soon disenchanted (it becomes a horse) and is eventually left behind like Una's lamb when the narrator reaches a point where "none might go but by himself" (p. 8). Indeed, by the time he approaches fairy-land, "foot-sore enough and weary" (p. 8), the voyaging ideal persists only in "improper" or displaced reminders of earlier adventures: "A sultry hour, and I wore a light hat, of yellow sinnet, with white duck trowsers— both relics of my tropic sea-going. Clogged in muffling ferns, I softly stumbled, staining the knees a sea-green" (p. 10).

Following this fall, the narrator sees "the fairy queen sitting at her fairy window," and although when he speaks she starts "like some Tahiti girl" (p. 10) she is obviously no Fayaway. Nor does she suggest Spenser's Gloriana. Rather she recalls the deserted and isolated figure of Tennyson's poem "Mariana." Like her poetic namesake, Melville's Marianna sits alone in an isolated, dilapidated, dreary house and laments her weary existence. Unlike the enchanted ground of Hawthorne's retreat, Marianna's surroundings possess no "slumberous influence" (p. 39), for she is tormented by "weariness and wakefulness together" (p. 14). And the picturesque "veil of woodbine" that adds to the idyllic atmosphere of the Old Manse ("The Old Manse," p. 33) is here the sign of decay: "This old house is rotting. That makes it so mossy" (p. 11).

The house that from the piazza had appeared as "one spot of radiance" has its "golden sparkle" (p. 5) disenchanted by the "strange fancies" of Marianna. Hers is a world of enigmatic shadows that lead not to essential forms but to other shadows. "The invading shadow gone the invaded one returns" (p. 12). Indeed, for Marianna "shadows are as things," as loving friends, for they are valued in themselves rather than as signs pointing to the things that cast them.

> But the friendliest one, that used to soothe my weariness so much, cooly quivering on the ferns, it was taken from me, never to return, as Tray did just now. The shadow of a birch. The tree was struck by lightning, and brother cut it up. You saw the cross-pile out-doors—the buried root lies under it; but not the shadow. That is flown, and never will come back, nor ever anywhere stir again. (p. 13)

This astonishing passage suggests the depth of Marianna's despair, for her lament ignores as irrelevant both the natural and human as-

pects of the "cross-pile of silver birch." Neither the lightning strike
nor the act of cutting has significance for her. And if the "cross-pile"
with the "buried root" beneath it suggests to her, as it does to the narrator, "some sequestered grave" (p. 9), it is neither an indication of
nostalgia for the natural object nor a sign that the influences of nature
can soothe us when "death is in our thoughts." [10] Her interest is not in
evidences of past life, for what was important to her was not alive.
Indeed what is now poignantly missing in her world might be said
itself to be simply the sign of an absence.

Marianna, however, is not completely without hope. For although
all other possible cures have failed to relieve her weariness, she believes that it would leave her if she could once "look upon whoever
the happy being is" (p. 14) who lives in the gleaming house at the bot-
tom of the mountain. Ironically, it is her belief in the power of that
happy house that permanently disenchants the narrator:

> —Enough. Launching my yawl no more for fairy-land, I stick to the
> piazza. It is my box-royal; and this amphitheatre, my theatre of San
> Carlo. Yes, the scenery is magical—the illusion so complete. And
> Madam Meadow Lark, my prima donna, plays her grand engagement
> here; and, drinking in her sunrise note, which, Memnon-like, seems
> struck from the golden window, how far from me the weary face be-
> hind it.
>
> But, every night, when the curtain falls, truth comes in with darkness.
> No light shows from the mountain. To and fro I walk the piazza deck,
> haunted by Marianna's face, and many as real a story. (pp. 14–15)

Once the narrator sees that Marianna's view of his "happy house"
(p. 14) is as poetic to her as her "fairy mountain house" (p. 10) has
been to him, he comes to understand the way the imagination seeks
to relieve the weariness and boredom of life by establishing the authority of illusion. And this understanding disenchants forever the
fiction of a fairy land by exposing it as a cruel and empty pretense.
Gone now is the desire for adventure that had transformed the piazza
into the "sleety deck" of a ship and generated the "inland voyage to
fairy-land," with the pleasant, haunted, picturesque perspective of
the early paragraphs of the sketch. The piazza is no longer seen as a
substitute pew, easy chair, or cozy lounge where the writer can sit like
Hawthorne in his "familiar room" and "dream strange things and

make them look like truth."[11] It has become a theatre-box, a place of deceiving appearances, of unreal falsifications. And with that change comes the return of a discredited authority. The narrator sits comfortably, even self-indulgently, in his "box-royal" enjoying the perspective of a privileged consciousness for whom both nature and other people have become merely elements in a representation. But along with this disenchanted vision comes a reversal of the traditional metaphorics that makes truth analogous to light and creativity to the act of seeing. "Truth comes in with darkness," the darkness that follows the fall of the stage curtain; and with it come ghostly presences quite unlike those that appear "without affrighting us" in Hawthorne's "familiar room." These are the presences that haunt the enchanted isles.

It is not surprising that much of the critical commentary on "The Encantadas" has focused on the problem of sources and allusions, for the sketches obsessively assert the importance of an authority of reference.[12] And yet at the same time they demonstrate the ways in which such an authority maintains itself through a variety of disguises and by way of "barren, bootless allusions."[13] The sketches are presented as the product of Salvator R. Tarnmore, a name that invokes the vocabulary of gothic theatricality as well as the tradition of the picturesque and sublime. It reminds us too of Melville's earlier use of that tradition in *Redburn*, where he describes the enigmatic Jackson in the following way: "Brooding there in his infernal gloom, though nothing but a castaway sailor in canvas trousers, this man was still a picture, worthy to be painted by the dark, moody hand of Salvator. In any of that master's lowering sea-pieces, representing the desolate crags of Calabria, with a midnight shipwreck in the distance, this Jackson's would have been the face to paint for the doomed vessel's figure head, seamed and blasted by lightning."[14] The name then appears in a curious way to be both full and empty of significance, for as an obvious pseudonym it raises the problem of authorial signature and equivocates the status of the sketches. In short, it introduces the problem of the literary and so suggests a context for Melville's account of the enchanted isles that differs significantly from the other context his contemporaries would have known, that of Charles Darwin's *Voyage of the Beagle*.

Nevertheless the narrator of the sketches emphasizes the fact that his descriptions depend not only on his memories of his own experiences but on the accounts of "three eye-witness authorities . . . Cowley, the Buccaneer (1684); Colnet, the whaling ground explorer (1798); Porter, the post captain (1813)." But these are all accounts by men who have long "hovered in the charmed vicinity of the enchanted group" (p. 171), and hence are the products of "spell-bound eye[s]" (p. 185). Surrounded by "deceptive vapours" (p. 165), victims of a "nameless magic" (p. 186), these eyewitnesses have their authority put into question by their exposure to the "self-transforming and bemocking isles" (p. 169). And the narrator, dependent at once on these enchanted accounts and on his own "wild nightmare" memories of the isles (p. 157), seems doubly spellbound. Unlike Bunyan's Christian, who heeds the warning to beware of the Enchanted Ground and resists the temptation to sleep, the narrator during his "far distant rovings in the baked heart of the enchanted isles" has been overcome by his weariness. "I can hardly resist the feeling," he writes, "that in my time I have indeed slept upon evilly enchanted ground" (p. 153). As a result, he is the victim of "ocular deceptions and mirages" (p. 169):

> Nor even at the risk of meriting the charge of absurdly believing in enchantments, can I restrain the admission that sometimes, even now, when leaving the crowded city to wander out July and August among the Adirondack Mountains, far from the influences of towns and proportionally nigh to the mysterious ones of nature; when at such times I sit me down in the mossy head of some deep-wooded gorge, surrounded by prostrate trunks of blasted pines and recall, as in a dream, my other and far-distant rovings in the baked heart of the charmed isles; and remember the sudden glimpses of dusky shells, and long languid necks protruded from the leafless thickets; and again have beheld the vitreous inland rocks worn down and grooved into deep ruts by ages and ages of the slow draggings of tortoises in quest of pools of scanty water; I can hardly resist the feeling that in my time I have indeed slept upon evilly enchanted ground.
>
> Nay, such is the vividness of my memory, or the magic of my fancy, that I know not whether I am not the occasional victim of optical delusion concerning the Gallipagos. For, often in scenes of social merriment, and especially at revels held by candle-light in old-fashioned mansions, so that shadows are thrown into the further recesses of an

angular and spacious room, making them put on a look of haunted un-
dergrowth of lonely woods, I have drawn the attention of my comrades
by my fixed gaze and sudden change of air, as I have seemed to see,
slowly emerging from those imagined solitudes, and heavily crawling
along the floor, the ghost of a gigantic tortoise, with "Memento
* * * * *" burning in live letters upon his back. (p. 153)

The retrospective moment described here at once suggests and contaminates a familiar romantic pattern where the poet nostalgically recalls the innocence and simplicity of an earlier self and moment. But
the moment recalled here is not an innocent childhood experience nor
even a time when nature seemed deceptively radiant and Edenic. Nor
is there a simple contrast between a state of enchanted dreaming and
one of waking on the cold hillside. Here there are two forms of enchantment, one suggested by the conventional poetic journey away
from the influences of towns toward the "mysterious ones of nature,"
by the familiar literary and painterly landscape of deep wooded gorge
and prostrate trunks of blasted pines, and by the gothic "revels held
by candle-light in old-fashioned mansions"; the other by the dream
that invades and disturbs these conventional scenes. Ambiguous
child of either fancy or memory or both, this enchantment is not the
product of romantic will or desire but appears as a repressed and deviant force that hollows out literary patterns and poses. As the apparent creations of a "malignant, or perhaps downright diabolical en-
chanter," the "spectre tortoises . . . emerging from [their] shadowy
recess" generate a "wild nightmare" vision in which the narrator finds
himself "lost . . . in volcanic mazes . . . sitting crosslegged upon [a
tortoise], a Brahmin similarly mounted upon either side forming a tri-
pod of foreheads which upheld the universal cope" (p. 157).

But the tortoises do not long retain their deviant energy. The narrator quickly naturalizes their strangeness by placing them within the
framework of the conventional and the ordinary. First they are given
an allegorical relation to the world by his emphasizing that "even the
tortoise, dark and melancholy as it is up the back, still possesses a
bright side" (p. 154); next their sinister qualities are accounted for by
his observation that "we had been broad upon the waters for five long
months, a period amply sufficient to make all things of the land wear
a fabulous hue to the dreamy mind" (p. 155); and finally they are com-

pletely familiarized by being transformed into steaks, stews, and cal-
apees. Still, not even the narrator's "firmest resolutions" (p. 154) can
completely erase the specter tortoise with its suggestion of an ironic
uncertainty at work beneath the surface play of cultural and literary
conventions, and its presence is felt in the echoes and allusions that
trouble the narrator's account of the enchanted isles.

"Sketch Third, Rock Rodondo" is structured by a familiar conflict
between appearance and reality as the narrator discusses the enchantment that caused the rock to be mistaken for a sail, as well as the process whereby the "enchanted frigate is transformed apace into a
craggy keep" (p. 159). Set against the "victimized confidence" of
"other voyagers" who are "taking oaths" that Rock Rodondo is a
"glad populous ship," is the disenchanted view of narrator and
reader who know it to be a "dead desert rock" (p. 162). In a world of
"ocular deceptions and mirages" (p. 169), however, such clear distinctions are difficult to sustain, and a disturbing uncertainty begins to
assert itself as the narrator leads the reader up Rock Rodondo. "How
we get there, we alone know" (p. 163). The title and epigraph of
"Sketch Fourth, A Pisgah View from the Rock" seem to establish a
series of ironic contrasts by setting the visions of ideal worlds against
that of a "land, not of cakes, but of clinkers, not of streams of spark-
ling water, but arrested torrents of tormented lava" (p. 167). The title,
of course, refers to Moses' vision of Palestine from the top of Mount
Pisgah, and the Spenserian epigraph describes the Red Crosse
Knight's experience in the House of Holinesse as he was led up the
Mount of Contemplation by "an aged holy man" and shown a vision
of "New Hierusalem." In Spenser, the lines immediately following
Melville's citation link the Mount of Contemplation with Mount Sinai,
the Mount of Olives, and Parnassus, a chain of associations that
would have caught Melville's eye. We know from *Pierre* that he identifies divine speech and prophetic vision with mountain tops. There he
links the "majestic mountain Greylock," ironic source of his artistic
vision, with Mount Sinai, meeting place of God and Moses; with the
divine mount that was the site of Christ's famous sermon; and with
Bunyan's Delectable Mountains, from which the celestial city may be
seen. Moses and Christ are then linked to other imposter philosophers who pretend that they are able to get a voice out of silence and
to discover the Talismanic secret that will reconcile man with the

world. Melville, in short, is deeply suspicious of Pisgah views, and in his world high places are often linked to deliberate attempts to blind and deceive. There is no doubt, of course, that Melville in this sketch is emphasizing the radical difference between the world as seen from Rock Rodondo and the promised worlds of the Old and New Testaments. But he is doing more than that. The world the narrator shows us is "grim and charred," but it is also enchanted, indeed in the case of Cowley's Enchanted Isle, doubly enchanted. And the "spell within a spell involved by this particular designation" (p. 168) suggests uncertainties that cloud the clear distinction between a fallen world and promised lands. "Self-transforming and bemocking" (p. 169), this isle appears in many forms, "one moment as a great city," and another as a "ruined fortification" (p. 168). That is to say the isle can generate both the fallen and the Pisgah perspectives, one no less deceptive than the other.

The name of the isle is "bestowed by that excellent Buccaneer himself" (p. 168), an act which doubles the spell and suggests a connection between the "nameless magic" (p. 186) of the place and a sinister magic of naming, for it links together the problems of naming, identity, and literature. "That Cowley linked his name with this self-transforming and bemocking isle," the narrator writes, "suggests the possibility that it conveyed to him some meditative image of himself. At least, as is not impossible, if he were any relative of the mildly-thoughtful and self-upbraiding poet Cowley, who lived about his time . . . for that sort of thing evinced in the naming of the isle runs in the blood, and may be seen in pirates as in poets" (p. 169). In linking his name to the enchanted isle Cowley implies that the idea of an essential self, like the "enigmatic craft" that is "American in the morning, and English in the evening" (p. 171), may be no more than a "strange delusion" (p. 152). He also initiates a chain of associations stretching to the narrator's fanciful genealogy coupling pirate and poet. Cowley's naming of the isle is the sign of something that "runs in the blood," like some pernicious genetic disorder with the effect of erasing individual differences. The name "Cowley," designating both adventurous pirate and self-upbraiding poet, not only reminds us that there may be nothing in a name but also suggests a disturbing connection between piracy and poetry.

Such connections trouble the "sentimental voyager" of "long ago"

(p. 173) whose account of his visit to Barrington Island is quoted at length by the narrator in "Sketch Sixth." Among the "fine old ruins" he finds there are "romantic seats," one of which seems "just such a sofa as the poet Gray might have loved to throw himself down upon." As a sentimentalist, he finds it "hard to impute the construction of these romantic seats to any other motive than those of pure peacefulness and kindly fellowship with nature" (p. 173). Hence he maintains that as long as "these ruins of seats . . . remain, the most singular monuments are furnished to the fact, that all the buccaneers were not unmitigated monsters" (p. 174). The seats are not the only ruins on the island, however. There are "signs" too of the "murderer" and "robber" as well as "trace[s]" of the reveller, suggesting the possibility that the buccaneers "robbed and murdered one day, revelled the next, and rested themselves by turning meditative philosophers, rural poets and seat-builders on the third" (p. 188). Like the word "Cowley," these signs or traces furnish us with no clear sense of the motives of the men that they represent, for they record textual rather than perceptual moments. Here as throughout the sketches, the narrator's present is inhabited by fragments of representations, relics from memory, words, sentences, passages from books, stories from shipmates "learned in the lore of outlandish life" (p. 175), gravestones, graveboards, half-mildewed documents and "doggeral epitaph[s]" (p. 207), a collection of rubbish that stands between himself and the world and precludes any original relationship to it.

The relation between the perceptual and the textual is a central issue in "Sketch Eighth, Norfolk Isle and the Chola Widow." More than any of the other sketches this one seeks to render the intensity, immediacy, and reality of human suffering, to portray an experience so profoundly moving to the narrator that it has transformed a "lone island" into a "sacred" spot (p. 180). And yet his account is prefaced with three epigraphs that situate it in a problematic and highly literary context. The first—"At last they in an island did espy/A seemly woman sitting by the shore,/That with great sorrow and sad agony/Seemed some great misfortune to deplore,/And loud to them for succor called evermore"—is from book 2 of *The Faerie Queene* and subversively associates Hunilla, the "lone shipwrecked soul" who has been treacherously abandoned on the island, with one of Spenser's sinister sirens, who through "womanish fine forgery" seeks to afflict man's "stubborne hart" with "fraile infirmity" (*Faerie Queene* 2.12.28). The second, from Thomas Chatterton's pseudo-medieval drama *Aella*—an obvious imitation of *Othello*, written in Rowleyan language and contaminated by the controversy surrounding its authenticity— is the song of a damsel mourning her swain; it reminds us of Hunilla's grief at the loss of her brother and husband, but in a way which robs it of its poignancy and intensity. The third epigraph (added to the first edition of *The Piazza Tales*) is from William Collins's *Dirge in Cymbeline*, and links this sketch to "The Piazza," prefaced by a fragment from the same passage of Shakespeare rewritten in the Collins poem. That passage, as we have seen, is subverted by one directly following it in Shakespeare's text.

The troubling distance which these passages open between experience or perception and its representations is increased by the narrator's emphasis on the distinction between his object and its image. "It is not artistic heartlessness, but I wish I could but draw in crayons; for this woman was a most touching sight; and crayon, tracing softly melancholy lines, would best depict the mournful image of the dark-damasked Chola widow" (p. 181). In addition to recalling the painterly associations suggested by the narrator's signature, this passage by contrasting the graphic powers of words and images calls attention to the difficulties of re-presenting. And indeed it is only Hunilla's external aspects that can be imaged by the narrator. His "little story" (p. 180) of "her story" (p. 181) is unable to convey her "nameless misery" (p. 184) or to represent the two "unnamed events" (p. 188) responsible for it. In "telling her own story" (p. 184) Hunilla simply recounts the events, making no attempt to represent herself. "From her mere words little would you have weened that Hunilla was herself the heroine of her tale. . . . She but showed us her soul's lid, and the strange ciphers thereon engraved; all within . . . was withheld" (p. 184). The narrator on the other hand, "sporting with the heart of him who reads" (p. 186), teases us with references to that which must remain unnamed and concludes with the sentimental assertion that "events, not books, should be forbid" (p. 186).

But the narrator's account of the death of Hunilla's brother and husband seems to put into question the very distinction between perception and representation, between events and their verbal or painterly images.

Before Hunilla's eyes they sank. The real woe of this event passed before her sight as some sham tragedy on the stage. She was seated on a
rude bower among the withered thickets, crowning a lofty cliff, a little
back from the beach. The thickets were so disposed, that in looking
upon the sea at large she peered out from among the branches as from
the lattice of a high balcony. But upon the day we speak of here, the
better to watch the adventure of those two hearts she loved, Hunilla
had withdrawn the branches to one side, and held them so. They
formed an oval frame, through which the bluely boundless sea rolled
like a painted one. And there, the invisible painter painted to her view
the wave-tossed and disjointed raft, its once level logs slantingly up-
heaved, as raking masts, and the four struggling arms undistinguisha-
ble among them; and then all subsided into smooth-flowing creamy waters, slowly drifting the splintered wreck; while first and last, no sound
of any sort was heard. Death in a silent picture, a dream of the eye; such
vanishing shapes as the mirage shows. (pp. 183–84)

In this remarkable passage the real appears as figure, perception as a
form of representation. The present, that which is maintained in front
of Hunilla's eyes, is already represented. And in the case of this "half
breed Indian woman" (p. 182) from Peru, the perspective cannot be
rationalized in terms of a mind burdened by the weight of books. In
her case the simple acts of selecting a seat and withdrawing some
branches transform the natural into the artificial. She experiences the
deaths of her loved ones as if they were painted figures in a Salvator
sea piece, or a work such as *The Slave Ship* or the *Raft of the Medusa*.
Melville's point seems to be that words and images tease and frustrate
the imagination by imposing a structure on the self and the world.
Not even our response to death is natural in the sense of being an underived and spontaneous reaction. It appears as picture, dream, or
mirage, and its truth manifests itself indirectly, as a spectral presence,
like Marianna's face and many as real a story.

❦

"The Piazza" and "The Encantadas," then, anticipate the tangle of
genealogical and representational metaphors that one finds in *The
Confidence Man*, and suggest some personal as well as literary reasons
why the knotted relationship in that novel should turn around the
concept of originality. The original man, of course, is one having the

quality of that which proceeds from himself, being without imitation or dependence on others. He is new, underived and hence capable of original ideas and actions. But original also pertains to origin, to the first and earliest, the primary, the primitive, innate, hence that from which everything else is derived. These are, of course, issues of genealogy, but the notion of originality also raises problems of representation: it suggests a thing or person in relation to something else that is a copy, imitation, or representation of it, or an object or a person by a picture or an image; or a writing or a literary work in relation to another that is a translation of it or that reproduces its statements. Melville, as one of my epigraphs suggests, is aware of all of these aspects. Even at the origin there is no originality. Adam at the beginning already lives with the burden of an absent Father whose words and acts he is doomed to repeat in a diminished key. The effect of this perception is to question the notion of an orderly, predictable movement between origin and image, a thing or self and its representation, and so to make possible the artifice of the confidence man. This man-charmer, who is deemed an original by the *Fidéle's* barber and his friends, knots together both the genealogical and representational aspects of originality from his first appearance. He appears, it would seem, *ex nihilo*; and yet as an "advent"[15] that appearance is associated with a number of other such manifestations. Specifically, it is linked to that of Manco Capac, a child of the sun, and hence seems to place the mute in a genealogical chain that complicates his status as a beginning character. And that status is confused further when he "chances to come to a placard nigh the captain's office, offering a reward for the capture of a mysterious impostor from the East; quite an original genius in his vocation, as would appear, though wherein his originality consisted was not clearly given; but what purported to be a careful description of his person followed" (p. 1). Here of course is the problem of representation raised, first by the nature of the relationship between the mute and the placard (is he the original represented by the careful description?); second by the connection between the placard and the mute's "small slate . . . held on a level with the placard, so that they who read the one might read the other" (p. 2); and finally by the fact that the crowd gathers around the placard "as if it had been a theatre bill" (p. 1). These issues are further entangled when the man in the gray coat observes that Black Guinea (who, we recall, as the loaf of black bread in the oven of a charitable baker is also a child of the sun) is to be trusted because nature "placarded" (p. 24) upon him the evidence of his claims.

These are of course only early links in a chain of associations that forms as the novel develops, and any reading must thread its way through related configurations of the genealogical and representational aspects of originality and their relation to the series of exchanges that constitute the novel. I will say here only that the final links are to be found in the penultimate chapter of the novel, where the narrator addresses the complex question of originality in his own voice. But, as the chapter title tells us, his discourse is not original but depends ambiguously on the words of the barber's friends: "In Which the Last Three Words of the Last Chapter Are Made the Text of Discourse, Which Will be Sure of Receiving More or Less Attention From Those Readers Who Do Not Skip It." To speak or to write is to repeat, and to repeat is to expose oneself to the arts of "some malignant sorceress" ("The Encantadas," p. 194), to give in to the charm of language. For Melville, the result of this spell is a world where ambiguity prevails, where the acts of reading and writing are contaminated by imposture and belatedness, and where the disenchanted, like Marianna, sit "never reading, seldom speaking, yet ever wakeful" (p. 13), doomed to a life of "weariness and wakefulness together" (p. 14).

Hawthorne's Genres:
The Letter of the Law Appliquée

PEGGY KAMUF

Man thinks woman profound—why? Because he can never fathom
her depths. Woman is not even shallow.
—Nietzsche, *The Twilight of the Idols*

Genres

Nietzsche's aphorism is set here as one place to begin a trajectory
through what for the moment I will call the feminist speculation of
literature. In the course of that speculation, it will no doubt become
necessary to renounce a simple feminist label as a remnant of the sort
of opposition which, in Nietzsche's phrase, "woman" confounds by
an unfathomable depth that is at the same time less than superficial,
"not even shallow." For the moment, however, let us claim the feminist title in order to signal at the outset a recognition of the historical
necessity to displace culture's consistent negation of that which is neither profound nor superficial but constitutive of the difference that
gives meaning to these terms. By following Nietzsche in naming this
difference "woman," one must bracket for the moment the obvious
fact that that name has its power to signify a stable entity already as
an effect of difference arrested in its movement between this term and
its implied other, "man."

To speak of "woman," then, as neither profound nor shallow but as
the suppressed vibration of the one term in the other is to textualize
that term—that is, to replace it in the signifying network that conditions meaning as a play of differences. Nietzsche's aphorism, therefore, is but a succinct textualization of "woman," one which leaves its
meaning suspended between the two extremes of unfathomable
depths and not-even-shallow surface. While this is a process we recognize as characterizing that textual production known as literature,
it is nonetheless the case that much of what is called literary theory
purports to explain this process, in effect, by opposing it—that is, by

69

positing a theoretical or critical discourse with which to account for literary production and which *in theory* operates outside the differential play of textualized meanings. In other words, some of the most concerted, serious efforts to account for textual practice have been informed by an initial resistance—sometimes even hostility—to that practice. In the course of the past decade, in North America, this resistance or hostility has been able to focus on the work of so-called textual theorists or thinkers who have asserted and affirmed the textualization one must engage in order to speak of literature. Because textual thought renders indistinct the distinctions among different genres of writing (in particular, fictional as opposed to nonfictional modes and also what we call literature and theory), the resistance to this thought has often taken the form of insisting that the laws of genre are not so easily revoked, and that therefore the literary or poetic claims of much current critical writing may be safely disregarded as pretentious deception. One native critic has gone so far as to suggest—only half-facetiously, it seems—that truth-in-advertising laws be invoked so as to suppress "fiction which presents itself in the guise of scholarly textual commentary."[1]

When the argument that genre exists as a true criterion is carried out in English, it is often set over against a countervailing notion of generic undecidability which has been formulated in another language—French, for example, as in Jacques Derrida's "La Loi du genre," translated as "The Law of Genre."[2] As the translation of this title reminds us, English has adopted the word "genre" from French in order to designate specifically categories of works of art: literature, painting, and so on. For distinctions within the world of nonart, English uses more English words (kind, sort, type, genus, species, etc.). Yet, for some reason, in order to talk about fine art, like fine *cuisine*, English-speakers need French words. In French, of course, the word *genre* has a much more general use, artistic *genre* being only one kind of a kind of thing. But also in French, the word *genre* has a sense it specifically does not have in English, at least not ordinarily, since this language has reserved that sense for another English word with the same Latin root—that word is gender, either sexual or grammatical. The use of "genre" in English makes a borrowing, then, which sets aside the category of gender and keeps the sexual separate from the textual.

However, just as one linguistic community cannot do without a persistent trade across its borders, even if the official state of a national language—like a national economy—might seem to be better off if it instituted a ban on foreign imports, so too the question of genre cannot sever so easily its connection to the question of gender. And in that case, perhaps the theoretical distinction of fiction from nonfiction derives part of its conviction from the distinction of the sexes which in English one might say is self-evident or, in French, *qui va de soi.* Thus in proposing to read what we call a literary or fictional text as nonfictional or theoretical, one risks provoking a resistance fueled by the culture's investment in a secure differentiation of the sexes. The risk may even increase if the text one reads in this fashion uses a non-gender-inflected language. English, for example, differs from many other Indo-European languages in that the gender distinction is pertinent only as a natural or self-evident attribute of the (usually animate) things denoted by words rather than as a grammatical, law-governed classification of words themselves which can ignore the gender or lack of gender of the thing denoted. When imported thought begins mixing up the genres and alarming our native thinkers, prompting them to cast about for a legal injunction against the practice, what may be at issue is a particularly Anglo-American form of the conviction that grammatical law follows natural law, an idea which is not too far from the notion that God, when he communicates to his creation, speaks—or writes—in English.

In any case, it is not the simple reversal of genre/gender oppositions which is in question here—fiction instead of textual commentary, female instead of male—since that kind of reversal, as everyone knows, leaves the oppositional dyad intact and unquestioned and the "natural" meanings of English plainly in place. Genre/gender oppositions, like the psychoanalytic distinction phallic/castrated, can be reversed as many times as one likes without upsetting the logic of identity or the economy of the same, of the presence or absence of the same. Because the feminine is neither phallic nor castrated if one takes those terms literally and can be either phallic or castrated if one takes those terms figuratively, it occurs as an admixture within the phallic economy of interpretation to which the phallic law can be applied only by suppressing a difference that exceeds it. For this reason, feminist criticism which has taken gender as an unquestioned ground of its practice has so far for the most part been unable to gain much critical leverage on phallic presuppositions.

It is not, then, in order to illustrate or apply a theory that I turn to Hawthorne's *The Scarlet Letter*. Rather, that text, because it stages the confrontation of a "feminine" art, a "feminine" thought, with the law of genre/gender, the phallic law of the truth of the same, also sets before us the terms within which to consider the question of its own genre or gender. And since, by its title, *The Scarlet Letter* assumes the name of that which is set in motion within its pages, it may be read as thinking the relation between the text of the letter—the literary text—and the letter of the law. That it does so in the form of a historical narrative where that law is situated at the origin of a specifically American cultural experience might just help to clarify whatever it is in a theoretical practice that invests national and linguistic boundaries with more than conventional meaning.

Before proceeding, however, a word is in order about Hawthorne's genre in the English sense, that is, about the distinction between romance and novel which the author invoked with a certain insistence. It would seem that this distinction served to indicate another differentiation which the unknown writer from Salem, Massachusetts, wished to make clear early in his career: Nathaniel Hawthorne did not want to be mistaken for a female scribbler of novels. *The Scarlet Letter*, therefore, is subtitled *A Romance*. I bring this up in part because it answers a certain expectation about Hawthorne's genres even though I do not propose to make any significant contribution to genre studies in general. As I suggested above, feminist literary thought which adopts genre/gender as its category has had too much obvious difficulty extracting itself from the phallocentric categories that have always ordered stories about gender. However, this may also be a promising space in which to turn up some textual evidence for what was earlier simply asserted: that genre (in the Anglo-American, formalist, aesthetic sense) preserves a link to *genre* (in the French, politicosexual sense). If Hawthorne can be taken as a model on this issue, then a question about the genre of titles will have to raise other questions about the distinction between feminine scribblings and masculine literature.

For example, Judith Fetterley, author of *The Resisting Reader: A Feminist Approach to American Fiction*,[3] has suggested that, if the canon of

American literature contains so few works by women, then it is in part because of this longstanding Hawthornian prejudice against novels in favor of romance. Moreover, Fetterley implies that this is because romance is such a highly symbolic genre, and that the erection of symbols of such dimension (scarlet letters, black cats, white whales) remains a male-centered enterprise.[4]

To survey this ground more closely, one would need to consider Hawthorne's apparent anxiety about his own *genre*—in the French sense—particularly as it surfaces in "The Custom-House," the preface to *The Scarlet Letter*. One would need, that is, to follow John Irwin's recent lead in addressing all the patriarchal spite which the "writer of story-books" fears will come down upon his head if he leaves his government sinecure at the Salem Custom-House for the business of literature.[5] The insistent metaphor of decapitation running through this preface seems clear enough language to put one on the track of a kindred sexual anxiety underlying Hawthorne's career choice. To scribble words on paper, to embroider extravagant, moonstruck fantasies instead of lending one's name to the customary laws of trade—what is that, after all, but to abdicate a masculine political privilege for an uncertain kind of literary title?

The subtitle of *The Scarlet Letter* is, as I said, *A Romance*. As is often the case, the second title tells one how to read the first, in the context of what genre, for example, one is meant to take the text. Its function here, moreover, would have to be doubly diacritical since *A Romance* was meant to be read as *Not a Novel* and *The Scarlet Letter*, therefore, as not a scribbling of feminine design.

For the Norton Critical Edition of *The Scarlet Letter* the cover design incorporates all sorts of information, including the names of no less than four editors and the phrase "an authoritative text." Nowhere, however, does it make room for Hawthorne's original subtitle. In fact, in this edition the subtitle only appears once in its indicated place following the title. Because *A Romance* has all but disappeared, one might not notice that, on the first page of the text and in his first note, the editor, Seymour Gross, refers to *The Scarlet Letter* as a "novel."[6] As if it made no difference. In effect, in the definitive Norton edition, *The Scarlet Letter* has been resubtitled "An Authoritative Text," even though the original title has thereby been changed. A tradition of literary scholarship has thus contrived virtually to wipe out certain traces which could lead one back to the politicosexual articulation of the text in question. As Fetterley and others have begun to notice, this authoritative aspect of the canon has contributed to the eclipse of what one might call the vast textile industry of homespun literary arts—including women's novels—on which New England's American Renaissance also rested. Yet it remains curious that someone who wields a significant authority over the canon (unlike feminist critics so far) can apparently disregard the difference between romance and novel. In this respect, the resisting reader turns out to be, as well, a more careful one. On the other hand, this reader's resistance may also have caused her to miss a slippage within the order of authority which has moved away from the terms of generic difference that Hawthorne invoked.[7] As a result perhaps of a crossing-over of resistances, one finds an authoritative editor of the canon reading *A Novel* while the extracanonical woman reads *A Romance*. What has occurred, then, is a reversal within the generic opposition which leaves phallogical authority undisturbed.

Turning now to Hawthorne's text, I find my gesture already outlined by the narrator of "The Custom-House" since, like the customs inspector, whoever would pick up the remnants of the tattered letter and try to figure out its design will have to become conversant with a ladies' mystery:

> It has been wrought, as was easy to perceive, with wonderful skill of needlework; and the stitch (as I am assured by ladies conversant with such mysteries) gives evidence of a now forgotten art, not to be recovered even by the process of picking out the threads. . . . [It] was a riddle . . . which I saw little hope of solving. And yet it strangely interested me. My eyes fastened themselves upon the old scarlet letter, and would not be turned aside. Certainly, there was some deep meaning in it, most worthy of interpretation, and which, as it were, streamed forth from the mystic symbol, subtly communicating itself to my sensibilities, but evading the analysis of my mind. (pp. 28–29)

Consider the "I" of this passage, which is to be read in the conjunction of autobiography with fictional story-books, something like "Hawthorne" in quotes: does anything in its discourse assure one of its gender in this moment of encounter with an "A"—a capital A, like Lacan's "Autre avec un grand A," the Other with a capital O which is not embodied by any other (small o)? But here, at least, the A has been embroidered upon by a feminine art, now forgotten. Retrieving, recovering it, cannot be the work of the analysis of I's mind nor even the material analysis of the letter itself. It is rather in their juncture that both I and A become worthy of interpretation—but in that juncture, who can tell I's gender or A's genre?

Taking apart the cross-stitch of *The Scarlet Letter* will not recover the answer to this kind of question: it may, however, undo certain familiar patterns of interpretation and lay bare an intersection with the "material" of alterity.

The Letter of the Law Appliquée

I said above that *The Scarlet Letter* may be read as thinking the relation between the text of the letter and the letter of the law, or, in other terms, between the written work and its interpretation according to the laws of genre. Thus, a relation which is generally conceived as subordinating written texts to externally independent rules for the classification of writing by genre cannot be so simply applied in this case. To indicate how Hawthorne's text thinks this relation differently, we'll consider briefly two parallel scenes in which the letter and the law of its interpretation are displayed together but with contrasting effect. Of the many passages in the text where interpretation of the letter is explicitly in question, I have chosen these because they inflect the difference they display with gender. The first scene, following the order of the narrative, is the initial exposure of Hester Prynne's scarlet letter on Boston's public scaffold; the second is Arthur Dimmesdale's self-exposure and reenactment of this first scene when he ascends the same scaffold, but at night. I will take up these scenes, however, in reverse order.

Dimmesdale's watch on the scaffold is marked by an event which, though insignificant in itself, produces an interpretation of significance. As he stood there "a light gleamed far and wide over all the muffled sky," which, the narrator conjectures, "was doubtless caused by one of those meteors . . . burning out to waste in the vacant regions of the atmosphere" (p. 112). Although the form of this conjecture points to the probable negative material significance of the phenomenon—it is but matter consuming itself in a vacuum—the light produced by the conversion of energy acts as well to transform the scene as described. This transformation is twice marked in the passage as a conversion of the meaningless into the significant by means of figurative language: first when we read that the "familiar scene of the street . . . [was] visible, but with a singularity of aspect that *seemed* to give another moral interpretation to the things of this world than they had ever borne before" (italics added); and then again at the end of the same paragraph, where we read that Dimmesdale, Hester, and Pearl "stood in the noon of that strange and solemn splendor, *as if it were* the light that is to reveal all secrets, and the daybreak that shall unite all who belong to one another" (italics added). This is only the beginning, however, of a metaphoric conversion or interpretation that will end up going well beyond the narrator's two carefully qualified suggestions. As the passage continues in the next paragraph, the narrator remarks that for the Puritans "nothing was more common, in those days, than to interpret all meteoric appearances . . . as so many revelations from a supernatural source" (p. 113). Bracketing for a moment the narrator's comments on this customary form of interpretation, we follow the passage as it moves to the zenith of the interpretive movement, the final conversion of nothingness into a fully meaningful sign. It is Dimmesdale who completes the circle, for while "looking upward to the zenith, [the minister] beheld there the appearance of an immense letter,—the letter A,—marked out in lines of dull red light."

These paragraphs—like the event they describe—seem to demand interpretation. Not because a hidden sense needs to be uncovered but, as Henry James has remarked, because of an excess of meaning. James singles out parts of this passage to illustrate what he thought was one of the work's few defects—what he calls "a certain superficial symbolism." He quotes at length from the narrator's description of the meteoric light in the initial paragraph and judges it "imaginative, impressive, poetic," but adds that this admirable effect is lost when, as he writes, "almost immediately afterwards" Hawthorne goes on to evoke the minister's vision of the letter in the sky. With that, writes James, "we feel he goes too far" and he comments: "Hawthorne is perpetually looking for images which shall place themselves in picturesque correspondence with the spiritual facts with which he is concerned, and of course the search is of the very essence of poetry. But in such a process discretion is everything, and when the image becomes importunate it is in danger of seeming to stand for nothing more serious than itself." Although James is for the most part a sympathetic and careful reader of Hawthorne, I think he has misread this passage—but with an interesting result. By following the letter of Hawthorne's text—but also by restoring the intervening paragraph, hidden behind James's hedging phrase "almost immediately afterwards"—one may find the terms of this critique well-chosen but poorly aimed. Perhaps this is because Hawthorne is not, as James implies, concerned with only "spiritual" facts.[8]

First, what James terms "a superficial conceit"[9] finds an echo in the narrator's remark that Dimmesdale's interpretation could only be the symptom of morbid self-contemplation (p. 113). There is indeed, as James suggests, a failure of discretion in the search for an image, since in that process Dimmesdale, in the narrator's terms, "extended his egotism over the whole expanse of nature." If, as James writes, an "image" is importunate here and "in danger of seeming to stand for nothing more serious than itself," then is it not in the sense of imitation, likeness, or reflection—a mirror image? Perhaps what imposes here—dangerously in James's judgment—is the image as "nothing more serious than" the mirror of interpretation. The minister's act, which conceives a written sign in the closed narcissistic circle from the guilty subject back to itself, is a failure of discretion in the sense that it does not discern the difference between the interpreter/subject and an exteriority of the material world on which that subject imposes itself as image. At that moment, the whole differentiated expanse of nature becomes the subject's likeness, or, rather, repeats the sign whereby the subject acknowledges his identity to himself, his secret interiority. A is for both Arthur and Adulterer, that other name which signals the corruption of the essence of identity, since to adulter or adulterate is "to render spurious or counterfeit by the admixture of baser ingredients" (OED).

However, the paragraph which James skips over in his summary of the passage links Dimmesdale's interpretive act to the practice of a community which read "natural phenomena . . . as so many revelations from a supernatural source." Of this belief in a transcendent meaning of community, the narrator remarks: "It was, indeed, a majestic idea, that the destiny of nations should be revealed, in these awful hieroglyphics, on the cope of heaven. A scroll so wide might not be deemed too expansive for Providence to write a people's doom upon. The belief was a favorite one with our forefathers, as betokening that their infant commonwealth was under celestial guardianship of peculiar intimacy and strictness." Dimmesdale's vision of the sign is then measured against this "majestic idea" and, like a telescope collapsing on itself, the transcendence of meaning is revealed to be a device with which the self addresses itself: "But what shall we say, when an individual discovers a revelation, addressed to himself alone, on the same vast sheet of record! In such a case, it could only be the symptom of a highly disordered mental state, when a man, rendered morbidly self-contemplative by long, intense, and secret pain, had extended his egotism over the whole expanse of nature, until the firmament itself should appear no more than a fitting page for his soul's history and fate."

Dimmesdale's symptom is the particularization, the individualization of the shared belief in the transcendent meaning of the commonwealth. As such, however, it points to the contradiction within communal meaning which the transcendent interpretation turns away from, disregards. This contradiction is put into relief at the end of the chapter whose central scene we've been considering: there, in the aftermath of the meteoric appearance, Dimmesdale is confronted with the community of interpretation. Its spokesman, the church sexton, says to the minister: "But did your reverence hear of the portent that was seen last night? A great red letter in the sky,—the letter A,—which we interpret to stand for Angel. For, as our good Governor Winthrop was made an angel this past night, it was doubtless held fit that there should be some notice thereof!" Dimmesdale's reply is an equivocation: "'No,' answered the minister. 'I had not heard of it.'" The "it" here may refer either to the symbol—A—or to the symbolized—Angel, either to the sign or to its interpretation. This equivocation in turn signals Dimmesdale's ambiguous identity within the interpretive community of which he is a privileged representative— both a part of it and outside it. Thus, the sexton's report confirms Dimmesdale's revelation at the same time as it denies what the revelation revealed. These several strands of ambiguity converge in the phrase "the letter A," which occurs first in the description of the minister's vision ("the appearance of an immense letter,—the letter A,—

marked out in lines of dull red light") and is then repeated, set off with the same double punctuation, in the sexton's description ("A great red letter in the sky,—the letter A,—which . . ."). The letter A joins the community in its manifest appearance only to divide it in its apparent significance, which alternates within paired oppositions: Adulterer or Angel, Abject or Adored, Arthur or Another. The letter A thus turns in a mirror of interpretation, its image infinitely reversible without a change in its appearance.

The reversibility of the letter, what the narrator earlier called its lack of "definiteness" (p. 113), is resolved in the theocratic Puritan state, as we have seen, by the common belief in the transcendent source of the letter's meaning. Arthur Dimmesdale not only shares this belief, he internalizes it and thus comes to exemplify it. Thereby, however, the minister also becomes in himself the locus of the contradiction which the concept of transcendent meaning seeks to remove from the community's midst. As the guilty subject of equivocation, the identity which hides its difference behind an appearance of sameness, his example to the community of its own belief must itself remain equivocal. Therefore in the penultimate chapter, "The Revelation of the Scarlet Letter," when Dimmesdale returns to the scaffold in the full light of day and uncovers his breast before the gathered citizenry, his revelation shatters rather than binds community. Interpretation of what one saw (or did not see) is then a matter of individual sensibility and contradiction is made manifest. When the narrator concludes the description of the final scaffold scene by turning its interpretation over to the reader—"The reader may choose among these theories. We have thrown all the light we could acquire upon the portent" (p. 182)—it is as if to remind one that, in a world of untranscended appearance, all that remains to give meaning to community is what we call literature.

In *The Scarlet Letter*, this remainder retains the form of the material letter which Hester Prynne, after the shattering dispersal of the last scaffold scene, returns to take up again. To be sure, Hester's letter also marks the place of the guilty subject as determined by the agency of Puritan law. Yet unlike the instances of a transcendent mark which make Arthur the locus of guilty contradiction, the material application of the letter to Hester reveals a contradiction at the very source of judgment. This displacement of the contradiction already appears in the different role assigned to interpretation in the scene of Hester's punishment.

To begin with, there is no question about what anyone saw, as in the above scene. The letter, as "the point which drew all eyes" (p. 44), is clearly discerned:

> On the breast of her gown, in a fine red cloth, surrounded with an elab-
> orate embroidery and fantastic flourishes of gold thread, appeared the
> letter A. It was so artistically done, and with so much fertility and
> gorgeous luxuriance of fancy, that it had all the effect of a last and fitting
> decoration to the apparel which she wore; and which was of a splendor
> in accordance with the taste of the age, but greatly beyond what was
> allowed by the sumptuary regulations of the colony. (p. 43)

While interpretation has little role here in the narrator's description, it does obtain in the question of which law is to be applied to the adulteress. Significantly, this question is raised by gossips present at the scene who quarrel about the magistrates' judgment on Hester, one arguing that "they should have put the brand of hot iron on [her] forehead," another that she should be put to death: "This woman has brought shame upon us all and ought to die. *Is there no law for it?* Truly there is, both in the Scripture and the statute-book" (p. 42; italics added). When Hester appears with "that *Scarlet Letter*, so fantastically embroidered and illuminated upon her bosom" (p. 44), the gossips are dismayed. Says one to her *commères:* "What is it but to laugh in the faces of our godly magistrates and make a pride out of what they, worthy gentlemen, meant for a punishment?"

The judgment on Hester—as strictly interpreted—is simply that of display. In the words of the town beadle who, as we read, represented "the whole dismal severity of the Puritanic code of law, which it was his business to administer in its final and closest *application* to the offender" (p. 43; italics added), Mistress Prynne "shall be set where man, woman and child may have a fair sight of her brave apparel, from this time till an hour past meridian." And he adds "A blessing on the righteous Colony of the Massachusetts, where iniquity is dragged out into the sunshine!" (p. 44).

By means of the counterpoint of the woman's chorus of gossips, which disputes the law as applied to Hester, and the official representation of the law, which drags iniquity out into the sunshine, a question is allowed to surface about the meaning of this punishment as an instance of the law's application. Towards the end of the description of the scene, the narrator suggests that this question can only be answered by the "solemn presence of men no less dignified than the Governor and several of his counsellors, a judge, a general and the ministers of the town. . . . When such personages could constitute *part of the spectacle,* without risking the majesty or reverence of rank and office, it was safely to be inferred that the infliction of a legal sentence would have an earnest and effectual meaning" (p. 46; italics added). In other words, it is the presence of the theocratic state's officials, their self-display on the balcony dominating the scaffold, that dissipates the potential ambiguity of this instance of the law's application of its mark upon the guilty subject. But with this suggestion, we see that the ambiguity has been not so much resolved as displaced upwards onto the personages who both guarantee the meaning of the spectacle as if from some transcendent position, and yet are themselves "part of the spectacle" they guarantee.

The effects of this displacement of ambiguity, from the guilty subject at the center of the spectacle onto the personages embodying the law at the margins of the scene of its application, can be traced to the letter itself, which, in applying the law of display of guilt to Hester's example, at the same time went "greatly beyond what was allowed by the sumptuary regulations of the colony." That is, the letter is an instance of display in two senses of the word, one of which the law invokes as the instrument of righteous truth in this "land where iniquity is searched out, and punished in the sight of rulers and people" (p. 49); the other of which the law—as sumptuary regulation—condemns as ostentatious expenditure. Thus, to make an ostentatious display of the law's display of guilt—as Hester's letter does—is to dissociate that law from itself in a fashion (the word is appropriate here) that leaves a doubt about the certain meaning of the symbol by which the law manifests itself to the community. In the face of this uncertainty, one may wonder how the simple presence of these dignified men could guarantee the effectual meaning of a legal sentence and what mark or sign assures the spectator that that presence in fact represents the legality of the law.

Unlike the meteor's immaterial light, which reveals the law to itself as in a mirror of interpretation and leaves no traces, the embroidery of the letter makes known the duplicity within the law itself. As both the prescription and proscription of display, the law shows itself to be infallibly a *scription*—a writing in a certain relation to the material exteriority of the sign. The law cannot take form except in the letter's difference—the very difference which is repressed by the narcissistic interpretation of signs as images of the interpreter. The articulation of the scarlet letter, in other words, discerns and displays the necessary complicity between the outlaw and the law, the design of difference and the sign of identity. To be sure, as John Irwin has observed, the position of the outcast wearer of the letter also figures the alienation of the self-conscious writer—"the feminine role of the artist in a Puritan, business-oriented society."[10] But Hawthorne's text, I believe, goes even further in relating the art of the lettered outcast to the central business of the community.

"It was the art—then, as now, almost the only one within a woman's grasp—of needlework" (p. 62). While Hester's "delicate and imaginative skill" should have found little use in a society where sumptuary laws restricted rich display, nevertheless we read that the products of her craft had a *necessary* function there.

> Public ceremonies, such as ordinations, the installation of magistrates, and all that could give majesty to the forms in which a new government *manifested itself* to the people, were, as a matter of policy, marked by a stately and well-conducted ceremonial, and a sombre, but yet a studied magnificence. Deep ruffs, painfully wrought bands and gorgeously embroidered gloves, were all deemed *necessary* to the official state of men assuming the reins of power; and were readily allowed to individuals dignified by rank or wealth, even while sumptuary laws forbade these and similar extravagances to the plebian order. . . .
>
> By degrees, nor very slowly, [Hester's] handiwork became what would now be termed the fashion. . . . Her needlework was seen on the ruff of the Governor; military men wore it on their scarfs, and the minister on his band. (p. 63; italics added)

Here one may pick out, with perhaps more precision than in the scene of Hester's punishment, what Hawthorne terms the *office* of the letter (p. 120) as illuminated by Hester's needlework. It is that which marks the law as law in its manifestation of itself but at the same time in contradiction with itself. As a supplementary device, embroidery designates the law with a sign of its own infraction. Thus we see that it is not the presence of these dignified men which guarantees the meaning of the law as applied to Hester, but the extravagant and extralegal mark on their persons of the law's manifest self-contradiction. There is, in other words, no guarantee of the letter's meaning as an instance of the law.

No formulation we might contrive of this inextricable relation between the manifest state and the extraneous design which is both cast out and "deemed necessary to the official state" can approach the economy of the text's own language. It was, we read, "as a matter of policy" that the new government marked its manifestation with a "studied magnificence"—a matter of *policy*, that is, and not of law. In the word Hawthorne chooses to designate this relation, a crossover has occurred between roots coming from the Greek *politeia/polis* (polity, state, political, police) and from the Latin *polītus* (polished, polite, refined, elegant). English has thus been left with a word which straddles a political division designating both "political sagacity; prudence, skill or consideration of expediency in the conduct of public affairs; statecraft" and "in a bad sense, political cunning, craftiness, dissimulation; a crafty device, stratagem, or trick" (*OED*).

Thus the office of the letter far exceeds its symbolic function of marking the guilty subject's exclusion from the center of law-governed society. According to the letter of Hawthorne's text, the policy of the mark situates as well a necessary inclusion of the unlawful accessory. The letter cannot be simply in the service of the law whose presence it signals only as an effect of absence. It is the office of the letter or the mark (in its extravagant wanderings over the manifest surface of the state's official aspect) to make known what the law does not, of itself, reveal: the policy of an unequal division and the accumulated disparities of power by which wealth signifies itself on the face of government as the negated logic of a sociopolitical order.

It is in this sense that Hester's art—the embroidery of the letter— may be read as a necessary difference which exceeds the law of the same. It is a speculation she embroiders on the position of the symbol of the guilty subject, the subject of nonidentity, the "woman" presented in social spectacle. This speculation of the letter overturns in its movement the narcissistic grounds of interpretation in the self-identical subject—as we may see, in conclusion, by turning to the chapter titled "Another View of Hester." Here, the narrator speculates on a certain speculation he ascribes to Hester as an "effect . . . of the position in respect to society that was indicated by the [letter]" (p. 118).

> A tendency to speculation, though it may keep woman quiet, as it does man, yet makes her sad. She discerns, it may be, such a hopeless task before her. As a first step, the whole system of society is to be torn down, and built up anew. Then, the very nature of the opposite sex, or its long hereditary habit, which has become like nature, is to be essentially modified, before woman can be allowed to assume what seems a fair and suitable position. Finally, all other difficulties being obviated, woman cannot take advantage of these preliminary reforms, until she herself shall have undergone a still mightier change; in which, perhaps, the ethereal essence, wherein she has her truest life, will be found to have evaporated. (p. 120)

This "speculation" cannot be specular, since the movement from the position of the thinking subject through "the whole system of society" back to itself does not close a circle but opens the possibility to thought of a woman who is essentially not a woman, as well as a man who is essentially not a man. If we may call such speculation feminist, then clearly it is only as a place to begin: a place at which to begin to think about both woman and man as other than guilty subjects which phallic law represses in its own midst.

Sexual Politics and Critical Judgment

Elizabeth A. Meese

Literature is no one's private ground; literature is common ground. Let us trespass freely and fearlessly and find our own way for ourselves.
—Virginia Woolf

A new scientific truth does not triumph by convincing its opponents and making them see the light, but rather because its opponents eventually die, and a new generation grows up that is familiar with it.
—Max Planck

From the beginning, women have been trespassers in the world's literary communities. We receive a vision of ourselves skating around the edges of groups of artistic and intellectual men, striking occasional relationships, enjoying fleeting patronages or glimmers of momentary recognition. Regardless of the literary mode or style we choose for our self-expression, regardless of our level of accomplishment, we remain the outsiders among insiders, the "Other" in Simone de Beauvoir's sense of the term. In a 1960 letter published in *The Winner Names the Age*, Lillian Smith offers a paradigmatic view of the woman writer's position in relation to the literary establishment:

> I have been curiously smothered during the past nine years; indeed, ever since *Killers of the Dream* (1949). When writers about "race" are discussed, I am never mentioned; when southern writers are discussed, I am not among them; when women writers are mentioned, I am not among them; when best-sellers are discussed, *Strange Fruit* (which broke every record for a serious book) is never mentioned. This is a curious amnesia; I have smiled at it, have laughed at it; but I know what it has done to me in sales and prestige.
> This is frank talk. Do not, I beg you, be embarrassed by it. I can still laugh it off most of the time; but now and then, I truly wonder. Whom, among the mighty, have I so greatly offended![1]

Smith aptly and painfully captures the woman writer's situation: when it comes to literary judgment, the overriding condition is invisibility resulting from sexual politics, exacerbated in her case by region and attitude toward race.

85

Of late it has become something of a commonplace among critics to acknowledge the political nature of the literary judgments used in constituting texts and in determining a writer's inclusion in or exclusion from the literary canon. There are politics of authorship (race, sex, ethnicity, and class), of form (undervaluation of short stories, letters, diaries, essays, oral testimonies), of region (every place but New York, California, and Boston), and of content as it reflects non-heterosexism, nonobjectivism, nonphallocentric heroism or any other nonexclusivist concern. (Clearly, it is easier to say what is not allowed, thus producing a reactive criticism, a criticism written from exclusion, than it is to elaborate what might be valued under a more inclusive politics of literary judgment.) The catalogue of injustices, abuses, and misrepresentations cited over the last decade by feminist critics is extensive.[2] While it bears repeating, ritualistically, in the way that chants and evocations do, it is my purpose to look at how criticism functions in relation to women writers, and why feminist literary criticism has not been more instrumental in changing the fundamental politics imbedded in method and judgment. I hope that, in the presentation of this particular view of the critical process, a clearer understanding of the challenge confronting feminist criticism might emerge.

How the critical community establishes literary reputation is at the heart of the problem for women writers and feminist critics. The complexity of the problem reveals itself easily in the questions it encompasses: What is great literature? How do we know when a book is a "classic"? What works comprise the literary canon and what principles inform the selection of texts? Who decides and by what means? The answers to these questions are, in theory, kept somewhat fluid. Obviously, certain writers like Chaucer, Shakespeare, and Milton enjoy permanence, but then there are numerous others whose reputations remain in a state of flux, waxing and waning in accord with the prevailing interests of the critical moment. In "Literature as an Institution: The View from 1980," Leslie Fiedler cynically observes: "We all know in our hearts that literature is effectively what we teach in departments of English; or conversely, what we teach in departments of English is literature. Within that closed definitional circle, we perform the rituals by which we cast out unworthy pretenders from our ranks and induct true initiates, guardians of the standards by which all song and story ought presumably to be judged."[3] The effects of this kind of exclusion are transparent: it places literature almost entirely in the service of white, male elite culture. The significance of works by writers outside of the mainstream is effectively diminished; as Tillie Olsen explains, "The rule is simple: whenever anyone of that sex, and/or class, and/or color, generally denied enabling circumstances, comes to recognized individual achievement, it is not by virtue of special capacity, courage, determination, will (common qualities), but because of chancy luck, combining with those qualities."[4] As most contemporary writers admit, albeit reluctantly, after the slings and arrows of the marketplace, it is the critics and teachers who create literary reputations, and critical neglect, whether occasioned by overt hostility or benign disinterest, produces the same result: women's works are not read, taught, studied, or discussed.

In a profound sense, the writer and the critic have been at odds with one another for centuries—at least since the secularization of literary forms, the increasing divergence of intellectual prose from other modes of discourse, and the changing function of criticism.[5] It remains the artist's role to challenge social conventions and to destroy artistic constraints in the process of making art. Unlike the artist, the critic too often serves the institutions of culture by assimilating the dissenting voices within only narrowly circumscribed limits; thus, George Stade notes:

> That literature has social functions is no longer news, although storytellers often deny it. They deny it because their private interests in their stories are at odds with the institutional ones—for humans differ from animals in that the interests of the individual human are often at odds with the interests of the group. Among such interests is the interest in stories. The private functions of literature . . . are at odds with the institutional functions, or there would be no need for critics, whose institutional function is to coopt private subversiveness for the public interest.[6]

Lagging behind, as categorizer, interpreter, ameliorator, as reactive rather than active, the critic is a conservator of culture, a perpetuator of the very traditions the artist is in the process of attacking. There is a circularity about this: by attacking old traditions, the artist creates the material out of which new traditions emerge; without a text, the critic has nothing to do; the artist without a critic (or worse, without a publisher) is silenced until one emerges. Both have their respective arenas of power.

☙

If we are to expand our consideration of literature beyond the traditional literary canon, we need to understand the critical dynamics underlying the perpetuation of conventions. In his collection of essays, *Is There a Text in This Class? The Authority of Interpretive Communities*, Stanley Fish presents a view of critical judgments as issuing from an interpretive community, which, when examined from a feminist perspective, provides a useful means of describing the nature of critical bias. Perhaps inadvertently, Fish helps us to see clearly what we have always intuited. A strong insider-outsider dynamic, taking the form of a gender-based literary tribalism, comes into play as a means of control. Critics who permit the possibility of variations in critical interpretation, as opposed to those seeking the *Ur*-reading, immediately face the problem of closing ranks against the extremes of relativism in interpretation. Otherwise, the authority of the mainstream literary tradition could be seriously threatened. Fish guards against this by invoking the concept of "community":

> What will, at any time, be recognized as literature is a function of a communal decision as to what will count as literature. All texts have the potential of so counting, in that it is possible to regard any stretch of language in such a way that it will display those properties presently understood to be literary. In other words, it is not that literature exhibits certain formal properties that compel a certain kind of attention; rather, paying a certain kind of attention (as defined by what literature is understood to be) results in the emergence into noticeability of the properties we know in advance to be literary. The conclusion is that while literature is still a category, it is an open category, not definable by fictionality, or by a disregard of propositional truth, or by a predominance of tropes and figures, but simply by what we decide to put into it.[7]

While it is true that Fish represents only one current in today's confluence, other critics who disagree with him in some respects seem to accept the concept of the authoritative community. Harold Bloom assumes such a community.[8] M. H. Abrams, in "How to Do Things with

Texts," observes: "Stanley Fish seems to me right in his claim that the linguistic meanings we find in a text are relative to the interpretive strategy we employ, and that agreement about meanings depends on membership in a community which shares an interpretive strategy."[9] Abrams then asserts his own position, maintaining that the text, invested with the author's meaning, is the source of control over the interpretations produced by the critic. Such a view grows problematic when the notion of the critic as the writer's linguistic heir proves as well that some have been disinherited.

Once the illegitimate children perceive the exclusivity masked in the illusion of objectivity that is perpetuated by this interpretive community, considerable bitterness results. Still resonant today is the outsider's view expressed by Virginia Woolf in *Three Guineas* (Olsen calls this work a "savage" essay emerging from "genius brooding on . . . exclusion"),[10] and epitomized in her fictitious "Outsiders' Society," an anonymous and secret society for the daughters of educated men. In the passage that follows, Woolf's persona is ironically the "insider" (occupant of domestic space) looking "sidelong from an upper window" at the "solemn sight" of the male community in all its awesome symbolic and real power, enrobed and ascendant. They move freely, related to each other in the procession of generations:

> There they go, our brothers who have been educated at public schools and universities, mounting those steps, passing in and out of those doors, ascending those pulpits, preaching, teaching, administering justice, practising medicine, transacting business, making money. It is a solemn sight always—a procession, like a caravanserai crossing the desert. Great-grandfathers, grandfathers, fathers, uncles—they all went that way, wearing their gowns, wearing their wigs, some with ribbons across their breasts, others without. One was a bishop. One was a professor. Another a doctor.[11]

They are self-perpetuating in their authority, these generations of powerful men. The ones who drop out of the procession are excluded in a manner similar to women. They are cloaked in silence, distant; or, divested of robes, wigs and ribbons, they wear shabby clothes and hold only menial jobs.

Critics like Fish, Bloom, and Abrams genuinely believe in their community of critics; they march in the procession, speaking the truth from their own positions of privilege but suggesting other truths to feminists, Marxists, and critics of the nonmajority culture. We see that the "interpretive community" is really the "authoritative community." Even though Fish regards criticism as an "open category," we are forced to see it, like his version of community, as a closed system which excludes us from the arena of its authority. In her time, Woolf perceived a similar circularity in the closed system of the great English universities: "With what other purpose were the universities of Oxford and Cambridge founded, save to protect culture and intellectual liberty? For what other object did your sisters go without teaching or travel or luxuries themselves except that with the money so saved their brothers should go to schools and universities and there learn to protect culture and intellectual liberty?"[12] The fact that literature is simply another cultural institution requiring protection dictates a process of circumscription.

Interpretive communities, like tribal communities, possess the power to ostracize or to embrace, to restrict or to extend membership and participation, and to impose norms—hence their authority. In her article "Dancing through the Minefield: Some Observations on the Theory, Practice and Politics of a Feminist Criticism," Annette Kolodny notes that "the power relations inscribed in the form of conventions within our literary inheritance . . . reify the encodings of those same power relations in the culture at large."[13] The system is mutually reinforcing—designed and chosen to mirror a system of power relationships. Thus, Fish states explicitly that credible interpretations issue not from just any critic but from members of the club: "The reader is identified not as a free agent, making literature in any old way, but as a member of a community whose assumptions about literature determine the kind of attention he pays and thus the kind of literature he 'makes.' . . . The act of recognizing literature . . . proceeds from a collective decision as to what will count as literature, a decision that will be in force only so long as a community of readers and believers continues to abide by it" (p. 11). His remarks contain the answer to the question, Why the failure of so many feminist commentaries aimed at demonstrating the stature of neglected works by women?

Fish sets the scene for this discussion in the introduction to his work *Is There a Text in This Class?* Here he argues that every native speaker essentially experiences the same text when reading a literary work. Variations manifest themselves at a secondary level, in the form of emotional responses to that basic perceptual experience, and result in discrepancies in critical response. Fish then concludes that various critics of a text share the same reading experience, but "that their critical preconceptions lead them either to ignore or devalue it" (p. 6). Although in principle critical argument occurs on the level of rational discourse, judgments are undeniably built upon affective responses, learned or spontaneous. It is difficult to imagine, for example, any feminist reader who could "value" Norman Mailer's judgment in *Advertisements for Myself*, the classic representation of man "thinking through his body":

> I have a terrible confession to make—I have nothing to say about any of the talented women who write today. . . . I can only say that the sniffs I get from the ink of women are always fey, old-hat . . . too dykily psychotic, crippled creepish, fashionable, frigid . . . or else bright and stillborn. Since I've never been able to read Virginia Woolf, and am sometimes willing to believe it can conceivably be my fault, this verdict may be taken fairly as the twisted tongue of a soured taste, at least by those readers who do not share with me the ground of departure—that a good novelist can do without everything but the remnant of his balls.[14]

Unlike many writers of criticism, Mailer makes his fundamental assumptions explicit. He is not obligated to feign objectivity. The object of his ridicule is viewed similarly by others who might not make such a public declaration but agree with him nonetheless.

Mailer's pronouncement points to the problem in Fish's scheme: the importance placed on persuasion as the means of establishing consensus as to what constitutes our shared assumptions. Fish knows that this is the sticking point, although he has found no way around it. He realizes that standards issue from assumptions which then determine the course of critical debate: "Assumptions do not stand in an independent relationship to verifying procedures, they determine the shape of verifying procedures, and if you want to persuade someone else that he is wrong you must first persuade him to the assumptions within which what you say will be convincing" (p. 296). By extension, assumptions do not exist in an independent relationship to literary judgments, yet few things are harder to change than beliefs forged around such fundamental factors as sex, race, ethnicity, and

class, perhaps because these attitudes issue from the critic's personal
and sometimes unarticulated belief system. A continuation of this
imaginary dialogue between Virginia Woolf and Stanley Fish (it would
do no good to talk with Mailer) throws the problem into relief. Woolf
claimed in *A Room of One's Own* that "when a subject is highly controversial—and any question about sex is that—one cannot hope to tell
the truth. One can only show how one came to hold whatever opinion
one does hold."[15] However, this is precisely what Mailer did in the
passage above. Fish and Woolf agree: when the differences are so
basic, the arguments go unheard. It is like shouting across the Grand
Canyon.

From Fish's viewpoint, however, the problem is not insurmount-
able; we agree every day, he maintains, on what interpretations are
acceptable and unacceptable. He argues for a "limited plurality" of
meanings determined by the subcommittees recognized by the reigning literary-critical establishment (pp. 342–44). But this particular
way around the critical impasse of conflicting interpretations places
the feminist critic right back at the same point of requiring communal
legitimization: one only gains acceptance and recognition for what
the community is willing to accept. Fish leads us to believe that if we
proceed according to certain conventions, recognition will be granted:
"Not only must what one says about a work be related to what has
already been said (even if the relation is one of reversal) but as a consequence of saying it the work must be shown to possess in a greater
degree than had hitherto been recognized the qualities that properly
belong to literary productions, whether they be unity and complexity,
or unparaphrasability, or metaphoric richness, or indeterminacy and
undecidability" (p. 351). In short, the new interpretation must reveal
that the work is other (possesses certain accepted qualities) than it has
previously been shown or understood to be. Of course, most critics,
feminists included, set out or think they are setting out to do precisely
what Fish describes. The more vigorously Fish argues to allay his colleagues' fears of rampant interpretive anarchy, the more clearly the
feminist critic perceives the power held by members of this interpretive community. They control the admissibility of facts, texts, and
evidence, as well as the norms constitutive of reasonableness in argu-
mentation. Out of commitment to the illusion of objectivity, they miss

an essential distinction that Camus apprehended: "There are crimes of passion and crimes of logic. The boundary between them is not clearly defined."[16]

Fish very cleverly catches all of us up in his critical net. Like it or not, we all play the game because, for him, there is no other. Even if we reject the rules we are still participants, because the rules themselves include the rejection of the rules—an inauspicious position for those who are not members of the authoritative community. You become a member when the community makes you one, and not necessarily by virtue of how well you perform critical acts. The truth that Fish fails to disclose is that membership is a privilege (conferred by those in power) rather than a right (earned by skill).

Fish's work is useful to feminist critics because he redirects our attention, away from the mystique of the text—from arguments concerning "facts," "truth," "beauty" and "universality"—toward the more political considerations of how literary value is legislated and culture thereby shaped. Because he speaks as a member of the authoritative community whose arguments in any contest of persuasion are invested with undeniable value, if not validity, he can honestly claim that disputes are settled by persuasion, that there is no position of privilege, and that one's argument will be considered, if not accepted. In contrast, the trespassers find themselves on shifting ground—trained on the one hand to construct arguments from textual and contextual evidence which then have little impact, and, on the other, to avoid unseemly debates, in reality the fundamental ones, predicated upon "extraliterary" assumptions concerning the nature of social and political reality, or the sexual politics of literary judgment. Ishmael Reed expresses similar frustration from the viewpoint of the black writer caught in the same system of judgment: "Art is what white people do. All other people are 'propagandists.'"[17]

❦

This brings us back to the real question: what difficulties are involved in attempting to change a community of Mailer-like authorities? Approaches to the problem have varied and continue to vary as we refine our understanding of the problem itself. In spite of her life-

long psychic and artistic struggle against "being despised," Virginia
Woolf, like some later feminist critics, was never certain that women
should join the authoritative community if they could:

> We have to ask ourselves, here and now, do we wish to join that pro-
> cession, or don't we? On what terms shall we join that procession?
> Above all, where is it leading us, the procession of educated men? The
> moment is short; it may last five years; ten years, or perhaps only a
> matter of a few months longer. But the questions must be answered;
> and they are so important that if all the daughters of educated men did
> nothing, from morning to night, but consider that procession, from
> every angle, if they did nothing but ponder it and analyse it, and think
> about it and read about it and pool their thinking and reading, and
> what they see and what they guess, their time would be better spent
> than in any other activity now open to them.[18]

Woolf has not been the only woman writer to explore the price of inclusion or the benefits of exclusion. Inclusion requires participation
in the perpetuation of what Michel Foucault calls the "'regime' of
truth."[19] Lillian Smith, whose words formed the basis for Adrienne
Rich's later exploration in "Disloyal to Civilization: Feminism, Racism,
Gynephobia," elaborates on the situation as follows: "Freud said once
that woman is not well acculturated; she is, he stressed, retarded as a
civilized person. I think what he mistook for her lack of civilization is
woman's lack of *loyalty* to civilization."[20] By virtue of her separateness,
woman develops immunities to certain ideological positions (segrega-
tion for Smith) and freedom from certain behavioral and attitudinal
compulsions (warmaking for Woolf and heterosexism for Rich). In the
best instances, a valuable perspective and critique of culture issues
from women's disengagement.

   At the same time, control by such a relatively homogeneous group
of critics has resulted in extremely narrow views of what great literature is and what criticism does, not so much because critics enjoy
seeing reflections of themselves and their values in what they praise
(though this is partially true), but because they pretend to equality,
objectivity, and universality. In terms suggested by Camus, such a
hegemony fosters dissent by employing "a theoretical equality [which]
conceals great factual inequalities."[21] The fundamental assumptions
underlying judgments are disguised, perhaps even from those who
adhere to them, and produce a distortion in the act of reading itself.

Margaret Atwood offers a characteristic description of the woman writer's experience with phallic criticism: "A man who reviewed my *Procedures for Underground* . . . talked about the 'domestic' imagery of the poems, entirely ignoring the fact that seven-eighths of the poems take place outdoors. . . . In this case, the theories of what women ought to be writing about, had intruded very solidly between the reader and poems, rendering the poems themselves invisible to him."[22] The result of criticism like this is that we need to consider everything anew, in a complete re-vision of women's work from text to theory. Annette Kolodny explains: "Whether its focus be upon the material or the imaginative contexts of literary invention; single texts or entire canons; the relation between authors, genres, or historical circumstances; lost authors or well-known names, the variety and diversity of all feminist literary criticism finally coheres in its stance of almost defensive re-reading."[23] By virtue of their pretense to critical objectivity, literary critics have created the need for a criticism of advocacy, espousing special values based on gender, ethnicity, race, and class. Woolf detected this intrusion of gender in critical assumptions at work; as the values of men and women differ in life, so these differences are reflected in literary judgment: "This is an important book, the critic assumes, because it deals with war. This is an insignificant book because it deals with the feelings of women in a drawing room. A scene in a battlefield is more important than a scene in a shop— everywhere and much more subtly the difference of value persists."[24] This axiological discrepancy creates the need for feminist criticism to base its work at times on different texts from those designated as the literary canon by representatives of the current regime of truth.

Fish is at least cognizant of the difficulty of effecting change in matters of belief; for after all, at issue is an ideology masked in the shape of a critical paradigm. He comments: "It is always possible to entertain beliefs and opinions other than one's own; but that is precisely how they will be seen, as beliefs and opinions *other than one's own*, and therefore as beliefs and opinions that are false, or mistaken, or partial, or immature, or absurd" (p. 361). Fish does not take this far enough. He clearly perceives the interplay between conflicting structures of belief, but stops short of questioning its implications. At this point, his position of privilege in the authoritative community appears to undercut his sense of urgency.

The most fortunate circumstance of women's writing in the Western world is that its production, though ignored, devalued, and misrepresented, could never be completely extinguished. Women could be denied education, employment, publication, and honest critical appraisal, but as Woolf keenly observed, ink and paper were the cheapest, most readily available tools for the practice of one's trade. She immediately detected this essential feature of the "profession of literature": "There is no head of the profession; no Lord Chancellor . . . no official body with the power to lay down rules and enforce them. We cannot debar women from the use of libraries; or forbid them to buy ink and paper; or rule that metaphors shall only be used by one sex, as the male only in Academies of music was allowed to play in orchestras." [25] Women could not be programmed or policed thoroughly enough to keep them out of the literary profession. They were saved by the very nature of the craft itself: the act of writing is solitary, accessible to anyone who is literate (still a fact of its elitism), and as such the institution of literature admits its own subversion.

☺

Feminist criticism is a monumental undertaking which involves changing the very structure/sex of knowledge, thereby attempting to liberate us from what Diana Hume George calls an "operational model that artificially . . . dualizes intellectual activity and sexuality." [26] The problem confronting us is both epistemological and political—each equally significant and inseparable from the other. For years feminist critics have hedged on both counts, wanting to believe on the one hand in that "theoretical equality," and fearing on the other the fragmentation that could result from definition and the articulation of methodology (an inchoate ideological map). Consciously or not, we have obscured the terms of the dispute, and with them the need to differentiate between criticism written by women and feminist criticism. Within feminist criticism, we have avoided both the political and the epistemological, as though there were no purpose in recapitulating the politics of gender (which threaten to separate women from men and from the institutions of culture).

In the mid-seventies, for example, very few feminist critics were sympathetic with the notion of "difference." The recent acceptance of poststructuralist approaches has provoked a reconsideration of this earlier position. Elizabeth Abel, in her introduction to the essays collected in *Writing and Sexual Difference*, explains that "the notion of difference has only recently emerged as a focus of feminist criticism. Initially, feminist theorists bolstered claims for equality with claims for similarity." The value she sees in this new focus is that it affords "the feminist critic a position closer to the mainstream of critical debate." [27] Beyond this dream of acceptability, there is no more reason to value the potential in the concept of "difference" now than there was to have rejected it seven years ago. Because of its nature and its origins, feminist critics should approach this current preoccupation cautiously. I am not arguing against deconstruction; rather, I am suggesting that we examine carefully the relationship between feminism and deconstruction before we commit ourselves to it.

When broad change has not been effected, it is as difficult to escape cynicism as to determine its appropriate object. At the English Institute session on canon formation, Fiedler, observing the "ultimate irony" of the situation, asks why members of "the elite guard" have volunteered to entertain this attack on their values: "Can it be because they believe in tolerance more? Or are they, on the off chance that one or more of us dissenters may be right, cannily hedging their bets? Or do they suffer us gladly, knowing that at this point, all dissent, whether populist, feminist, Marxist, or Third World, can be assimilated, neutralized, sterilized . . . ?" [28] Fiedler poses nagging questions that return us to the issue at hand: how can we ever expect to transform assumptions and judgments? Critics and philosophers, reflecting their essential idealism, espouse a commitment to change. Fish reveals his own idealism when he says that the critic is not "trapped forever in the categories of understanding at one's disposal (or the categories at whose disposal one is), but that the introduction of new categories or the expansion of old ones to include new (and therefore newly seen) data must always come from the outside or from what is perceived, for a time, to be outside" (pp. 314–15). Still, it is never clear how criticism itself, employing its own favored methodologies and working within its own constraints, ever transforms the "extrinsic" into the "intrinsic."

Some proponents of poststructuralism, engaged in their own attack on the ideological character of discourse, believe that criticism has finally freed itself of its orientation toward objectivity and universality. It is tempting to regard the poststructuralist position as pervasive, characteristic of criticism of the past decade. And yet, far from epitomizing critical activity today, poststructuralists have made only a beginning in their attack on the historically rooted traditions of criticism. In his discussion "Conventional Conflicts," Hayden White suggests the complexity of efforts to reform the theory and practice of criticism: "Any appeal to the 'interpretive community' must fail for the more fundamental reason that there is no such thing as *the* interpretive community but rather a hierarchy of such communities, each with its own conventions and all more or less antagonistic to the rest."[29] White's observation discloses the inherent limitation of basing revisionary efforts on a monolithic approach to the critical community. His point further reinforces the view that the only real common denominator underlying today's various interpretive schools is the patriarchal substructure of the discipline of criticism as a whole. The political nature of the struggle is heightened further when coupled with the realization that, as White puts it, "it is the privilege of devotees of dominant conventions either to pay attention or not to any new practice appearing on the horizon of a discipline."[30] Just as the masters are never obliged to learn the language of the slave, the hierarchy of critical communities will continue to resist feminist, black, and Marxist criticism as long as the power configuration upon which it rests remains undisturbed.

The records of the new and newly seen are accumulating in a swiftly mounting challenge to the old structures of knowledge. As Foucault suggests in *Power/Knowledge*, "The essential political problem for the intellectual is . . . that of ascertaining the possibility of constituting a new politics of truth. The problem is not changing people's consciousnesses—or what's in their heads—but the political, economic, institutional regime of the production of truth."[31] In other words, prevailing paradigms reflect and are reflected in the current regime of truth. Truth does not hold an independent relationship to systems of power. It results from or is coincident with the very power which structures knowledge itself. Thus, our effort as feminist critics necessarily becomes highly political when approaching a paradigm from the outside. Foucault explains, "It's not a matter of emancipating truth from every system of power (which would be a chimera, for truth is already power) but of detaching the power of truth from the forms of hegemony, social, economic and cultural, within which it operates at the present time."[32] Foucault's observation speaks directly to those functioning outside of the literary critical establishment. It is clear that those excluded from the terms of truth are the very ones who perceive the inadequacies of the paradigm and experience the sense of urgency required to address it. A diffusion of the experience of discontinuity, beyond the ring of outsiders/trespassers, is needed before significant changes can occur. Such a generalized discomfort—the guilt or uncertainty that includes at least one novel by a woman in a course or invites feminist and other minority critics to the English Institute—marks the transitional phase toward paradigm revolution.

It has never been the obligation of literary critics, masked by the pretense of objectivity, to explicate the political origins and implications of their judgments. As a result, feminist critics need to question vigorously the methods and techniques of the inherited critical tradition. For example, Fish, in his notion of the interpretive (authoritative) community, proffers equality: literature is an open system, admitting any text (within reason); variations in interpretation are permitted (within reason); and persuasion is the means by which (reasonable) critics establish consensus. When he reinvests the authority for determining the limits of the reasonable in the profession as it is now constituted, Fish reinscribes the politics of exclusion he might have undone by defining literature as an open category and defending interpretive pluralism. But inherent in Fish's approach is the fact that the right to reason and the power of determination are located where power and reason have always rested in Western civilization—within the community of elite white men. He thereby preserves theoretical access at the expense of actual change. It makes sense to suspect, as Marxist critics have always noted from their vantage point, that our conceptual frameworks mirror ideology. The principle task of feminist criticism, in providing a necessary re-vision of the politics of "truth," is to make its own ideology explicit. If we seek to transform the structures of authority, we must first name them, and in doing so, unmask and expose them for all to see. As we forge a new criticism, our theories and assumptions must stay clear of a hegemonic role reversal that results from unending deconstructions of oppositions like male/female and insider/outsider, where the second term simply replaces the first in an infinite regression within an economy of oppression. The future of feminist criticism rests on defying the oppositional logic currently fostering the very concept of privilege.

In "When Our Lips Speak Together," Luce Irigaray warns us of the failure to extricate ourselves from this phallogocentric system: "If we continue to speak the same language to each other, we will reproduce the same story. Begin the same stories all over again. . . . If we continue to speak this sameness, if we speak to each other as men have spoken for centuries, as they taught us to speak, we will fail each other."[33] But the transformation of literature and criticism as cultural institutions demands a language of defiance rather than the silent complicity required of us for the perpetuation of phallogocentrism. Feminist criticism, if it is any good, is guaranteed to offend the mighty. This is essential to its value, a barometer of its ultimate effectiveness. A new politics, based not on negation but on the positive construction of woman through the solidarity of feminist practitioners, should yield a new theory as well as a new praxis.

Having reached the end, I return to the epigraphs. We are trespassing and creating our own way, as Woolf advises. The path is made clearer and the journey more urgent when the assumptions masking the actual with the theoretical are exposed: the case of Woolf versus Fish. The second epigraph for this article talks about the process of profound change in scientific knowledge, another set of fictions fused with power. While my discussion made no reference to science, Max Planck's remark could be taken as a comment on a question posed repeatedly in this article but never answered. The epigraphs might better serve as postscripts, reminders of what is required of us.

Shakespeare and the Exorcists

STEPHEN GREENBLATT

Between the spring of 1585 and the summer of 1586, a group of English Catholic priests led by the Jesuit William Weston, alias Father Edmunds, conducted a series of spectacular exorcisms, principally in the house of a recusant gentleman, Sir George Peckham of Denham, Buckinghamshire. The priests were outlaws—by an act of 1585 the mere presence in England of a Jesuit or seminary priest constituted high treason—and those who sheltered them were guilty of a felony, punishable by death. Yet the exorcisms, though clandestine, drew large crowds, almost certainly in the hundreds, and must have been common knowledge to hundreds more. In 1603, long after the arrest and punishment of those involved, Samuel Harsnett, then chaplain to the Bishop of London, wrote a detailed account of the cases, based upon sworn statements taken from four of the demoniacs and one of the priests. It has been recognized since the eighteenth century that Shakespeare was reading Harsnett's book, *A Declaration of Egregious Popish Impostures*, as he was writing *King Lear*.[1]

My concern is with the relation between these two texts, and the reader may well wonder what such a conventional concern has to do with "the role of theory in the study of literature." Source study is, as we all know, the elephants' graveyard of literary history, a graveyard situated at the farthest remove from the glamorous spiral of names, from Heidegger to Althusser, that adorns the present volume. My own work, moreover, has consistently failed to make the move that can redeem such unpromising beginnings: the move from a local problem to a universal, encompassing, and abstract problematic within which the initial concerns are situated. For me the study of literature is the study of contingent, particular, intended, and historically embedded works; if theory inevitably involves the desire to escape from contingency into a higher realm, a realm in which signs are purified of the slime of history, then this paper is written *against* theory.[2]

But I am not convinced that theory necessarily drives toward the abstract purity of autonomous signification, and even when it does,

101

its influence upon the study of literature may be quite distinct from its own designs. Indeed, I believe that the most important effect of contemporary theory upon the practice of literary criticism, and certainly upon *my* practice, is to subvert the tendency to think of aesthetic representation as ultimately autonomous, separable from its cultural context and hence divorced from the social, ideological, and material matrix in which all art is produced and consumed. This subversion is true not only of Marxist theory explicitly engaged in polemics against literary autonomy, but also of deconstructionist theory, even at its most hermetic and abstract. For the undecidability that deconstruction repeatedly discovers in literary signification also breaks down the boundaries between the literary and the nonliterary. The intention to produce a work of literature does not guarantee an autonomous text, since the signifiers always exceed and thus undermine intention. This constant exceeding (which is the paradoxical expression of an endless deferral of meaning) forces the collapse of all stable oppositions, or rather compels interpretation to acknowledge that one position is always infected with traces of its radical antithesis.[3] Insofar as the absolute disjunction of the literary and the nonliterary had been the root assumption of mainstream Anglo-American criticism in the mid-twentieth century, deconstruction emerged as a liberating challenge, a salutary return of the literary text to the condition of all other texts and a simultaneous assault on the positivist certitudes of the nonliterary, the privileged realm of historical fact. History cannot be divorced from textuality, and all texts can be compelled to confront the crisis of undecidability revealed in the literary text. Hence history loses its epistemological innocence, while literature loses an isolation that had come to seem more a prison than a privilege.

The problem with this theoretical liberation, in my view, is that it is forced, by definition, to discount the specific, institutional interests served both by local episodes of undecidability and contradiction and by the powerful if conceptually imperfect differentiation between the literary and the nonliterary. Deconstruction is occasionally attacked as if it were a satanic doctrine, but I sometimes think that it is not satanic enough; as John Wesley wrote to his brother, "If I have any fear, it is not of falling into hell, but of falling into nothing."[4] Deconstructionist readings lead too readily and predictably to the void; I would argue that in actual literary practice the perplexities into which one is led are not moments of pure, untrammeled *aporia* but localized strategies in particular historical encounters. Similarly, it is important to expose the theoretical untenability of the conventional boundaries between facts and artifacts, but the particular terms of this boundary at a specific time and place cannot simply be discarded. On the contrary, as I will try to demonstrate in some detail, these impure terms that mark the difference between the literary and the nonliterary are the currency in crucial institutional negotiations and exchange. This institutional economy is one of the central concerns of the critical method that I have called cultural poetics.

Let us return to Samuel Harsnett. The relation between *King Lear* and *A Declaration of Egregious Popish Impostures* has, as I have remarked, been known for centuries, but the knowledge has remained almost entirely inert, locked in the conventional pieties of source study. From Harsnett, we are told, Shakespeare borrowed the names of the foul fiends by whom Edgar, in his disguise as the bedlam beggar Poor Tom, claims to be possessed. From Harsnett too the playwright derived some of the language of madness, several of the attributes of hell, and a substantial number of colorful adjectives. These and other possible borrowings have been carefully catalogued, but the question of their significance has been not only unanswered but unasked.[5] Until recently, the prevailing model for the study of literary sources, a model in effect parcelled out between the old historicism and the new criticism, blocked such a question. As a free-standing, self-sufficient, disinterested art work produced by a solitary genius, *King Lear* has only an accidental relation to its sources: they provide a glimpse of the "raw material" that the artist fashioned. Insofar as this "material" is taken seriously at all, it is as part of the work's "historical background," a phrase that reduces history to a decorative setting or a convenient, well-lighted pigeonhole. But once the differentiations upon which this model is based begin to crumble, then source study is compelled to change its character: history cannot simply be set against literary texts as either stable antithesis or stable background, and the protective isolation of those texts gives way to a sense of their interaction with other texts and hence to the permeability of their boundaries. "When I play with my cat," writes Montaigne, "who knows if I am not a pastime to her more than she is to me?"[6] When Shakespeare borrows from Harsnett, who knows if Harsnett has not already, in a deep sense, borrowed from Shakespeare's theater what Shakespeare borrows back? Whose interests are served by the borrowing? And is there a larger cultural text produced by the exchange?

Such questions do not lead, for me at least, to the *O altitudo!* of radical indeterminacy. They lead rather to an exploration of the institutional strategies in which both *King Lear* and Harsnett's *Declaration* are embedded. These strategies, I suggest, are part of an intense and sustained struggle in late sixteenth- and early seventeenth-century England to redefine what Edward Shils calls the "central zone in the structure of society."[7] This zone is coterminous with the central value system, a system constituted by the general standards of judgment and action and affirmed by the society's elites. At the heart of the central value system is an affirmative attitude toward authority which is endowed, however indirectly or remotely, with a measure of sacredness. "By their very possession of authority," Shils writes, elites "attribute to themselves an essential affinity with the sacred elements of their society, of which they regard themselves as the custodians" (p. 5). In early modern England, these sacred elements are most often explicitly religious, and hence rivalry among elites competing for the major share of authority is expressed in struggles over religious doctrine and practice.

Harsnett's *Declaration* is a weapon in one such struggle, the attempt by the established and state-supported Church of England to eliminate competing religious authorities by wiping out pockets of rivalrous charisma. Charisma, as Shils redefines Weber's famous concept, is "awe-arousing centrality" (p. 257), the sense of breaking through the routine into the realm of the "extraordinary," and hence the sense of making direct contact with the ultimate, vital sources of legitimacy and authority (p. 130). Exorcism was for centuries one of the supreme manifestations in Latin Christianity of this charisma; "in the healing of the possessed," Peter Brown writes, "the *praesentia*" of the saints "was held to be registered with unfailing accuracy, and their ideal power, their *potentia*, shown most fully and in the most reassuring manner."[8] By late sixteenth-century England, neither the *praesentia* nor the *potentia* of the exorcist were reassuring to religious authorities.

In the *Declaration* Harsnett specifically attacks exorcism as practiced by Jesuits, but he had earlier levelled the same charges at the Puritan exorcist John Darrel.[9] And he does so not, as we might expect, to

claim a monopoly on the practice for the Anglican Church, but to expose exorcism itself as fraud. On behalf of established religious and
secular authority, Harsnett wishes, in effect, to cap permanently the
great rushing geysers of charisma released in rituals of exorcism. Spiritual *potentia* will henceforth be distributed with greater moderation
and control through the whole of the Anglican hierarchy, a hierarchy
at whose pinnacle is placed the sole legitimate possessor of absolute
charismatic authority, the monarch, Supreme Head of the Church in
England.

The arguments that Harsnett marshalls against exorcism have a ra-
tionalistic cast that may mislead us, for despite appearances we are
not dealing with a proto-Enlightenment attempt to construct a rational faith. Harsnett denies the presence of the demonic in those
whom Father Edmunds claimed to exorcise, but finds it in the exorcists themselves:

> And who was the deuil, the brocher, herald, and perswader of these
> vnutterable treasons, but *Weston* [*alias* Edmunds] the Iesuit, the chiefe
> plotter, and . . . all the holy Couey of the twelue deuilish comedians in
> their seuerall turnes: for there was neither deuil, nor vrchin, nor Elfe,
> but themselues. (pp. 154–55)

Hence, writes Harsnett, the "Dialogue between *Edmunds,* & the deuil"
was in reality a dialogue between "the deuil *Edmunds,* and *Edmunds*
the deuil, for he played both parts himselfe" (p. 86).

This strategy—the reinscription of evil onto the professed enemies
of evil—is one of the characteristic operations of religious authority in
the early modern period and has its secular analogues in more recent
history when famous revolutionaries are paraded forth to be tried as
counter-revolutionaries. The paradigmatic Renaissance instance is the
case of the *benandanti,* analyzed brilliantly by the historian Carlo
Ginzburg.[10] The *benandanti* were members of a Northern Italian folk
cult who, in dreams, believed that their spirits went forth to battle
with fennel stalks against their enemies, the witches. If the *benandanti*
triumphed, their victory assured the peasants of good harvests; if
they lost, the witches would be free to work their mischief. The Inquisition first became interested in the practice in the late sixteenth
century; after conducting a series of lengthy inquiries, the Holy Office
determined that the cult was demonic, and in subsequent interroga-

tions attempted, with some success, to persuade the witch-fighting *benandanti* that they were themselves witches.

Harsnett does not hope to persuade exorcists that they are devils; he wishes to expose their fraudulence and relies upon the state to punish them. But he is not willing to abandon the demonic altogether, and it hovers in his work, half-accusation, half-metaphor, whenever he refers to Father Edmunds or the pope. Satan served too important a function to be cast off lightly by the early seventeenth-century clerical establishment. The same state church that sponsored the attacks on superstition in the *Declaration of Egregious Popish Impostures* also cooperated, in this period as for generations before, in the prosecution of witches. These prosecutions significantly were handled by the secular judicial apparatus—witchcraft was a criminal offense like aggravated assault or murder—and hence reinforced rather than rivalled the bureaucratic control of authority. The eruption of the demonic into the human world was not denied altogether, but the problem would be processed through the proper, secular channels. In cases of witchcraft, the devil was defeated in the courts through the simple expedient of hanging his human agents and not, as in cases of possession, compelled by a spectacular spiritual counterforce to speak out and depart.

Witchcraft then was distinct from possession, and though Harsnett himself is skeptical about accusations of witchcraft, his principal purpose is to expose a nexus of chicanery and delusion in the practice of exorcism.[11] By doing so he hopes to drive the practice out of society's central zone, to deprive it of its prestige and discredit its apparent efficacy. In late antiquity, as Peter Brown has demonstrated, exorcism was based upon the model of the Roman judicial system: the exorcist conducted a formal *quaestio* in which the demon, under torture, was forced to confess the truth.[12] Now, after more than a millenium, this power would once again be vested solely in the state.

Harsnett's efforts, backed by his powerful superiors, did seriously restrict the practice of exorcism. Canon 72 of the new Church Canons of 1604 ruled that henceforth no minister, unless he had the special permission of his bishop, was to attempt "upon any pretense whatsoever, whether of possession or obsession, by fasting and prayer, to cast out any devil or devils, under pain of the imputation of imposture or cozenage and deposition from the ministry."[13] Since special permission was never granted, exorcism had, in effect, been ruled illegal. But it proved easier to drive exorcism from the center to the periphery than to strip it entirely of its power. Exorcism had been a process of reintegration as well as a manifestation of authority; as the ethnographer Shirokogorov observed of the shamans of Siberia, exorcists could "master" harmful spirits and restore "psychic equilibrium" to whole communities as well as individuals.[14] The pronouncements of English bishops could not suddenly banish from the land inner demons who stood, as Brown puts it, "for the intangible emotional undertones of ambiguous situations and for the uncertain motives of refractory individuals."[15] The possessed gave voice to the rage, anxiety, and sexual frustration that built up particularly easily in the authoritarian, patriarchal, impoverished, and plague-ridden world of early modern England. The Anglicans attempted to dismantle a corrupt and inadequate therapy without effecting a new and successful cure. In the absence of exorcism Harsnett could only offer the possessed the very slender reed of Jacobean medicine; if the recently deciphered journal of the Buckinghamshire physician, Richard Napier, is at all representative, doctors in the period struggled to treat a substantial number of cases of possession.[16]

But for Harsnett the problem does not really exist, for he argues that the great majority of cases of possession are either fraudulent or subtly called into existence by the ritual designed to treat them. Eliminate the cure and you eliminate the disease. He is forced to concede that at some distant time possession and exorcism were authentic, for, after all, Christ himself had driven a legion of unclean spririts out of a possessed man and into the Gadarene swine (Mark 5:1–19); but the age of miracles has passed, and corporeal possession by demons is no longer possible. The spirit abroad is "the spirit of illusion" (p. A3), and where there was once a holy ritual, there is now only *theater*.

In the most powerful artistic practice of his age, Harsnett finds the analytical key to disclosing the degradation of the ancient spiritual practice: exorcisms are stage plays fashioned by cunning clerical dramatists and performed by actors skilled in improvisation. Some of the participants are self-conscious professionals like Father Edmunds or the Puritan Darrel; others (mostly impressionable young serving-women and unstable, down-at-heels young gentlemen) are amateurs cunningly drawn into the demonic stage business. Those selected to play the possessed are in effect taught their roles without realizing at first that they are roles.

The priests begin by talking conspicuously about the way successful exorcisms abroad had taken place and describing in lurid detail the precise symptoms of the possessed. They then await occasions upon which to improvise: a servingman "beeing pinched with penurie, & hunger, did lie but a night, or two, abroad in the fieldes, and beeing a melancholicke person, was scared with lightning, and thunder, that happened in the night, & loe, an euident signe, that the man was possessed" (p. 24); a dissolute young gentleman "had a spice of the *Hysterica passio*" or, as it is popularly called, "the Moother" (p. 25), [17] and that too is a sign of possession. An inflamed toe, a pain in the side, a fright taken from the sudden leaping of a cat, a fall in the kitchen—all are occasions for the priests to step forward and detect the awful presence of the demonic, whereupon the young "scholers," as Harsnett wryly terms the naive performers, "*frame* themselues iumpe and fit vnto the Priests humors, to mop, mow, iest, raile, raue, roare, commend & discommend, and as the priests would haue them, vpon fitting occasions (according to the differences of times, places, and commers in) in all things to play the deuils accordinglie" (p. 38).

The theatrical aspect of exorcism, to which the *Declaration* insistently calls attention, has been repeatedly noted by modern ethnographers who do not share Harsnett's reforming zeal. In an illuminating study of possession among the Ethiopians of Gondar, Michel Leiris notes that the healer carefully instructs the *zar*, or spirit, who has seized upon someone, how to behave: the types of cries appropriate to the occasion, the expected violent contortions, the "decorum," as Harsnett would put it, of the trance state. [18] The treatment is in effect an initiation into the performance of the symptoms which are then cured precisely because they conform to the stereotype of the healing process. One must not conclude, writes Leiris, that there are no "real"—that is, sincerely experienced—cases of possession, for many of the patients (principally young women and slaves) seem genuinely ill, but at the same time there are no cases that are exempt from artifice (pp. 27–28). Between authentic possession, spontaneous and involuntary, and inauthentic possession, simulated to provide a show or extract some material or moral benefit, there are so many subtle shadings that it is impossible to draw a firm boundary (pp. 94–95).

Possession in Gondar *is* theater, but theater that cannot confess its own theatrical nature, for this is not "theater played" but "theater lived," lived not only by the spirit-haunted actor but by the audience. Those who witness a possession may at any moment be themselves possessed, and even if they are untouched by the *zar*, they remain participants rather than passive spectators. For the theatrical performance is not shielded from them by an impermeable membrane; possession is extraordinary but not marginal, a heightened—but not separate—state. In possession, writes Leiris, the collective life itself takes the form of theater (p. 96).

Precisely those qualities that fascinate and charm the ethnographer disgust Harsnett: where the former can write of "authentic" possession in the unspoken assurance that neither he nor his readers actually believe in the existence of *zars*, the latter, granted no such assurance, struggles to prove that possession is by definition inauthentic; where the former sees a complex ritual integrated into the social process, the latter sees "a *Stygian* comedy to make silly people afraid" (p. 69); where the former sees the theatrical expression of collective life, the latter sees the theatrical promotion of specific and malevolent institutional interests. And where Leiris's central point is that possession is a theater that does not confess its own theatricality, Harsnett's concern is to enforce precisely such a confession: the last 102 pages of the *Declaration* reprint the "severall Examinations, and confessions of the parties pretended to be possessed, and dispossessed by *Weston* the Iesuit, and his adherents: set downe word for word as they were taken vpon oath before her Maiesties Commissioners for causes Ecclesiasticall" (p. 172). These transcripts prove, according to Harsnett, that the solemn ceremony of exorcism is a "play of sacred miracles," a "wonderful pageant" (p. 2), a "deuil Theater" (p. 106).

The force of this confession, for Harsnett, is to demolish exorcism. Theater is not the disinterested expression of the popular spirit but the indelible mark of falsity, tawdriness, and rhetorical manipulation. And these sinister qualities are rendered diabolical by that which so appeals to Leiris: exorcism's cunning concealment of its own theatricality. The spectators do not know that they are responding to a powerful if sleazy tragicomedy; hence their tears and joy, their transports of "commiseration and compassion" (p. 74), are rendered up not to a troupe of acknowledged players but to seditious Puritans or to the supremely dangerous Catholic church. The theatrical seduction is not, for Harsnett, merely a Jesuitical strategy; it is the essence of the Church itself: Catholicism is a "Mimick superstition" (p. 20).

Harsnett's response is to try to compel the Church to become the theater, just as Catholic clerical garments—the copes and albs and amices and stoles that were the glories of medieval textile crafts— were sold during the Reformation to the players.[19] When an actor in a history play took the part of an English bishop, he could conceivably have worn the actual robes of the character he was representing. This is less realism than rhetoric: a vivid, a wry reminder that Catholicism, as Harsnett puts it, is "the Pope's playhouse."[20] Hence the *Declaration* takes pains to identify exorcism not merely with "the theatrical"—a category that scarcely exists for Harsnett—but with the actual theater; at issue is not so much a metaphorical concept as a functioning institution. For if Harsnett can drive exorcism into the theater—if he can show that the stately houses in which the rituals were performed were playhouses, that the sacred garments were what he calls a "lousie holy wardrop" (p. 78), that the terrifying writhings were simulations, that the uncanny signs and wonders were contemptible stage tricks, that the devils were the "cashiered wooddenbeaten" Vices from medieval drama (pp. 114–15), and that the exorcists were "vagabond players, that coast from Towne to Towne" (p. 149)—then the ceremony and everything for which it stands will, as far as he is concerned, be emptied out. And with this emptying out, Harsnett will have driven exorcism from the center to the periphery—in the case of London quite literally to the periphery, where the law had already driven the public theaters.[21]

Indeed it is the Renaissance sense of the theater's marginality and emptiness—the sense that everything the players touch is thereby rendered hollow—that underlies Harsnett's theatrical analysis of the Catholic church. Demonic possession is a particularly attractive cornerstone for such an analysis, not only because of its histrionic intensity but because the theater itself is by its very nature bound up with possession. Harsnett did not have to believe that the cult of Dionysius out of which the Greek drama evolved was a cult of possession; even the ordinary and familiar theater of his own time depended upon the apparent transformation of the actor into the voice, the actions, and the face of another.

With his characteristic opportunism and artistic self-consciousness, Shakespeare in his first known play, *The Comedy of Errors* (1590), was already toying with the connection between theater, illusion, and spurious possession. Antipholus of Syracusa, accosted by his twin's mistress, imagines that he is encountering the devil: "Sathan, avoid. I charge thee tempt me not" (4.3.48). The Ephesian Antipholus's wife, Adriana, dismayed by the apparently mad behavior of her husband, imagines that the devil has possessed him, and she dutifully calls in an exorcist: "Good Doctor Pinch, you are a conjurer, / Establish him in his true sense again." Pinch begins the solemn ritual—

> I charge thee, Sathan, hous'd within this man,
> To yield possession to my holy prayers,
> And to thy state of darkness hie thee straight:
> I conjure thee by all the saints in heaven!—

only to be interrupted with a box on the ears from the outraged husband: "Peace, doting wizard, peace! I am not mad." For the exorcist, such denials only confirm the presence of an evil spirit: "The fiend is strong within him" (4.4). At the scene's end, Antipholus is dragged away to be "bound and laid in some dark room."

The false presumption of demonic possession in *The Comedy of Errors* is not the result of deception; it is an instance of what Shakespeare's contemporary, George Gascoigne, calls a "suppose"—an attempt to make sense of a series of bizarre actions gleefully generated by the comedy's screwball coincidences. Exorcism is the kind of straw people clutch at when the world seems to have gone mad. In *Twelfth Night*, written some ten years later, Shakespeare's view of exorcism, though still comic, has darkened. Possession now is not a mistaken "suppose" but a fraud, a malicious practical joke played upon Malvolio. "Pray God he be not bewitched" (3.4.94), Maria piously intones at the sight of the cross-gartered, leering gull, and when he is out of earshot, Fabian laughs, "If this were played upon a stage now, I could condemn it as an improbable fiction" (3.4.119–20). The theatrical self-consciousness is intensified when Feste the clown is brought in to conduct a mock-exorcism; "I would I were the first that ever dissembled in such a gown," he remarks sententiously as he disguises himself as Sir Topas the curate. If the jibe had a specific reference for the play's original audience, it would be to the Puritan exorcist Darrel, who had only recently been convicted of dissembling in the exorcism of William Sommers of Nottingham.[22] Now, the scene would suggest, the tables are being turned on the self-righteous fanatic. "Good Sir Topas," pleads Malvolio, "do not think I am mad. They have laid me here in hideous darkness." "Fie, thou dishonest Sathan," Feste replies; "I call thee by the most modest terms, for I am one of those gentle ones that will use the devil himself with courtesy" (4.2.29–33).

By 1600 then Shakespeare had clearly marked out possession and exorcism as frauds, so much so that in *All's Well That Ends Well*, a few years later, he could casually use the term "exorcist" as a synonym for illusion-monger: "Is there no exorcist / Beguiles the truer office of mine eyes?" cries the King of France when Helena, whom he thought dead, appears before him; "Is't real that I see?" (5.3.301–3). When in 1605 Harsnett was whipping exorcism toward the theater, Shakespeare was already at the entrance to the Globe to welcome it.

Given Harsnett's frequent expressions of "the anti-theatrical prejudice," this welcome may still seem strange, but in fact nothing in the *Declaration* necessarily implies hostility to the theater as a professional institution. On the contrary, what the work attacks is a form of theater that pretends that it is not entertainment but sober reality. Harsnett's polemic virtually depends upon the existence of an officially designated commercial theater, marked off openly from all other forms and ceremonies of public life precisely by virtue of its freely acknowledged fictionality. Where there is no pretense to truth, there can be no *imposture*: it is this argument that permits so ontologically anxious a figure as Sir Philip Sidney to defend poetry—"the poet doth nothing affirm and hence doth nothing lie."

In this spirit Puck playfully defends *A Midsummer Night's Dream*:

If we shadows have offended,
Think by this, and all is mended,
That you have but slumb'red here
While these visions did appear.
And this weak and idle theme,
No more yielding but a dream.

(5.1.423–28)

With a similarly frank admission of illusion Shakespeare can open the theater to Harsnett's polemic. Indeed, as if Harsnett's momentum carried *him* into the theater along with the fraud he hotly pursues, Shakespeare in *King Lear* stages not only exorcism, but Harsnett *on* exorcism:

> Five fiends have been in poor Tom at once; as Oberdicut, of lust; Hober-didance, prince of dumbness; Mahu, of stealing; Modo, of murder; Flib-bertigibbet, of mopping and mowing; who since possesses chamber-maids and waiting-women. (4.1.58–62)

Those in the audience who had read Harsnett's book or heard of the notorious Buckinghamshire exorcisms would recognize in Edgar's lines an odd, joking allusion to the chambermaids, Sara and Friswood Williams, and the waiting woman, Ann Smith, principal actors in Father Edmunds' "Devil Theater." The humor of the anachronism here is akin to the Fool's earlier quip, "This prophecy Merlin shall make; for I live before his time" (3.2.95–96); both are bursts of a cheeky self-consciousness that dares deliberately to violate the historical setting in order to remind the audience of the play's conspicuous doubleness, its simultaneous distance and contemporaneity.

A Declaration of Egregious Popish Impostures supplies Shakespeare not only with an uncanny anachronism but with the model for Edgar's histrionic disguise. For it is not the *authenticity* of the demonology that the playwright finds in Harsnett—the usual reason for authorial recourse to a specialized source (as, for example, to a military or legal handbook)—but rather the inauthenticity of a theatrical role. Shakespeare appropriates for Edgar then a documented fraud, complete with an impressive collection of what the *Declaration* calls "vncouth non-significant names" (p. 46) that have been made up to sound exotic and that carry with them a faint but ineradicable odor of spuriousness.

In Sidney's *Arcadia*, which provided the outline of the Gloucester subplot, the good son, having escaped his father's misguided attempt to kill him, becomes a soldier in another land and quickly distinguishes himself. Shakespeare insists not only on Edgar's perilous fall from his father's favor but upon his marginalization: Edgar becomes the possessed Poor Tom, the outcast with no possibility of working his way back in toward the center. "My neighbors," writes John

Bunyan in the 1660s, "were amazed at this my great conversion from prodigious profaneness to something like a moral life; and truly so well they might for this my conversion was as great as for a Tom of Bethlem to become a sober man."[23] Of course, Edgar is only a pretend Tom-o-Bedlam and hence can return to the community when it is safe to do so, but the force of Harsnett's argument is to make mimed possession even more marginal and desperate than the real thing.

Indeed Edgar's desperation is bound up with the strain of "counterfeiting," a strain he has already noted in the presence of the mad and ruined Lear and now, in the scene from which I have just quoted, feels still more intensely in the presence of his blinded and ruined father. He is struggling with the urge to stop playing or, as he puts it, with the feeling that he "cannot daub it further" (4.1.51). Why he does not simply reveal himself to Gloucester at this point is entirely unclear. "And yet I must" is all he says of his continued disguise, as he recites the catalog of devils and leads his despairing father off to Dover.[24]

The subsequent episode—Gloucester's suicide attempt—deepens the play's brooding upon spurious exorcism. "It is good *decorum* in a Comedie," writes Harsnett, "to giue vs emptie names for things, and to tell vs of strange Monsters within, where there be none" (p. 142); so too the "Miracle-minter" Father Edmunds and his fellow exorcists manipulate their impressionable gulls: "The priests doe report often in their patients hearing the dreadful formes, similitudes, and shapes, that the devils vse to depart in out of those possessed bodies . . . : and this they tell with so graue a countenance, pathetical termes, and accommodate action, as it leaues a very deepe impression in the memory, and fancie of their actors" (pp. 142–43). Thus by the power of theatrical suggestion the anxious subjects on whom the priests work their charms come to believe that they too have witnessed the devil depart in grotesque form from their own bodies, whereupon the priests turn their eyes heavenward and give thanks to the Blessed Virgin. In much the same manner Edgar persuades Gloucester that he stands on a high cliff, and then after his credulous father has flung himself forward Edgar switches roles and pretends that he is a bystander who has seen a demon depart from the old man:

As I stood here below methought his eyes
Were two full moons; he had a thousand noses,
Horns whelk'd and wav'd like the enridged sea:

It was some fiend; therefore, thou happy father,
Think that the clearest Gods, who make them honours
Of men's impossibilities, have preserved thee.

(4.6.69–74)

Edgar tries to create in Gloucester an experience of awe and wonder
so intense that it can shatter his suicidal despair and restore his faith
in the benevolence of the gods: "Thy life's a miracle," he tells his father. For Shakespeare as for Harsnett this miracle-minting is the product of specifically histrionic manipulations; the scene at Dover is
simultaneously a disenchanted analysis of religious and theatrical illusions. Walking about on a perfectly flat stage, Edgar does to
Gloucester what the theater usually does to the audience: he persuades his father to discount the evidence of his senses—"Methinks
the ground is even"—and to accept a palpable fiction: "Horrible
steep." But the audience, of course, never absolutely accepts such fictions: we enjoy being brazenly lied to, we welcome for the sake of
pleasure what we know to be untrue, but we withhold from the theater the simple assent that we grant to everyday reality. And we enact
this withholding when we refuse to believe that Gloucester is on a cliff
above Dover Beach.

Hence in the midst of Shakespeare's demonstration of the con-
vergence of exorcism and theater, we return to the difference that
enables *King Lear* to borrow comfortably from Harsnett: the theater
elicits from us complicity rather than belief. Demonic possession is
responsibly marked out for the audience as a theatrical fraud, designed to gull the unsuspecting: monsters such as the fiend with the
thousand noses are illusions most easily imposed upon the old, the
blind, and the despairing; evil comes not from the mysterious other-
world of demons but from this world, the world of court and family
intrigue. In *King Lear* there are no ghosts, as there are in *Richard III,
Julius Caesar,* or *Hamlet;* no witches, as in *Macbeth;* no mysterious music of departing daemons, as in *Antony and Cleopatra.*

King Lear is haunted by a sense of rituals and beliefs that are no
longer efficacious, that have been *emptied out.* The characters appeal
again and again to the pagan gods, but the gods remain utterly silent.[25] Nothing answers to human questions but other human voices;
nothing breeds about the heart but human desires; nothing inspires
awe or terror but human suffering and human depravity. For all the

invocation of the gods in *King Lear*, it is quite clear that there are no devils.

Edgar is no more possessed than the sanest of us, and we can see for ourselves that there was no demon standing by Gloucester's side. Likewise Lear's madness does not have a supernatural origin; it is linked, as in Harsnett, to *hysterica passio*, exposure to the elements, and extreme anguish, and its cure comes not at the hands of an exorcist but of a doctor. His prescription involves neither the religious rituals of Catholicism nor the fasting and prayer of Puritanism, but tranquillized sleep:

> Our foster-nurse of nature is repose,
> The which he lacks; that to provoke in him,
> Are many simples operative, whose power
> Will close the eye of anguish.[26]

(4.4.12–15)

King Lear's relation to Harsnett's book then is essentially one of reiteration, a reiteration that signals a deeper and unexpressed institutional exchange. The official church dismantles and cedes to the players the powerful mechanisms of an unwanted and dangerous charisma; in return the players confirm the charge that those mechanisms are theatrical and hence illusory. The material structure of Elizabethan and Jacobean public theaters heightened this confirmation, since unlike medieval drama with its fuller integration into society, Shakespeare's drama took place in carefully demarcated playgrounds. *King Lear* offers then a double corroboration of Harsnett's arguments: within the play, Edgar's possession is clearly designated as a fiction, while the play itself is bounded by the institutional signs of fictionality: the wooden walls of the play space, payment for admission, known actors playing the parts, applause, the dances that followed the performance.

This theatrical confirmation of the official position is neither superficial nor unstable. And yet, I want now to suggest, Harsnett's arguments are alienated from themselves when they make their appearance on the Shakespearean stage. This alienation may be set in the context of a more general observation: the closer Shakespeare seems to a source, the more faithfully he reproduces it on stage, the more devastating and decisive his transformation of it. Let us take, for a small, initial instance, Shakespeare's borrowing from Harsnett of the unusual adjective "corky"—i.e., sapless, dry, withered. The word appears in the *Declaration* in the course of a sardonic explanation of why, despite the canonists' declaration that only old women are to be exorcised, Father Edmunds and his crew have a particular fondness for exorcising young women. Along with more graphic sexual innuendos, Harsnett observes that the theatrical role of a demoniac requires "certain actions, motions, distortions, dislocations, writhings, tumblings, and turbulent passions . . . not to be performed but by supplenesse of sinewes. . . . It would (I feare mee) pose all the cunning Exorcists, that are this day to be found, to teach an old corkie woman to writhe, tumble, curvet, & fetch her Morice gamboles" (p. 23).

Now Shakespeare's eye was caught by the word "corkie," and he reproduces it in a reference to Gloucester. But what had been a flourish of Harsnett's typically bullying comic style becomes part of the horror of an almost unendurable scene, a scene of torture that begins when Cornwall orders his servant to take the captive Gloucester and "bind fast his corky arms" (3.7.28). The note of bullying humor is still present in the word, but it is present in the character of the torturer.

This one-word instance of repetition as transvaluation may suggest in the tiniest compass what happens to Harsnett's work in the course of *Lear*. The *Declaration*'s arguments are loyally reiterated but in a curiously divided form. The voice of skepticism is assimilated to Cornwall, to Goneril, and above all to Edmund, whose "naturalism" is exposed as the argument of the younger and illegitimate son bent on displacing his legitimate older brother and eventually on destroying his father. The fraudulent possession and exorcism are given to the legitimate Edgar, who is forced to such shifts by the nightmarish persecution directed against him. Edgar adopts the role of Poor Tom not out of a corrupt will to deceive, but out of a commendable desire to survive. Modu, Mahu, and the rest are fakes, exactly as Harsnett said they were, but they are the venial sins of a will to endure. And even "venial sins" is too strong: they are the clever inventions that enable a decent and unjustly persecuted man to live. Similarly, there is no grotesque monster standing on the cliff with Gloucester—there isn't even any cliff—but Edgar, himself hunted down like an animal, is trying desperately to save his father from suicidal despair.

All of this has an odd and unsettling resemblance to the situation of the Jesuits in England, if viewed from an unofficial perspective. The resemblance does not, I think, resolve itself into an allegory in which Catholicism is revealed to be the persecuted, legitimate elder brother forced to defend himself by means of theatrical illusions against the cold persecution of his skeptical bastard brother Protestantism. But the current of sympathy is enough to undermine the intended effect of Harsnett's *Declaration*: an intensified adherence to the central system of official values. In Shakespeare, the realization that demonic possession is a theatrical imposture leads not to a clarification—the clear-eyed satisfaction of the man who refuses to be gulled—but to a deeper uncertainty, a loss of moorings, in the face of evil.

"Let them anatomize Regan," Lear raves, "see what breeds about her heart. Is there any cause in nature that makes these hard hearts?" (3.6.76–78). We know that there is no cause *beyond* nature; the voices of evil in the play—"Thou, Nature, art my goddess"; "What need one?"; "Bind fast his corky arms"—come from the unpossessed. Does it make it any better to know this? Is it a relief to understand that the evil was not visited upon the characters by demonic agents but released from the structure of the family and the state by Lear himself?

Edgar's pretended demonic possession, by ironic contrast, is of the homiletic variety; the devil compels him to acts of self-punishment, the desperate masochism of the poor, but not to acts of viciousness. On the contrary, like the demoniacs in Harsnett's contemptuous account who praise the Mass and the Catholic church, Poor Tom gives a highly moral performance:

> Take heed o' th' foul fiend. Obey thy parents; keep thy word's justice; swear not; commit not with man's sworn spouse; set not thy sweet heart on proud array. Tom's a-cold. (3.4.80–83)

Is it a relief to know that Edgar is only miming this little sermon?

All attempts by the characters to explain or relieve their sufferings through the invocation of transcendent forces are baffled. Gloucester's belief in the influence of "these late eclipses in the sun and moon" (1.2.107) is decisively dismissed, even if the spokesman for the dismissal is the villainous Edmund. Lear's almost constant appeals to the gods—

> O Heavens,
> If you do love old men, if your sweet sway

> Allow obedience, if you yourselves are old,
> Make it your cause; send down and take my part!
>
> (2.4.192–95)

are constantly left unanswered. The storm in the play seems to several characters to be of more than natural intensity, and Lear above all tries desperately to make it *mean* something (a symbol of his daughters' ingratitude, a punishment for evil, a sign from the gods of the impending universal judgment), but the thunder refuses to speak. When Albany calls Goneril a "devil" and a "fiend" (4.2.59, 66), we know that he is not identifying her as a supernatural being—it is impossible, in this play, to witness the eruption of the denizens of hell into the human world—just as we know that Albany's prayer for "visible spirits" to be sent down by the heavens "to tame these vile offences" (4.2.46–47) will be unanswered.

In *King Lear*, as Harsnett says of the Catholic church, "neither God, Angel, nor deuil, can be gotten to speake" (p. 169). For Harsnett this silence betokens a liberation from lies; we have learned, as the last sentence of his tract puts it, "to loath these despicable Impostures, and returne vnto the truth" (p. 171). But for Shakespeare the silence leads to the desolation of the play's close:

> Lend me a looking-glass;
> If that her breath will mist or stain the stone,
> Why, then she lives.
>
> (5.3.261–63)

The lines give voice to a hope by which the audience has been repeatedly tantalized: a hope that Cordelia will not die, that the play will build toward a revelation powerful enough to justify Lear's atrocious suffering, that we are in the midst of what the Italians called a *tragedia di fin lieto*, that is, a play where the villains absorb the tragic punishment while the good are wondrously restored. Lear invokes, in effect, the romance conventions of a theater that requires the audience at the close of a play to will imaginatively a miraculous turn of events, often against the evidence of its own senses (as when the audience persuades itself that the two actors playing Viola and Sebastian in *Twelfth Night* really *do* look identical, in spite of the ocular proof to the contrary). But in *King Lear* there is an ironic reversal of these conventions, because in order to believe Cordelia dead, the audience, insofar as it can actually see what is occurring on stage, must work against the evidence of its own senses. After all, the actor's breath would have misted the stone, and the feather held to Cordelia's mouth must have stirred. But we remain convinced that Cordelia is, as Lear first says, "dead as earth." [27]

In the wake of Lear's first attempt to see some sign of life in Cordelia, Kent asks, "Is this the promis'd end?" Edgar echoes the question: "Or image of that horror?" And Albany says, "Fall and cease." By itself Kent's question has an oddly literary quality, as if he were remarking on the end of the play, either wondering what kind of ending this is or implicitly objecting to the disastrous turn of events. Edgar's response suggests that the "end" is the end of the world, the Last Judgment, here conceived not as a "promise"—the punishment of the wicked, the reward of the good—but as a "horror." But like Kent, Edgar is not certain about what he is seeing: his question suggests that he may be witnessing not the end itself but a possible "image" of it, while Albany's enigmatic "Fall and cease" empties even that image of significance. The theatrical means that might have made something magical out of this moment are abjured; there will be no imposture, no histrionic revelation of the supernatural.

Lear repeats this miserable emptying out of the redemptive hope in his next lines:

> This feather stirs; she lives! if it be so,
> It is a chance which does redeem all sorrows
> That ever I have felt.
>
>   (5.3.265–67)

Deeply moved by the sight of the mad king, a nameless gentleman had earlier remarked, "Thou hast one daughter / Who redeems Nature from the general curse / Which twain have brought her to" (4.6.201–3). Now in Lear's words this vision of universal redemption through Cordelia is glimpsed again, intensified by the king's own conscious investment in it. What would it mean to "redeem" Lear's sorrows? To buy them back from the chaos and brute meaninglessness they now seem to signify, to reward the king with a gift so great that it outweighs the sum of misery in his entire long life, to reinterpret his pain as the necessary preparation—the price to be paid—for a consummate bliss. In the theater such reinterpretation would be represented by a spectacular turn in the plot—a surprise unmasking, a sudden reversal of fortunes, a resurrection—and this dramatic peripeteia, however secular, would almost invariably recall the consummation devoutly wished by centuries of Christian believers. This consummation had in fact been represented again and again in medieval resurrection plays which offered the spectators ocular proof that Christ had risen.[28] Despite the pre-Christian setting of Shakespeare's play, Lear's craving for just such proof—"This feather stirs; she lives!"—would seem to evoke precisely this theatrical and religious tradition, only in order to reveal itself, in C. L. Barber's acute phrase, as "post-Christian."[29] *If it be so*: Lear's sorrows are not redeemed; nothing can turn them into joy, but the forlorn hope of an impossible redemption persists, drained of its institutional and doctrinal significance, empty and vain, cut off even from a theatrical realization, but like the dream of exorcism, ineradicable.

The close of *King Lear* in effect acknowledges that it can never satisfy this dream, but the acknowledgment must not obscure the fact that the play itself has generated the craving for such satisfaction. That is, Shakespeare does not simply inherit and make use of an anthropological given; rather, at the moment when the official religious and secular institutions were, for their own reasons, abjuring the rituals they themselves had once fostered, Shakespeare's theater moves to appropriate this function. On stage the ritual is effectively contained in the ways we have examined, but Shakespeare intensifies as theatrical experience the need for exorcism, and his demystification of the practice is not identical in its interests to Harsnett's.

Harsnett's polemic is directed toward a bracing anger against the lying agents of the Catholic church and a loyal adherence to the true, established Church of England. He writes as a representative of that true church, and this institutional identity is reinforced by the secular institutional imprimatur on the confessions that are appended to the text. The joint religious and secular apparatus works to strip away imposture and discover the hidden reality which is, Harsnett says, the theater. Shakespeare's play dutifully reiterates this discovery: when Lear thinks he has found in Tom-o-Bedlam "the thing itself," "unaccommodated man," he has in fact found a man playing a theatrical role. But if false religion is theater, and if the difference between true religion and false religion is the presence of theater, what happens when this difference is enacted in the theater?

What happens, as we have already begun to see, is that the official position is *emptied out*, even as it is loyally confirmed. This "emptying out" bears a certain resemblance to Brecht's "alienation effect" and still more to Althusser and Macherey's "internal distantiation." But recent Marxist literary theory tends to underestimate the extent to which "internal distance" is perfectly compatible with the interests of the ruling elite. In Shakespeare's use of Harsnett, it is less the Marxists' "internal distance" than the deconstructionists' principle of excess, now revealed ironically to be a principle of evacuation, that accounts for the felt differentiation between art and ideology. And this differentiation is in the interest less of political subversion than of the power of the theater.

Edgar's possession is a theatrical performance, exactly in Harsnett's terms, but there is no saving institution, purged of theater, against which it may be set, nor is there a demonic institution which the performance may be shown to serve. On the contrary, Edgar's miming is a response to a free-floating, contagious evil more terrible than anything Harsnett would allow. For Harsnett the wicked are corrupt individuals in the service of a corrupt church; in *King Lear* there are neither individuals nor institutions adequate to contain the released and enacted wickedness; the force of evil in the play is larger than any local habitation or name. In this sense, Shakespeare's tragedy reconstitutes as theater the demonic principle demystified by Harsnett. Edgar's fraudulent, histrionic performance is a response to this principle: exploded rituals, drained of their original meaning, are preferable to no rituals at all.

Shakespeare does not counsel, in effect, that one accept as true the fraudulent institution for the sake of the dream of a cure—the argument of the Grand Inquisitor. He writes for the greater glory and profit of the theater, a fraudulent institution that never pretends to be anything but fraudulent, an institution that calls forth what is not, that signifies absence, that empties out everything it represents. By doing so the theater makes for itself the hollow round space within which it survives. The force of *King Lear* is to make us love the theater, to seek out its satisfactions, to serve its interests, to confer upon it a place of its own, to grant it life by permitting it to reproduce itself over generations. Shakespeare's theater has outlived the institutions to which it paid homage, has lived to pay homage to other, competing institutions which in turn it seems to represent and empty out. This complex, limited institutional independence, this illusion of autonomy, arises not out of an inherent, formal self-reflexiveness but out of the ideological matrix in which Shakespeare's theater is created and recreated.

Why has our culture embraced *King Lear*'s massive display of mimed suffering and fraudulent exorcism? Because the judicial torture and expulsion of evil have for centuries been bound up with the display of power at the center of society. Because we no longer believe in the magical ceremonies through which devils were once made to speak and were driven out of the bodies of the possessed. Because the play recuperates and intensifies our need for these ceremonies, even though we do not believe in them, and performs them, carefully marked out for us as frauds, for our continued consumption. Because with our full complicity, Shakespeare's company and scores of companies that followed have catered profitably to our desire for spectacular impostures.

And also perhaps because the Harsnetts of the world would free us from the oppression of false belief only in order to reclaim us more firmly for the official state church, and this "solution"—confirmed by the rechristening, as it were, of the devil as the pope—is hateful. Hence we embrace an alternative that seems to confirm the official line and thereby take its place in the central system of values, yet that works at the same time to unsettle all official lines. "Truth to tell," writes Barthes, "the best weapon against myth is perhaps to mythify it in its turn, and to produce an *artificial myth*: and this reconstituted myth will in fact be a mythology."[30] Shakespeare's mythology empties out the center that it represents, and in its cruelty—Edmund, Goneril, Regan, Cornwall, Gloucester, Cordelia, Lear: all dead as earth—paradoxically creates in us the intimation of a fullness that we can only savor in the conviction of its irremediable loss:

> We that are young
> Shall never see so much, nor live so long.

Auerbach's Mimesis:
Figural Structure and Historical Narrative

Timothy Bahti

Intellectual debates represent the most public aspects of changes within intellectual disciplines; these changes themselves often only reflect impulses and challenges issuing from thinkers and forces that may not reside within these disciplines' boundaries. As such a derivative phenomenon, our debates are not always an accurate barometer of what is actually going on in a way of thinking; they tend to exaggerate the importance of the new, and to underestimate the recently past. But even when they might be shown to be incorrect in their assessments, intellectual debates can serve to alert one to the perceived import of a shift within a discipline, and to the names and values being attributed to the antagonists.

I have in mind here the debates currently devoted to literary theory, a discipline of thought that scarcely existed in this country two decades ago but that today seems to dominate many journals, departmental decisions, and professional meetings. And my introductory remarks concern the character of public dissatisfaction with such literary theory. A decade or so ago, the accusations tended to be ethical or aesthetic in kind. The new theory, then still called "structuralism," was said to be antihumanist in preferring structure to substance, signs to reference, varieties of otherness to the surety of the self. This seemed to make it particularly pernicious, a kind of *trahison des clercs* or betrayal from within the very bastions of academic humanism. The aesthetic accusation was not unrelated to this ethical one. The more that textual meaning was said to be "open," "polyvalent," or "plural," the more the literary work of art lost its status as a unified product and artifact, along with its singular intent and meaning. What was at stake here was the image of a unified literary work as the correlative to either the unitary producer and producing period, or the similarly stable and reassured audience, the appreciative observer or reader. The ethical and aesthetic objections may thus be seen as two sides of the same coin, each imprinted with certain values of unity, and put into public circulation to counter what was perceived as a threat to the literary work or its "workers"—its authors and critics.

Now we know that ethical humanism is a historical development arising with the Renaissance, and one of such tenacious staying power that even much later movements that would think of themselves as revolutionary—such as Marxism or existentialism—have seen fit to declare themselves "humanisms." But it is more important here to recall that Renaissance humanism is not only a historical development, but a development that arises from doing history, that is, from historical philology directed toward the distant past of the classics. Likewise, the aesthetic investment in the unity of the work of art is also a historical phenomenon—with Aristotelian and Horatian antecedents, but with its real efflorescence in the Renaissance and after—but in its most persuasive form in Kant's third *Critique*, it, too, is of a piece with a *historical* project, the project of guaranteeing a historical teleology of moral freedom. Thus, the two principal kinds of attacks upon recent literary theory—aesthetic and ethical—shared a historical foundation uniting formal properties and moral proprieties in a common narrative about the past and future.

This point, only briefly sketched and asserted here, allows me to turn toward the final remark I would make in introduction, and it concerns an apparent change in the critique of literary theory. As if the accusers had worked their way beyond the surfaces of the past attacks and arrived at the implicit assumptions that are at work there, the criticism today seems to be that much contemporary literary theory is ahistorical or even antihistorical. A critique such as Frank Lentricchia's *After the New Criticism* is organized historically, from its title and contents through its "method" of claiming to uncover the theorists' real sources and thus the real origins of their problems; and it proposes a revamped historical criticism as its alternative, an option proffered, for instance, in the chapter-heading "History or the Abyss."[1] (One recalls the comedian's rejoinder: "Are those my only choices?") Other examples come readily to mind. Gerald Graff's *Literature against Itself* similarly would wish literature and literary criticism to be more responsive to their historical worlds once again.[2] In the *New York Times Book Review* Robert Langbaum chides J. Hillis Miller for "rejecting that unfashionable discipline" of literary history while also still "doing" it in some sense, almost despite himself.[3] Frederick

Crews recently had a public pique, in which he complained that a "progress from historically informed interpretation to vapid attitudinizing could stand for the fate of much 'advanced' academic discourse over the past two decades."[4] And this pronouncement of lost historical thought does not only occur in the mode of accusation; sometimes it takes the more revealing form of an admission. Paul de Man's book *Allegories of Reading* begins with the confession that he set out to write a historical study of romanticism, and wound up with a theory of ahistorical reading instead.[5] Likewise, it is sometimes the very dissenters from new trends in literary theory who acknowledge doubts about the viability of literary-historical criticism. Thus René Wellek is at once one of our most determined literary historians—in the realm of the history of criticism—*and* one who has come to despair of literary history's possibilities and potential: his late essay "The Fall of Literary History" frames symmetrically a career that began with such optimistic titles as "The Theory of Literary History" and *The Rise of English Literary History*.[6]

What I mean this collection of symptoms to suggest is neither a simplistic historical backlash to complex imported theory, nor an indisputable decline in historical writing and in faith in the historical; rather, these phenomena of our contemporary scene suggest how once again a battle between theoretical reflection and interpretive practice is being fought within a conventional opposition between history and the nonhistorical. This battle was fought by a previous generation in our Anglo-American context between the so-called New Critics and more materialist or Marxist historical critics; it was fought in France for decades between the university literary historians and a succession of antagonists, including the "Geneva School" phenomenologists, the French structuralists, and today's so-called "poststructuralists." In fact, this battle of and for the books is an ancient, as well as modern, quarrel: a frustration with literary theory takes recourse to "history"; a frustration with literary history finds theoretical justification, solace, or adventure in theory.

Rather than join in either a blind, polemical dispute about the virtues or naivetés of old-fashioned literary history, or a self-deluding complacency with regard to our knowledge that such disputes always go on, we might take the occasion of this apparent struggle between literary theory and literary history and pause to reflect upon their interaction in an exemplary case: Erich Auerbach's *Mimesis: The Representation of Reality in Western Literature*, from the Germany of the first half of this century. My claim that Auerbach's *Mimesis* is exemplary as literary history is not only that Auerbach's work is one of the few historically organized works of literary criticism that, like M. H. Abrams's *The Mirror and the Lamp*, for example, still deserves and receives wide readership twenty-five or thirty-five years after its publication—in other words, that it stands a certain test of time as historical writing. Nor is my claim simply that the book stands as a monument to that postwar phenomenon that may be called "NATO humanism" and that survives in the countless "Great Books" courses of our curricula: the organization and teaching of a politicocultural view of the West as a continuous and ultimately consistent body of thought and discourse, the hallmarks of which are historical progress, democratic liberalism, a faith in individual man, and a tolerance of multiple gods. In this context, Auerbach's *Mimesis* continues to do service as an immensely useful—indeed, uncontested—pedagogic tool in this popular dissemination of literary high culture.

Instead, my claim for the work's exemplary status rests primarily on a recognition of its particular disciplinary or institutional achievements as a literary-historical argument. *Mimesis* established a term and concept—that of the "levels of style" and their mimetic power—as an indispensible element, at once thematic and methodological, in our literary-critical vocabulary. Considered thematically, the notion of "levels of style" is a key cog—apparently (and by his own word) *the* key cog—in Auerbach's machine of historical continuity. He traces the now well-known path from the classical doctrine of strictly distinguishable levels of style to that doctrine's initial disruption by the *sermo humilis* of the New Testament and its story of Christ's incarnation and passion. His narrative then moves on to the theoretical development of *sermo humilis* under Jerome, Augustine, and the exegetical method of figural interpretation; to the combination of mixed styles and figural representation in Dante; to the further levelling and inmixing of stylistic differences in such figures as Rabelais and Montaigne, Shakespeare and Schiller; until the final destruction of distinct levels of style is achieved, along with the fullest representation of contemporary social reality, by nineteenth-century French realism.

But this enormous accomplishment—the historical argument about the mixing and levelling of levels of style for which *Mimesis* is probably best known—is, as I hinted, only one side of the book's critical achievement, the thematic side, that is. The other side is the *methodological* employment of style in Auerbach's work: not the historical theme of style as an object of study, then, but the critical practice of *stylistics* as a surprisingly elastic method. One recalls how almost every chapter begins with a stylistic analysis of a brief passage, and how Auerbach can then move from the passage to the work in question, from the work to the author, from the author to the period, and from the period to the history of all periods. This method—one might call it a synecdoche turned into metonymy's revenge—offers as powerful and influential a critical tool *qua* method as does Auerbach's argument regarding levels of style and representations of reality *qua* historical themes; and one may remark that in this metonymic elasticity of stylistics, his method represents philology at its most ambitious, implying a methodological continuum that extends from the smallest etymon or morphological unit to the largest dimensions of the histories of languages and literatures.[7]

I do not wish to contest Auerbach's demonstrable achievements; they are what give *Mimesis* its critical value and make it worthy of critical scrutiny in its own right. Rather, in what follows I wish to expose and consider the structure whereby Auerbach comes to tell his historical story and arrive at these effects. But first let me situate Auerbach's work in its German intellectual milieu. Germany is exemplary of the problem of history and theory because the so-called "crisis" or "loss of faith" in historiography, and in literary history in particular, played itself out earlier and more decisively there than elsewhere in the West. Our own non-Germanic perspective may prevent our recognition of the stakes involved. French historians today are perhaps more positivistic, and more self-assured in their positivism, than ever; in America, we have many models—psychohistory, cliometrics, demographics, etc.—that professional historians employ with confidence. But since the war years, there have been virtually no outstanding German literary historians or "true believers" in the efficacy of literary historiography: instead there have been "work-immanent" interpreters, theoretical or Hegelian "Frankfurt School" analysts, or religious brooders on the one hand, and more or less vulgar historical materialists on the other. In fact, one can say that the most ambitious literary-historical projects by Germans were undertaken in states of exile: Benjamin's unfinished studies of Baudelaire and Paris in the nineteenth century, written in Paris; Curtius's *European Literature and the Latin Middle Ages*, written in what he called an "inner exile" within Hitler's Germany; Auerbach's *Mimesis*, written in Istanbul, followed by other historical studies written in this country. Indeed, it is my contention that even as Germany was the country that believed most profoundly and productively in the centrality of historical thinking in the nineteenth century, this heritage—largely the work of Hegel, Ranke, and Dilthey—runs aground or decays from within the German intellectual context at about the same time that it is being most powerfully absorbed into the larger Western context. As literary history flourished in France, England, Italy, and America from the 1860s to the early twentieth century, Germany witnessed the general and devastating critique of historicism delivered by Nietzsche and then Heidegger, and such specific and interestingly failed attempts at literary *history* as Nietzsche's *Birth of Tragedy*, Lukács's *Theory of the Novel*, and Benjamin's late studies.

Auerbach was aware of this "crisis" in German historical thinking after Hegel and the nineteenth century. On the one hand, he remained devoted to the tradition and saw his discipline of Romance philology as its heir; on the other hand, he sought alternative models for rejuvenated historical studies. As I have written elsewhere,[8] Auerbach found such an alternative model in an amalgam of Vico's *New Science* with biblical and medieval figural interpretation. These two concerns—both as objects of historical study and as models for historiography—were in turn associated by Auerbach with the Hegelian problem of the "sublation" (*Aufhebung*) of historical change. The sublation of historical temporality involves the recuperation of change, loss, negation, and sheer difference through their systematic elevation from contingency to proper—that is, philosophic—meaning.[9] Historical change is sublated within the philosophic process into the form and concept of *its meaning*; most succinctly, the truth of time—time's true meaning—manifests itself as the presence of truth, or absolute knowledge. I will have to summarize several points from this earlier essay before we turn to Auerbach's *Mimesis* to examine the construction of its history and the figural structure of its narrative. My first point is that Vico's apparent understanding of human nature—its languages, its institutions, its history (what he called its *cose*)—postulated at one and the same time the immanent unfolding of historical change *and* the providential *storia ideale eterna*. This synthesis is crucial to Auerbach's understanding of his project as a philologist and a literary historian. A second point is that Auerbach's understanding of Vico, while avowedly an attempt to distinguish him from German idealism and historicism, was nonetheless a highly Hegelian understanding, a fact explainable by the assimilation of Vico into post-Hegelian idealism before Auerbach, as well as by Auerbach's own Hegelian leanings. And a third point is that if Auerbach did not explicitly understand Vico's *New Science* as a treatise on the rhetorical *method* of historical construction and interpretation—as a work of rhetorical *historiography* in the sense of the figurative construction and operation of history in its narration and interpretation—this is because he did not need to: having already in hand his understanding of *figura* as a rhetorical structure at work within historiography.

Now what are the main points of Auerbach's understanding of *figura*?[10] Briefly they are as follows. First, and essential to bear in mind, is his historical and philological thesis about *figura*. *Figura* could not have developed its exegetical and representational meaning and power without having first unfolded from its service as a philosophic term for the translation of the Greek *schēma* and *typos*. From this, *figura* becomes a rhetorical term for the verbal distinctions between the real and the apparent or seeming, the straightforward and the stylized, the model and the copy, the true and the concealing—most basically, the distinction between the literal and the figurative. In other words, one cannot raise the objection that Auerbach's historical understanding of *figural* interpretation might have little to do with the theory of *figurative* language; on the contrary, "figural" in Auerbach's historical sense is grounded upon "figurative" in our conventional sense. A second crucial point may be made by juxtaposing several of Auerbach's definitional remarks on *figura* in the sense of figural biblical interpretation as it was developed by Tertullian, Jerome, Augustine, and other early church fathers. On the one hand, the relational understanding of the *figura* as an event (in the Old Testament, and in history more broadly) that is prefigural or prophetic of a spiritual event and meaning (in the New Testament, and in Christian or salvation history more broadly) that would fulfill the figure[11]—this relation between the figure and its fulfillment must be, Auerbach insists, between two equally real, concrete, historical events. "Real historical figures are to be interpreted spiritually, but the interpretation points to a carnal, hence historical fulfillment—for the truth has become history or flesh" (F, p. 34).

> Figural interpretation establishes a connection between two events or persons, the first of which signifies not only itself but also the second, while the second encompasses or fulfills the first. . . . Both, being real events or figures, are within time, within the stream of historical life. Only the understanding of the two persons or events is a spiritual act, but this spiritual act deals with concrete events whether past, present, or future . . . since promise and fulfillment are real historical events, which either have happened . . . or will happen. (F, p. 53)

And in a third quotation, this time from the epilogue to *Mimesis*, we read that "an occurrence on earth signifies not only itself but at the same time another, which it predicts or confirms, without prejudice to the power of its concrete reality here and now."[12] Auerbach's main point regarding figural interpretation is precisely that the "figural schema permits both its poles—the figura and its fulfillment—to retain the characteristics of concrete historical reality . . . so that figure and fulfillment—although the one 'signifies' the other—have a significance which is not incompatible with their being real" (p. 195). But if this is his main point, Auerbach must also recognize that the second pole, event, or sign is necessarily privileged over the first. He writes: "The fulfillment is often designated as *veritas* . . . and the figure correspondingly as *umbra* or imago"; but against the obvious disjunction and difference thus established between one event or sign as truthful, the other as merely shadow or image (or, in another patristic formulation, as merely *imitatio veritatis*, "the imitation of truth"), Auerbach then immediately adds: "But both shadow and truth are abstract only in reference to the meaning first concealed, then revealed; they are concrete in reference to the things or persons which appear as vehicles of the meaning" (F, p. 34). Truth and its shadow or foreshadowing are each concretely situated in the real, historical events which are the "vehicles of their meaning," and this despite the implied tension in the concept of *figura* as a relation between two signs, both of which are to remain real and historical, but the latter of which is to be the truth of the former's mere prefiguration.

The character of this tension may be further indicated by reference to two more aspects of Auerbach's essay "Figura." For one thing, Auerbach makes explicit the rhetorical or, more precisely, the *figurative* structure which underwrites this interpretive ambivalence between figural truth and its mere prefiguration:

> Beside the opposition between *figura* and fulfillment or truth there appears another, between *figura* and *historia; historia* or *littera* is the literal sense or the event related; *figura* is the same literal meaning or event in reference to the fulfillment cloaked in it, and this fulfillment is *veritas*, so that *figura* becomes a middle term between *littera-historia* and *veritas*. (F, p. 47)

In other words, the tension between prefiguration and fulfillment— wherein the latter, as truth, would make the former be less than true, thereby endangering its value as concrete, historical reality—this tension is reduplicated in, or, more accurately, is already implied in the *rhetorical* structure of figural interpretation: one event, the *figura*, is historically literal but interpretively figural; the second, fulfilling event, also a historical event, is figuratively the truth (*veritas*) of the *figura*. Thus, there is already a first opposition between literal and figural in the *figura* or prefiguration itself; this then reappears as an opposition between the *figura* as historical sign, and the later figural truth (*veritas*) which "fulfills" it, or which reveals the "true" figurative meaning of that first figure.

The last aspect to which I would call attention in Auerbach's "Figura" essay regards this same point, and helps move our discussion back toward *Mimesis* and the question of its historiography. Auerbach must repeatedly attempt to explain how the fulfillment of a previous figure can avoid annihilating the value of the former's historical reality; he once writes that the latter term "fulfills and annuls" (*erfüllt und aufhebt*, F, p. 51) the former; twenty pages later, he writes that the *veritas* will "unveil and preserve" (*enthüllend und bewahrend*, F, p. 72) the *figura*. Cancel and preserve—this implies all the difficulty of sublation or *Aufhebung* in its speculative, Hegelian meaning. The initial *figura* has the double structure of *littera-historia and* spiritual meaning, although that meaning is not fulfilled until the advent of the *veritas* (say, Moses as a historical figure and as the sign of the Christ to come). Within the *figura*, then, the operation of cancelling-and-preserving the literal-historical event in the production of a spiritual sign seems to obey the economy of sublation. In the same manner, the *veritas* or fulfillment of this historical *figura* follows the pattern of the Hegelian "idealization" of phenomenal and historical experience, and so the *veritas* cancels-and-preserves the historical reality of the previous *figura* in fashioning truth through this elevation-and-negation. Yet that initial *figura*, as we have seen, itself displays the double structure of the figurative sign, that is, it is both literal and figurative. What would it mean for the *veritas* to cancel-and-preserve this sublation of the literal into the figurative which occurs *within* the very *figura* which the *veritas* fulfills? What is sublated, what is cancelled-and-yet-preserved, is precisely this first rhetorical sublation of the historical, the very double structure already at play within the beginning *figura*. Whatever the prior historical event might be, when it is taken to prefigure some later meaning, it becomes doubled (literal and figural), but the later "fulfillment" of the former's prefigural meaning must at once preserve the former's figural character—as the latter's sign, after all, as its prefiguration—*and* cancel it, render it nothing but a mere *littera*, annihilate it into a non-thing, a dead letter or a corpse. This is, I will now argue, the structure and operation of *Mimesis*: history, as historical reality and as the history of its realistic literary representation, is the *historia et littera* which, rendered figurative in the hands of Auerbach's figural interpretation, must at one and the same time perpetuate or preserve its figural character in a later fulfillment, and—*as this very fulfillment*—cancel itself to the extent that it is then merely the dead letter of some other figural meaning of "history."

I take as the operative instances of *Mimesis*'s literary history the chapters on Dante and Flaubert: they are privileged by Auerbach in his epilogue as the two decisive moments, medieval and modern, in realism's overcoming of the doctrine of the levels of style; but as I shall show, Dante and Flaubert are also, in the exact language and texture of Auerbach's chapters, related to one another as prefiguration and fulfillment. When Dante is said by Auerbach to fulfill the structure of figural *representation* implied in the Christian and medieval concept of *figura*, and thereby to overcome the very concept which prizes the

fulfillment over the literal figure, the spiritual truth over the literal historical event or life, he is also seen to carry over the structure of *figura*
toward Flaubert, so that Dante prefigures the "real" fulfillment of
Western realism in nineteenth-century French realism: Dante becomes the figure for Flaubert's truth. But if the fulfillment of figural
interpretation by Dante is supposed to preserve and value the real *historia et littera* of the fulfilled figure, then when Flaubert fulfills the *figura* of Dante, there occurs necessarily the cancellation of Dante's apparent "truth" (now mere prefiguration or *figura*) and the revelation
of a different *veritas* behind that "first" truth of Dante's fulfillment.
This new *veritas* would be the realization of a lived *historia et littera*.
There are, in other words, three figural moments in this story of Auerbach's about Dante and Flaubert: Dante's realism as figural fulfillment,
Flaubert's realism as such, and the figural relation between the two.

   Readers of the Dante chapter will recall the exquisite stylistic analysis which is so patiently sustained in the initial treatment of the encounter between the Dante-pilgrim and Farinata and Cavalcante in
canto ten of *Inferno* (it is perhaps the best such example of applied
stylistics in *Mimesis*, and certainly among the best studies of Dante's
style that we have in Dante criticism). After Auerbach recounts the
nearly "incomprehensible miracle" and "unimaginable" achievement
of Dante's mixing of styles in this passage, and after his discussion
accounts more largely for the mixture of the sublime and the trivial or
comic which the *Commedia* represents, his discourse turns thematic:

> The *Commedia* . . . [is] a literary work which imitates reality and in
> which all imaginable spheres of reality appear: past and present, sub-
> lime grandeur and vile vulgarity, history and legend, tragic and comic
> occurrences, man and nature. . . . Yet, in respect to an attempt at the
> elevated style, all these things are not so new and problematic as in
> Dante's undisguised incursion into the realm of a real life neither se-
> lected nor preordained by aesthetic criteria. And indeed, it is this con-
> tact with real life which is responsible for all the verbal forms. (p. 189)

Auerbach now begins to argue that the *Commedia*, with its subject of
the *status animarum post mortem*, represents "God's design in active
fulfillment," and yet these dead souls, represented as judged for eternity by God, "produce the impression not that they are dead—though
that is what they are—but alive." "Here," Auerbach continues,

we face the astounding paradox of what is called Dante's realism. Imitation of reality is imitation of the sensory experience of life on earth—among the most essential characteristics of which would seem to be its possessing a history, its changing and developing. Whatever degree of freedom the imitating artist may be granted in his work, he cannot be allowed to deprive reality of this characteristic, which is its very essence. But Dante's inhabitants of the three realms lead a "changeless existence." [Auerbach borrows here a phrase from Hegel's *Aesthetik*, *wechselloses Dasein*, and continues with Hegel as he adds:] Yet into this changeless existence Dante "plunges the living world of human action and endurance and more especially of individual deeds and destinies." (p. 191)

As Auerbach characterizes it, the existence of the personae is "final and eternal, but they are not devoid of history. . . . We have left the earthly sphere behind, . . . and yet we encounter concrete appearance and concrete occurrence" (p. 191). Though not yet named here, the basis of Auerbach's Dante interpretation is obviously his understanding of figural interpretation—already foreshadowed in his much earlier book on Dante,[13] and introduced in the last section of his "Figura" essay. The characters are more themselves, more fulfilled in "reveal[ing] the nature proper to each" here in their state of eternal judgment than they were in their real, historical lives: "We behold an intensified image of the essence of their being, . . . behold it in a purity and distinctness which could never for one moment have been possible during their lives upon earth" (p. 192). Auerbach first explains these claims within the context of the poem's theological thematics: God has judged Farinata and Cavalcante, and "not until He has pronounced that judgment has He fully perfected it and wholly revealed it to sight" (p. 192). But when Auerbach then writes of Cavalcante that "it is not likely that in the course of his earthly existence he ever felt his faith in the spirit of man, his love for the sweetness of light and for his sons so profoundly, or expressed it so arrestingly, as now, when it is all in vain" (pp. 192–93)—this statement is saved from absurdity (a "man" more real in literature than in life?) by two particular facts: that Cavalcante, like Farinata, was indeed a real, historical persona; and that the theological thematics of Dante's poem do indeed confirm Auerbach's judgment that the characters' lives are more fulfilled in God's eternal world than they could have been in their real, earthly, historical lives.

Here, with the examples of human beings represented as more real and more fully themselves after death than in life, thereby retaining "earthly historicity in [the] beyond" as "the basis of God's judgment [and] the absolute realization of a particular earthly personality in the place definitively assigned to it" (p. 193), Auerbach finally and explicitly announces the figural "conception of history" as "the foundation for Dante's realism, this realism projected into changeless eternity" (p. 194): "It is precisely [the] 'full notion of their proper individuality' which the souls attain in Dante's beyond by virtue of God's judgment; and specifically, they attain it as an actual reality, which is in keeping with the figural view. . . . [The dead in Dante represent] the relation of figure fulfilled . . . in reference to their own past life on earth" (p. 196). Auerbach then refers to that feature of the figural conception which I mentioned above, the privileging of the fulfillment as truth over the figure as mere prefiguration: "Both figure and fulfillment possess . . . the character of actual historical events and phenomena. The fulfillment possesses it in greater and more intense measure, for it is, compared with the figure, *forma perfectior*. This explains," Auerbach concludes, "the overwhelming realism of Dante's beyond" (p. 197).

But with the phrase "*overwhelming* realism of Dante's beyond," something is set in motion. For the remaining pages now stand this thematic and theologically orthodox understanding on its head as Auerbach goes on to preserve the literal and historical reality *beyond* the realism of its spiritual fulfillment in Dante's depiction of the afterlife. Auerbach asserts that, in personae such as Farinata and Cavalcante, "never before has this realism been carried so far; never before . . . has so much art and so much expressive power been employed to produce an almost painfully immediate expression of the earthly reality of human beings" (p. 199). Beyond the thematic and theological justification, then, Auerbach refocuses on Dante's style and its "expressive power."

> Figure surpasses fulfillment, or more properly: the fulfillment serves to bring out the figure in still more impressive relief. . . . What actually moves us is not that God has damned them, but that the one [Farinata] is unbroken and the other [Cavalcante] mourns so heartrendingly for his son and the sweetness of the light. (p. 200)

In other words, as fulfillment overcomes or surpasses its *figura*'s literal, historical, *real* life, it also preserves and even elevates that *figura* to the point where it surpasses its fulfillment. Auerbach seizes upon this counter-surpassing of the fulfillment (the thematic, theological representation of divine judgment) by the *figura* (the stylistic realism of Dante's representation of the characters' lives in the afterlife) to conclude with these three crucial points. First, this "impression" of the realism of life beyond its thematic fulfillment ("the listener is all too occupied by the figure in the fulfillment," he writes)—this impression "is so rich and so strong that its manifestations force their way into the listener's soul *independently of any interpretation*" (p. 201). Second,

> the principle, rooted in the divine order, of the indestructibility of the whole historical and individual man turns *against* that order, makes it subservient to its own purposes, and obscures it. The image of man eclipses the image of God. Dante's work made man's Christian-figural being a reality, and destroyed it in the very process of realizing it (p. 202).

Third—as if the previous point were not Hegelian enough—Auerbach closes the chapter by saying: "In [the] fulfillment, the figure becomes independent. . . . We are given to see, in the realm of timeless being, the history of man's inner life and unfolding [*wir erfahren . . . im zeitlosen Sein das innergeschichtliche Werden*]" (p. 202).

These three closing points of Auerbach's thus expound two kinds of "independence" enacted by a quasi-dialectical *Aufhebung* on the far side of figural representation: the lived, historical realism of that figural representation of an ahistorical, eternal afterlife becomes so powerful as to be "independent of any interpretation"; the *figura* as such consequently becomes "independent" of its spiritual meaning in fulfillment. Both of these effects are brought about by the "dialectic" of figural representation itself: an "obscuring," "eclipsing" or *concealing* of revelation *in* revelation; a "destruction" of fulfilled truth *in* its "realization"; the figure free of fulfillment *in* the fulfillment itself; or the literal and historical—the real—returning *in* its having been turned into the figural and ahistorical or eternal. Auerbach's figural understanding of Dante can therefore be summarized as follows: the historical reality (the past lives of real, historical characters) is made to serve as the *figura* for its fulfillment in divine judgment, but the representation of this fulfillment by its *figura* is so realistic—more real than life, history, reality itself—that the fulfillment becomes in turn a figure whose fulfillment is the realism of—but now *independent of*—the figural representation; the fulfillment of that historical reality itself in its realism. *Figura* in its Christian, spiritual interpretation thus becomes lived reality "independent of any interpretation."

It should already be clear how this conclusion to Auerbach's chapter on Dante foreshadows his treatment of French realism as the fulfillment of Western literature's development toward the objective representation of contemporary social reality. Briefly, the real, historical world whose representation is promised by Dante's achievement (the realism promised by reality set free) no longer receives its literary representation *within* the domain of figural fulfillment—the spiritual setting of the afterlife in Dante's *Commedia*—but rather is now fulfilled by the realism of the French novelist, a realism not of an afterlife larger and more real than life as *lived*, but of the real social-historical lived world itself. No longer would there be a *décalage* between figure and fulfillment; rather, the real, historical world of nineteenth-century France will be both *littera* and *figura* for the novels, the realism of which—like Dante's realism—will now be that literal figure's fulfillment within the very letters of literal figures. Such realistic representation of historical reality is also, then, *Mimesis*'s fulfillment of the *figura* of Dante in Flaubert. Most generally, this unfolding of the "independence" of the *figura* from its fulfillment and from its spiritualist interpretation is, in Auerbach's literary history, the enactment of Western history according to a double-edged structure of secularization. That is, the argument for the historical secularization of literary realism is coextensive with a writing of literary history according to the model of figural representation, of *figura* (Dante as medieval figural realism) and fulfillment (Flaubert as modern social-historical realism). Thus, a history of literary secularization is a figural writing of history, a *literary* history with the accent on the adjective—an *allegory* of history as its own literalization.

But the matter is not this simple. The tensions between *figura* and fulfillment are between the literal *figura* (Dante's liberated realism of life) and the figural meaning of literal representation (the letters of French realism made figurative of a higher meaning in Auerbach's interpretive construction of Flaubert's place in history). We need to investigate these tensions more closely now by turning to the chapter on French realism. In striking antithesis to the beginning of the Dante chapter, it begins without a word of stylistic commentary, offering instead several pages of historical information on 1830 and its preceding years as background material necessary for an understanding of a passage extracted from Stendhal's *Le Rouge et le Noir.* But this antithesis is not at all surprising; it is rather the first sign of the chapter's figural relation to the Dante chapter. If there one began and ended with literary *style* as the locus of realism, prior to and finally beyond the poem's thematics of fulfilled judgment, then here one begins with real social-historical detail as the beginning *and* end, *figura* and fulfillment, of the novel's realism. But a second contrast to the Dante chapter is perhaps more genuinely surprising, and it foreshadows things to come. While the Dante chapter began and ended by extolling the passionate and vital expression of the characters' fullest possible lives—"We cannot but admire Farinata and weep with Cavalcante," Auerbach wrote (p. 200)—here Auerbach begins with a discussion of boredom:

> No ordinary boredom . . . [no] fortuitous personal dullness, [but] a phenomenon politically and ideologically characteristic of the Restoration period . . . an atmosphere of pure convention, of limitation, of constraint and lack of freedom . . . mendaci[ty] . . . [people] no longer themselves believ[ing] in the thing they present . . . talk[ing] of nothing but the weather . . . unashamed baseness . . . fear . . . pervading boredom. (pp. 455–56)

This is all in the first paragraph. What has happened here, where the history of realistic Western literature is to reach its triumphant fulfillment? When the chapter, after sections on Stendhal and Balzac, finally arrives at its treatment of Flaubert, the discussion focuses immediately, for the third time and again in the first paragraph, on Emma Bovary's situation of "mediocrity . . . boredom . . . unrest and despair . . . cheerlessness, unvaryingness, grayness, staleness, airlessness, and inescapability" (p. 483). What has happened to Auerbach's argument? Here his analysis must be followed in precise detail.

In remarking upon the selected passage—Emma and her husband at dinner in Tostes ("toute l'amertume de l'existence lui semblait servie sur son assiette")—Auerbach first comments that the reader "sees [directly] only Emma's inner state; he sees what goes on at the meal indirectly, from within her state, in the light of her perception" (p. 483). But if the reader sees through Emma, Auerbach then notes that Emma sees through Charles:

> When Emma looks at him and sees him sitting there eating, he becomes the actual cause of the *elle n'en pouvait plus*, because everything else that arouses her desperation—the gloomy room, the commonplace food, the lack of a tablecloth, the hopelessness of it all—appears to her, and through her to the reader also, as something that is connected with him, that emanates from him, and that would be entirely different if he were different from what he is. (p. 484)

With this reference to Charles as the "actual cause" of what Emma sees, and of what the reader therefore also sees, one must ask whether it is Auerbach's own voice or his imitation of Flaubert's *style indirect libre*—that is, of Emma's consciousness—that says all "would be entirely different if he were different from what he is." Is it Emma, in the plot of the novel, wishing Charles were different so that her life might be different as well? Or is it Auerbach imagining that if Charles were different, Emma would be, too, and the reader—Auerbach— would see a different world? The question is especially germane since the suggestion of a possibly different life that could be available for representation recalls that larger, fuller, more vital life represented in Farinata and Cavalcante by Dante.

The next paragraph answers our question, and does so with a sentence I find the most bizarre in all of *Mimesis*. Auerbach begins by recapitulating: "We are first given Emma and then the situation through her," but not in "a simple representation of the content of Emma's consciousness, of *what* she feels *as* she feels it"; rather, "the light which illuminates the picture proceeds from her, [but] she is yet herself part of the picture. . . . Here it is not Emma who speaks, but the writer" (p. 484). Indeed, if the reader gets the scene through Emma, and Emma gets it through Charles, the reader actually gets both through Flaubert. Well enough; but then—in contrast to Flaubert's felicitously phrased expressions, says Auerbach—Emma

> would not be able to sum it all up in this way . . . if she wanted to express it, it would not come out like that; she has neither the intelligence

nor the cold candor of self-accounting necessary for such a formulation. To be sure, there is nothing of Flaubert's life in these words, but only Emma's; Flaubert does nothing but bestow the power of mature expression upon the material which she affords, in its complete subjectivity. (p. 484)

Auerbach's remarks about Emma's lack of self-expression, "intelligence," and "candor" still conform to the critic's conventional thematic commentary on the representation of a character; but then he speaks of her "life" and her "subjective material." And now the bizarre sentence: "If Emma could do this herself, she would no longer be what she is, she would have outgrown herself and thereby saved herself" (p. 484).

"She would no longer be what she is." She would no longer be Emma, the unhappy and doomed heroine of Flaubert's novel. Perhaps—surely in part—Auerbach means she would be a different character, less unhappy, less doomed. But who is "she"? "She" is not, as Farinata or Cavalcante was, a once real and historical person. "She" is the "real" Emma Bovary who is not. A realistic representation of a fictional character is taken by Auerbach as a person—a "complete subjectivity"—who might have been otherwise than she is, that unhappy fiction. And to be real—"she would no longer be what she is"—would be to develop ("outgrow herself") and to be fulfilled ("save herself").

I can now move rapidly to my conclusion. In Dante, realistic representation translates historical lives into the apotheosis of their actuality, until this fullness of representation saves them from their thematic depiction as dead souls in the afterlife of hell; to recall Auerbach's formulation, they "produce the impression not that they are dead—though that is what they are—but alive" (p. 191). The *figurae* of their thematic fulfillment surpassed and cancelled their own spiritual fulfillment, and were *refigured* as literal, living, historical figures. Now, with Flaubert, the opposite occurs. The power of the realistic representation of a fictional life set in real, social-historical circumstances appears to Auerbach as the unfulfilled promise of a more spiritually real life that might have been—really, historically, literally. That absent fulfillment would "save" Emma, who is otherwise an inauthentic, unfulfilled, fictional yet realistic *figura*. To adapt Auerbach, she produces the impression not that she is fiction—though that is what she is—but real. Her *figura*, as the letters on the pages of

Madame Bovary producing (signifying, representing) the figure of a real person, would be fulfilled (surpassed, overcome, cancelled) in her becoming more (but also less) than she is—in her becoming *dis-figured* as a figure (a representation of a reality), and being made literal, historical, real. The move, in other words, from Dante to Flaubert is from real historical life transformed into a literature which is more than a reality, to a realistic fictional life transformed into a reality which would be more, should be more, but *is* not: *plus de réal-ité*—more, and no more, reality.

Thus, when Auerbach moves, on the next page, to speak of Flaubert's artistic practice, he speaks of "selecting events and translating them into language" as if they were already there, like real, historical lives or a real history, a real past; and he adds: "This is done in the conviction that every event, if one is able to express it purely and completely, interprets itself far better and more completely than any opinion appended to it could do" (p. 486). This exact echo of the claim made for Dante—realism "independent of any interpretation"—is made here in the absence of an authorial judgment: the self-sufficient truth of verbal representation, or what Auerbach calls "a profound faith in the truth of language" (p. 486). But the truth of language here, its *veritas*, is the fulfillment or unveiling of Flaubert's *figure*—Emma—as *letters*; not as a literal, historical being ("a complete subjectivity"), but as *litterae* or letters. The truth of literary realism becomes the revelation of the falseness, the fictionality, of its rhetorical or figural representation in and through literal letters.

The truth of modern realism is the "no more reality" that disfigures the "more reality" figured in the representation of a person *who is not* except as a *personage* who is "her" letters. It is this truth that surfaces in the final pages of Auerbach's chapter, less as a guilty conscience, perhaps, than as a guilty unconscious. For as his language—in paraphrasing a letter of Flaubert's—still echoes that which he used to praise Dante ("subjects are seen as God sees them, in their true essence" [p. 487]), this truth without interpretation is not that of the plenitude of lived, historical lives, but rather of "a chronic discomfort, which completely rules an entire life. . . . The novel is the representation of an entire human existence which has no issue. . . . Nothing happens, but that nothing has become a heavy, oppressive something" (p. 488). He insists that, as with Dante, this interpretation is immanent ("The interpretation of the situation is contained in its description" [p. 489]), but he then goes on not in praise, but in a final, mounting tirade: Emma and Charles

> have nothing in common, and yet they have nothing of their own, for the sake of which it would be worthwhile to be lonely. For, privately, each of them has a silly, false world, which cannot be reconciled with the reality of his situation, and so they both miss the possibilities life offers them. What is true of these two, applies to almost all the other characters in the novel; each of the many mediocre people who act in it has his own world of mediocre and silly stupidity . . . each is alone, none can understand another, or help another to insight; there is no common world of men, because it could only come into existence if many should find their way to their own proper reality, the reality which is given to the individual—which then would be also the true common reality. . . . [But instead it is] one-sided, ridiculous, painful, and . . . charged with misunderstanding, vanity, futility, falsehood, and stupid hatred. (p. 489)

A "silly, false world" which is not reconcilable with reality and which misses life's possibility; stupidity and nothingness, falsehood and misunderstanding, as "what is true" of the characters; and the absence of "true reality" due to the absence of the character's "own proper reality, the reality given to the individual." This, then, is the fulfillment of Dante's promise of the history of Western realism: representation without reality or so much as the possibility of life; truth as falsehood and nothingness; characters lacking both fulfillment *and* prefiguration of "their own proper reality" except in their figural fulfillment as signifying letters.

Alphabetic characters of inanimate material? Dead letters? *Litterae* as the corpse, the heavy, oppressive nothing of *historia*? When Auerbach attempts to turn, at the end of the paragraph I have been quoting, from his dyspeptic tantrum—"In his book the world consists of pure stupidity, which completely misses true reality, so that the latter should properly not be discoverable in it at all" (p. 489)—he attempts to make this turn with a sudden epiphany: "Yet [true reality] is there; it is in the writer's language, which unmasks the stupidity by pure statement; language, then, has criteria for stupidity and thus also has a part in that reality of the 'intelligent' which otherwise never appears in the book" (p. 489). Auerbach's phrasing here is precisely right even as his meaning is profoundly wrong. The "true reality" that cannot be fulfilled or revealed in realistic representation—for what is revealed is falsehood and nothingness—is nonetheless to be revealed and fulfilled somewhere; but if it is not in the realistic representation, it is not "*in* the writer's language" or "*in* the book" either, as if it were some thematic or semantic representation of meaning to be revealed, fulfilled, and made real in an act of understanding. Rather, it *is* the language and *is* the book: the "true reality" of the letters which unmask—literally, "re-veal"—their representational stupidity and nothingness by their pure statement, as if to say, we are the *littera* and its *figura, historia* and its meaning, which now fulfill and reveal the history of our representations of reality by the pure statement of its stupidity and nothingness—its corpse.

And what can we draw from this "exemplary" case of literary history as the literalization of historical letters? The corpse of Flaubert's language is one thing; as for the language of Auerbach's *Mimesis*, I come not to bury, but to honor it. I have tried to demonstrate how the figural model of interpretation and representation structures and operates upon the historical narrative of Auerbach's study of literary realism. Literally the figural model structures, and is operative within, his narrative of the two-tiered triumph of the representation of lived, historical reality in Dante and Flaubert. But figuratively, Auerbach's historiography disfigures the literal narrative and its *figura* by fulfilling them as the letters in a *literary* history, letters that represent the stupidity and nothingness of the real history that thought itself, in this literary mode, to be more real—but is, alas, no more real—than its representation as letters. In its intellectual context, this is a Hegelian allegory: the allegory of historical meaning (as phenomenal appearance) being preserved-and-cancelled, left behind in the uncovering of its truth and yet retained as the mere letter of this significance.

I understand this as one kind of allegory of history, what may be called the allegory of the nihilism of historical meaning: the meaning of historiography being that historical reality is cancelled or annihilated in its fulfillment in literature, including those genres called history and literary history. What this means is that to write and think the historical is to enter into allegory, to enact a literary, and specifically a rhetorical, mode of discourse. It is fortuitous, not merely accidental, that Auerbach's title and object of study is *mimesis*, for the insight that lies therein is the same one that I have tried to expose within the book's historical narrative: history itself is *mimesis*, the representation of the dead past, and the figurative structure that appears when history is done is already implied in the rhetorical structure of its ontology, indeed, of its name. The term names two notions, ontologically opposed as origin and representation, and the confusion between the two unfolds whenever historical narrative is attempted. "History" is literally the past, figuratively its meaning as the history that is thought and written. And this history—what we conventionally intend when we use and think the term—must always reduce history as an ontological object into a dead letter, so that it might be "meaningful," the literal sign for an allegorical meaning.

An alternative allegory of history which suggests itself—Walter Benjamin comes to mind—might then be called the allegory of the *eschatology* of historical meaning: the meaning of historiography being not the *re*presentation, but the *pre*sentation of reality, as and in history, in its ongoing deferral of fulfillment; reality preserved, that is, as signs to be read, preserved as literature to be read, including history and literary history. But to speak of alternate allegories of history is not necessarily to invoke any question of choice in the matter; the meaning of my study of Auerbach's historiography may perhaps be that the letter always grasps, even to the point of throttling, the figure of its own historical life. Rather, the apparent "choice" with which I began lay between nonhistorical literary theory and the possibility of literary history. The senses of the alternate allegories of history—nihilism or eschatology, dead meaning or meaning deferred—might be borne in mind today whenever literary history would be so blithely opposed to the labyrinths of literary theory.

Between Dialectics and Deconstruction: Derrida and the Reading of Marx

ANDREW PARKER

For Stephen Melville

In general terms, this essay asks of Marxism a question which hitherto has been posed solely in connection with psychoanalysis: can a theory of conflict escape the effects of the object it seeks to describe? Some of Freud's best recent readers, such as Samuel Weber, have argued persuasively that such a question can be answered only in the negative, for the inherent instability of the unconscious seems inevitably to rebound upon the very theory that would specify systematically the properties of such an object.[1] In accordance with this insight, Freud's writings have begun to be read not simply as theoretical accounts of psychic conflict but as textual exemplifications of such conflict as well. The phrase "theory of conflict" thus might stand as an appropriate motto for this revised, "deconstructive" understanding of the conditions of psychoanalytic possibility: at once the explanation and the site of conflict, Freudian theory now finds itself replicating internally the condensations and displacements it sought merely to delineate. One casualty of this reading would be, of course, the traditional practice of "applied psychoanalysis," for if Freud's writing is traversed by the movements of its objects—if it repeats within itself the rhetorical operations of the texts (whether "psychic" or "literary") that it would analyze—then psychoanalysis begins to lose its ostensible coherence as a discrete, self-identical body of knowledge different in kind from the unstable phenomena it seeks simply to read.

Such a line of questioning has never been brought systematically to bear upon that *other* "theory of conflict"—Marxism. To extend to the realm of Marxist theory a problematic first developed in relation to psychoanalysis is certainly *not* to invite renewed attempts at an elusive "Freud-Marx synthesis," nor is it to advocate the creation of something which might be called a "psychoanalysis of Marxism."

Rather, it is simply to contend that Marx still awaits his poststructuralist readers and that the conflicts characteristic of Marxism as a systematic theory have yet to receive the attention they deserve. There are, to be sure, sound reasons for this reluctance to submit Marx's texts to the kind of critical reading that distinguishes recent analyses of Freudian theory. Foremost among these, perhaps, is a recognition of the political stakes involved: at a time when, in this country, Marxism has little discernible impact as a force of popular resistance, one might hesitate to contribute to its further weakening by calling its principles into question. It might be argued, however, that the present moment precisely requires just such a careful analysis— especially if the strategic failures of the past are not to be repeated blindly. If, indeed, there are signs that Marxist theory is now beginning to be *read* rather than simply memorized and recited—if a "commitment to Marxism" can no longer proceed without a rigorous understanding of the letter of Marx's text—we might very well conclude that a deconstructive reading of Marxism would be less an evasion of the political (as might be charged) than a timely attempt to construe the political *otherwise*.

This essay is an initial attempt to supply protocols for that critical task, to begin marking the internal limits of Marxist theory by describing how the inversions and distortions that form its ideological object ultimately are reproduced within the discourse that would master these effects. Reading what is now commonly referred to as "the crisis of Marxism," it will suggest not only that this crisis is fundamentally "rhetorical" in nature but also that Marx's rhetorical practice might be the best guide for the analysis of (his own) crises. Such a conclusion—which will undermine the assumptions shared by the various extant forms of "semiotic Marxism"—will also raise by implication the question of the relationship between Marxism and deconstruction, a question generating at present a heated debate between the advocates of each discourse. By reformulating this relationship in terms of *supplementarity*, the essay finally will argue that Marx and Derrida may be viewed most productively as neither antithetical nor complementary figures, thereby opening up a space of interimplication that will redefine as one of its effects the stakes of the current controversy.

The Crisis of Theory

Contemporary Marxist theory appears to be suffering from a severe crisis of confidence. As many of its current and former partisans are acknowledging with increasing frequency, Marxism's power as an explanatory model has been damaged irreparably by its inability either to predict or to comprehend the full complexities of twentieth-century history. In 1892, at the time of the Second International, Karl Kautsky still could maintain with conviction the "orthodox" view that

> capitalist society has failed; its dissolution is only a question of time; irresistible economic development leads with natural necessity to the bankruptcy of the capitalist mode of production. The erection of a new form of society in place of the existing one is no longer merely desirable; it has become something inevitable.[2]

Subsequent events, however, have belied the adequacy—and the implicit optimism—of any such notion of "natural necessity"; indeed, if the trajectory of history in our century has demonstrated anything, it is that the "laws" of historical materialism have shown themselves fallible. Contrary to expectations, the proletariat in the West has not emerged as "the identical subject-object of the historical process" or as the self-conscious agent of revolutionary practice.[3] The rise of Fascism in the guise of a "workers' movement" and the postwar integration of organized labor into the mainstream of economic life are merely two of the many anomalies that Marxist theory could in no way foresee, could account for only by way of retrospection. The ultimate irony, of course, is that when class struggle *did* culminate in revolution, it did so in the least likely of places—Russia, where, moreover, the excesses committed in the name of socialism should not have occurred (in theory) once the private ownership of property formally had been abolished. Given the manifest irregularity of such developments—phenomena whose "contradictory" character has proven highly resistant to dialectical sublation—it seems easy to agree with Stanley Aronowitz's conclusion that "the theoretical basis of Marxism [has been] called into question by historical reality," that Marxism's "underlying prophetic value" has been compromised decisively by the very object it purports to comprehend.[4]

For many observers, the current crisis of historical materialism—the diminution of its powers "as a scientific discipline and as a guide to political practice"—derives ultimately from Marx's preponderant emphasis on the categories of political economy.[5] Our era of post-industrial capitalism (so these arguments run) has witnessed the formation of a gap between base and superstructure on such an unprecedented scale that the mode of production cannot fulfill its traditional function as the ground of historical determination. Ideology, in our century, seems to have claimed a recalcitrant specificity all its own, while cultural forms and practices appear to evolve in a "relative autonomy" that no longer reflects with any accuracy the conditions of the infrastructure. The feminist and civil rights movements have also contested the primacy that Marxism grants to the mode of production, for the transhistorical existence of sexual and racial oppression cannot be explained entirely by reference to the economic "last instance."[6] Faced with this mounting evidence of theoretical inadequacy, various Marxists have argued for a modification of the base/superstructure model that would allow for multiple and indirect determinations while still reserving ultimate dominance for the economy. Others, however, have attacked even this revised model for its residual economism, claiming that Marxism's very emphasis on the concept of production—the cornerstone of historical materialism—is itself the offspring of nineteenth-century capitalism, an ideological remainder that defines Marxism as a part of the system against which it would contend. If any weight is to be accorded this latter view, then the title of a recent work of Marxist theory—*Is There a Future for Marxism?*—must be read as other than narrowly rhetorical. All signs thus point to what seems an inescapable diagnosis: "Western Marxism is in crisis."[7]

This widening consensus concerning the crisis of historical materialism is an important development if only because it indicates the willingness of contemporary Marxism to examine itself critically. What is surprising about such acknowledgments, however, is their own failure to recollect that Marxism is itself a *theory of crisis*—of the periodic fluctuations of supply and demand that destabilize the capitalist economy. George Lichtheim has outlined the fundamental properties of these cyclical business crises:

Capitalist accumulation is regulated by the search for profit, while the satisfaction of wants comes in only incidentally. Production is thus divorced from consumption, and though the two are brought together by the mechanism of the market, the latter operates in such a way as to ensure equilibrium between supply and demand only at the cost of periodic upheavals, in which "superfluous" capital is destroyed and large numbers of uncompetitive firms are driven to the wall. Since purchases are divorced from sales, the "law of markets" represents an abstraction to which nothing corresponds in reality.[8]

Crisis, in other words, results when "the split between the sale and the purchase [of commodities] becomes too pronounced," a development which reflects an underlying lack of correspondence between production and consumption: "Nothing could be more childish than the dogma that because every sale is a purchase, and every purchase a sale, therefore the circulation of commodities implies an equilibrium of sales and purchases."[9] Marx's essential contribution to the understanding of this "disequilibrium" is his demonstration of its *necessity* for the self-regulation of capitalism: "Crises are always but momentary and forcible solutions of existing contradictions. They are violent eruptions which for a time restore the disturbed equilibrium."[10] Capitalism thus generates within itself an economic dehiscence in which the production of commodities regularly exceeds the possibility of their consumption; the crisis point is reached when the unequal ratio between supply and demand surpasses acceptable levels of toleration.

Can this brief overview of the Marxist theory of crisis help us to reformulate the issues involved in the crisis of Marxist theory? This question might be answered affirmatively if the theory of crisis were read, in effect, as an implicit theory of figuration. Such a suggestion is not as extravagant as it first may appear, for Marx's account of the relationship between production and consumption under capitalism resembles nothing so much as the relationship between figural and literal language as elaborated consistently throughout the history of Western philosophy. Just as the "law of markets" in the capitalist system constitutes an "abstraction to which nothing corresponds in reality," so, too, has philosophy traditionally condemned the "excesses" of rhetoric as an improper departure from the literal truth. The inherent possibility that production might proliferate without any necessary connection to consumption finds its parallel, moreover, in philosophy's recurrent fear that figures might flourish in the absence of their referents, that tropes might wander aimlessly without coming to rest at a stable source of meaning. This potential for rhetorical aberration seems as intolerable to philosophy as it is to capitalism: in both cases, the drift toward "free play" must be corrected no matter the cost; errancy must be suppressed if each system is to preserve its essential integrity.[11]

If the Marxist theory of crisis therefore reveals a *rhetorical* fissure at the heart of the capitalist economy, this very gap will allow us to reappraise the crisis of Marxist theory. For if Marxism takes rhetoric as its implicit *object* in its analysis of the business cycle, it will also become *subject* to figural instability to the extent that it construes itself as a science of historical development—a science which, by definition, cannot admit the wanderings of (its own) rhetoric. Philosophy's worst anxiety, it has been argued, concerns the potential lack of correspondence between the figural and the literal. Marxism's greatest fear similarly derives from the possibility that a rhetorical gap might intervene between base and superstructure—that political, ideological, and cultural practices might not be grounded firmly in the mode of production. As an "objective" model of historical explanation, Marxism must foreclose this potential disharmony, must bring the free play of the superstructure into conformity with the "literal" base. This capacity of the superstructure to develop in "relative autonomy" is not, however, simply a contingency that could be rectified by means of a more "scientific" analysis; it is rather a rhetorical schism of the kind already identified by Marxism in its theory of business crises. Marxism, in other words, seems unable to escape from the figural object of its own theorization, for the disequilibrium encountered at the level of production ultimately rebounds upon the base/superstructure paradigm as well, forcing the latter to repeat within itself these very rhetorical disjunctions.

Viewed in this manner, the crisis of Marxist theory may be redefined as a tendency to overproduce rhetorical anomalies, to generate a supply of superstructural phenomena that exceeds the demands of the economic base. Marxism's "crisis" is thus not merely a contemporary condition but one which results from a figural "drifting" [*dérive*] intrinsic to the theory as such. For at its most powerful, Marxism has *always* acknowledged this implicit ability to go astray in the rhetorical gaps it discloses: in *The Eighteenth Brumaire of Louis Napoleon,* for example, Marx confronts explicitly the eruption of uncanny forces that undermine the correspondences between base and superstructure on which his theory is staked.[12] When, however, Marxism mistakes itself for a science of historical reality—when it cannot recognize itself in the errancy of its objects—the theory indeed risks complicity with its capitalist adversary, borrowing the latter's techniques of containment in an effort to preserve its own systematic integrity.[13]

The Ends of Mediation

There are many ways for Marxism to mistake itself for a science, to avoid an acknowledgment of its inherent capacity to stray from itself. Foremost among these, perhaps, are the theories of mediation developed in recent years in an attempt to provide "Marxism's missing link between infrastructure and superstructure."[14] Focusing on *language* as the essential connection between the economic and the political, many Marxists have borrowed heavily from the fields of linguistics and semiotics, claiming that "ideology is made of language in the form of linguistic signs" and thus that it is incumbent upon Marxism to produce a theory of language in order to account more precisely for ideological formations.[15] Such a turn towards language nevertheless should strike us as inherently surprising, for Marx left only a few scattered remarks on the subject—nothing, in short, that would warrant the central role that language has come to play recently in Marxist analyses of culture and society. As late as 1971, for example, Roland Barthes still could express his admiration for Brecht in terms of the latter's idiosyncratic interest in the dynamics of language:

> What makes Brecht exemplary for me is properly speaking neither his Marxism nor his aesthetic (although both are very important) but the conjunction of the two: namely of Marxist analysis and thinking about meaning. He was a Marxist who reflected upon *effects of the sign*: a very rare thing.[16]

Also in 1971, Fredric Jameson could characterize Walter Benjamin's writings on the rhetoric of memory in the following way: "Strange reflections, these—strange subjects of reflection for a Marxist."[17] If these statements indicate the comparative marginality of language in relation to Marxism's more traditional concerns, then we must ask why many contemporary Marxists have chosen linguistics as the solution to the problem of mediation.

This question might be addressed in terms of the fact that "never as much as at the present has [the problem of language] invaded, *as such*, the global horizon of the most diverse researches and the most heterogeneous discourses."[18] If, in other words, our century has been marked by an all-pervasive "linguistic turn"—if most philosophical questions have since been redefined as questions of language—it perhaps was inevitable that Marxism would attempt to keep abreast of the changing *epistēmē* by allying itself with the developing linguistic sciences.[19] Now as never before a properly Marxist theory of language is widely viewed as the only possible remedy for the implicit shortcomings of the base/superstructure paradigm; historical materialism is suddenly thought to be "impossible without an adequate theory of language."[20] The absence of such a theory is now held to be responsible for the failings of traditional Marxist criticism. Georg Lukács, for example, is currently charged with the crime of treating language as a largely instrumental medium, as a transparent reflection of historical relationships, rather than—as his recent critics would argue—the very site at which such relationships are themselves produced. According to the new consensus, however, Marxism's linguistic gap could be bridged (and Lukács's criticism corrected) if sufficient attention were directed to the semiotic component of cultural production—for, in the words of Julia Kristeva, it is the signifying dimension "without which no linkages between 'base' and 'superstructure' can exist."[21] Although Althusser has contended that any serious investigation into the linguistic nature of ideology must break with the base/superstructure model itself, it is nevertheless fair to say that most varieties of contemporary Marxism share a commitment to the linguistic sciences as the preferred manner of mediating between the domains of production and ideology.

A common linguistic orientation hence can be shown to underlie the otherwise distinct projects of such theorists as Raymond Williams, who maintains that "a fully historical semiotics would be very much the same thing as cultural materialism";[22] Fredric Jameson, whose entire career to date might be described as a "search for a [linguistic] method," for a semiotic model that would combine "the findings of narrative analysis, psychoanalysis, and traditional as well as modern approaches to ideology";[23] Ferruccio Rossi-Landi, for whom sign systems occupy "an intermediate position between modes of production and ideological institutions";[24] and the now defunct *Tel Quel* group, whose former goal was to inaugurate a properly "materialist" semiotics.[25] This catalogue of theorists is not, of course, intended to be exhaustive; the point is simply that, despite genuine differences in method, all of these writers fully subscribe to the view that *some* form of linguistic model is necessary in order to resolve "l'impasse de langage dans le marxisme" and to establish, thereby, an adequate theory of mediation.[26]

There are, however, several reasons to doubt the ultimate viability of this attempt to remedy the faults of Marxism by employing the tools of linguistics. In the first place, it is simply not self-evident that a "theory of language" is, in fact, absent from Marx's writings. Although such a theory would not, of course, find expression in any explicit or systematic form, it nevertheless might be located in the characteristic (if unpredictable) ways his texts perform *rhetorically*. We have seen above, for example, that Marx's theory of crisis can be read as an implicit theory of figuration. *Capital* is similarly not about language in any overt or sustained manner, yet in its description of the commodity form as "a social hieroglyphic" [*eine gesellschaftliche Hieroglyphe*], we encounter another rhetorical crux around which much of this text can be said to (un)hinge.[27] By thus reading Marx as a "rhetorical theorist"—by examining in detail the tropological *labor* of his writing (etymologically, its "slippage," its "sliding")—we might succeed in elaborating a general economy of Marxist figuration that could reopen, among its many possibilities, the question of Marxism's repressed "literary" heritage: the early poetic and dramatic works which, according to the leading Marxologists, supposedly were "transcended" [*aufgehoben*] by Marx in his later writings.

A second reservation concerning Marxism's linguistic turn is, perhaps, more substantial, for the very notion that language can be used to cure the deficiencies of the base/superstructure model seems inherently dubious. This is surely *not* to say that the paradigm is without serious shortcomings, that there is no gap between its two poles.

What I would argue, rather, is that this gap cannot be bridged by language since it is itself the *product* of language—of an inversion between cause and effect accomplished through the figure of metalepsis. Marxism necessarily thinks of the infrastructure as its *first* principle, as the cause ("in the final instance") of the superstructure's effects. The primacy of the base could be challenged, however, if one were to acknowledge that

> the first is not the first if there is not a second to follow it. Consequently, the second is not that which merely arrives, like a latecomer, *after* the first, but that which permits the first to be the first. The first cannot be the first unaided, by its own properties alone: the second, with all the force of its delay, must come to the assistance of the first. The "second time" thus has priority of a kind over the "first time": it is present from the first time onwards as the prerequisite of the first's priority.

The base, in other words, might now be regarded less as an original, self-identical entity than as the rhetorical effect of a *prior* effect—of the superstructure. Marxism's most elementary principle thus has undergone inversion, for if the superstructure allows the base to become the base, then it is the superstructure which must be counted as the fundamental term, as the base's condition of possibility.[28] This inversion of cause and effect—the characteristic feature of the figure of metalepsis—will preclude definitively *any* possible linguistic correction of Marxism, for the discontinuity between base and superstructure can now be construed as a product of language in the "first" place. The remedy therefore turns out to be the disease it attempted to cure; "constituted by the very distances and differences it seeks to overcome," language is not Marxism's solution to the problem of mediation but the name of this problem itself.[29]

Marxism Versus Deconstruction?

To suggest, as I have done, that Marxism can stray from itself—that it avoids the consequences of this drifting insofar as it relies on theories of linguistic mediation—is, by implication, to raise the question of the relationship between Marxism and deconstruction. Much has been written of late on the subject of this relationship, most of which has taken a highly predictable form. Although Michael Ryan has argued at length that Marxism and deconstruction are complementary discourses, both of which offer powerful critiques of the principle of self-evidence, most theorists have chosen simply to defend one "side" against the other, arguing that Marxism and deconstruction are mutually exclusive in their implications.[30]

There is much, in fact, to substantiate this claim that Marxism and deconstruction are antithetical practices. If, as Paul Ricoeur puts it, "the task of hermeneutics . . . has always been to read a text and distinguish the true sense from the apparent sense, to search for the sense under the sense, to search for the intelligible text under the unintelligible text," we then can state unequivocally that Marxism has always construed itself as a critical hermeneutics—a discipline devoted to the demystification of the ideological through the unconcealment of its buried truth.[31] "It is always," writes Marx, "the direct relationship of the owners of the conditions of production to the direct producers . . . which reveals *the innermost secret, the hidden basis* of the entire social structure."[32] This notion of truth (*alētheia*) as the unveiling of a disguised presence comprises, however, precisely one of deconstruction's main targets, leading Derrida to insist that his is not a critical, hermeneutic enterprise: "Deconstruction is not a critical operation; criticism is its object. Deconstruction aims, at one moment or another, at the confidence expressed in the critical instance, in the critico-theoretical, that is, deciding instance, in the ultimate possibility of decidability itself." Since the Marxist conception of ideology constitutes one such "deciding instance," Derrida can detect in it "a certain logic of representation, of consciousness, of the subject, of the imaginary, of mimesis"—a logic that will always confer on the notion of fetishism a negative valuation. For Derrida, however, there has never been anything *but* fetishism: no simple, pure, originary state that subsequently could be degraded into alienation. Though he recognizes "the necessity of the problematic *domain* designated by the Marxist conception of ideology," he nevertheless maintains his distance from Marxism insofar as it continues to view itself as a foundationalist enterprise:

> To the extent that it includes a system named dialectical materialism, doesn't Marxism present itself as a philosophy (whether elaborated or

to be elaborated), as a *founded* philosophical practice, as a "construction"? . . . I haven't known any Marxist discourse—considered as such or said to be such—which would respond negatively to this question. Nor even, I might add, which poses or recognizes this *as* a question.[33]

Where, then, Marxism subscribes to "a sense of society as a totality" which would "allow social phenomena once again to become transparent,"[34] deconstruction would contend that any "totality" is undermined by its irreducible lack of self-identity, that social phenomena have always already lost their putative transparency. Where Marxism necessarily remains committed to a notion of history as the *history of sense*—a history guaranteed by the operation of the dialectic as it transforms local contradictions into universal truths—Derrida would linger over the detritus that resists dialectical sublation, producing as a result "another concept or conceptual chain of 'history'": a history inherently different from itself. Where, finally, production constitutes Marxism's fundamental category, deconstruction would argue that "everything begins with reproduction."[35]

By all appearances, then, Marxism and deconstruction remain opposed to one another. This is, indeed, the common verdict reached by the majority of supporters of each of these discourses: Hillis Miller "views as naive the millennial or revolutionary hopes still present in one way or another even in sophisticated Marxism"; Terry Eagleton claims that "many of the vauntedly novel themes of deconstructionism do little more than reproduce some of the most commonplace topics of bourgeois liberalism"; Jacob Rogozinski maintains that Marxism's belief in proletarian revolution is merely "the last avatar of political metaphysics"; Andreas Huyssen contends that "Derridean deconstruction . . . remains indifferent to its own historical moment, let alone that of the texts it reads."[36] For each of these partisans, then, Marxism and deconstruction are inherently incompatible; one must choose sides between them.

Derrida, however, does not make this "choice." Although he has written on the texts of Marx and of Marxism only in passing—an "omission" that has generated a plethora of commentary—he nevertheless indicated relatively early in his career that the absence of Marx in his writings represents not an objection to Marxism per se but a constellation of lacunae explicitly calculated "to mark the loci of a theoretical elaboration which, from my standpoint in any case, remains yet to come."[37] More than a decade after this statement, however, Derrida's readings of Marx remain *á venir*—and might very well be deferred endlessly. Marxism did form an occasional topic explored by Derrida and his interviewers in the 1970s, and Marx is analyzed very briefly both in *Dissemination* and in *Glas*. In recent years, moreover, Derrida seems to be thinking increasingly of Marxism, affirming that "there is some possible articulation between an open Marxism and what I am interested in," and that "Marxism is not to be attacked like such and such other theoretical comfort" [*comme tel ou tel autre confort théorique*].[38] But despite the good will expressed by these suggestive comments, the question remains as to why Marx continues to be absent from Derrida's texts. How *can* we account for Derrida's reticence on the subject? Will an answer to this question help us to reformulate the relationship between Marxism and deconstruction in a way that avoids the usual reductive *choices*?

In the Crypt

As typically conducted, the debate between Marxists and deconstructionists has turned on the issue of Who encompasses Whom, of which theory can incorporate a wider range of phenomena (including, of course, the other). Marxists, for example, regularly charge that deconstruction does not know its *place*, its own limitations relative to Marxism—a position defended by Michael Ryan, for whom deconstruction literally is *comprehended* by Marxist theory:

> Deconstruction can derive from Marxism the broad political and socio-historical outlines which it now lacks. Like bourgeois feminism which dictates its own limits—limits which Marxist-feminists are beginning to overcome—deconstruction as it exists projects limits which can only be overcome by placing its *at once more local and more general* undertaking (because the critique of logocentrism is limited in comparison to social theory, but it nevertheless deals with a phenomenon that characterizes all western, not only bourgeois, rationality) within the framework of a broader revolutionary theory.

Deconstruction, in other words, is inherently lacking, is limited with respect to Marxism's greater powers of explanation. Although Ryan adds that Marxism, too, can "benefit" from its encounter with deconstruction (he finds the latter "a means of detecting and correcting residual idealism in Marxist theory itself"), his argument nevertheless typifies the terms of the current controversy in its attempt to rank these theories hierarchically, to draw discernible and stable boundaries between them—even if the asymmetry of "at once more local and more general" offers a troubling, though momentary, pause.[39]

The claim that Marxism incorporates deconstruction—that the latter is far more limited than the former—surfaces as well in the last three interviews collected in *Positions* (between Derrida and the *Tel Quel* Marxists Jean-Louis Houdebine and Guy Scarpetta). Like Ryan, Houdebine contends that deconstruction is already contained within the practice of Marxist-Leninism, that Derrida's "concept" of *différance* in fact can be assimilated to "the motif of heterogeneity [which] is the motif of a—the?—basic dialectical materialist contradiction."[40] The interview in which this allegation occurs, however, is marked by a bizarre *pas de deux*: Houdebine and Scarpetta insist repeatedly that Derrida define his position with respect to Marxism (as if it were a matter of asking him, Are you *for* or *against*?); each of these demands elicits a lengthy response from Derrida which, strangely enough, only seems to reinforce his interviewers' frustration (thereby prompting them to reiterate their question to him in a slightly altered form). If, in general, the intent of an interview is the facilitation of direct communication between two discrete parties, then the sheer *perversity* of these exchanges between Derrida and his Marxist critics—their evident lack of communicative success—seems to call out for a psychoanalytic reading that would account for the insistence of the pattern. In what follows such a reading will be undertaken in an effort to displace the kind of territorial warfare currently afflicting the dialogue between Marxists and deconstructionists; we might, in this way, discover that the two theories ultimately cannot be "comprehended" in the form of a stable hierarchy—that, indeed, the borders between them are far less secure than previously had been imagined.

In reading the *Positions* interview, one may be struck by the curious fact that the questions put to Derrida resemble, in their blind insistency, nothing so much as the Freudian "compulsion to repeat" [*Wiederholungszwang*]—for if the interviewers remain unsatisfied despite receiving answers fitted to their questions, then theirs is a com-

pulsion that "cannot ultimately be reduced to . . . the interplay between the pleasure principle and the reality principle." Nor can this
compulsion to repeat be understood simply as a desire to master deconstruction—to subject Derrida to the mastery of Marxism:

> What then is this function of traumatic repetition if nothing—quite the
> reverse—seems to justify it from the point of view of the pleasure prin-
> ciple? To master the painful event, someone might say—but who mas-
> ters, where is the master here, to be mastered? Why speak so hastily
> when we do not know precisely where to situate the agency that would
> undertake this operation of mastery?[41]

Neither, however, can Derrida assume this position of mastery, for his
is literally a "defensive" position—a stance characterized by a rhetoric of defense [Abwehr]: "There is what you call this 'encounter' [with
Marx] which has seemed to me indeed, for a long time, absolutely necessary. *You may well imagine that I was not completely unconscious of it.*"[42]
This defensive tone marks as well a discussion in *La Carte
postale* in which Derrida objects to the translation (in a recent French edition of
The German Ideology) of the phrase *aufgelöst werden können* as *peuvent
être déconstruites*. The passage in question is a famous one in which
Marx distinguishes between the merely intellectual analysis of ideological forms and a truly revolutionary practice that overthrows the
real determining structures of material production. The new translation quietly places "deconstruction" in the former category. Derrida
protests: "Once the amalgam is accomplished, the appropriation in-
corporated [*incorporée*], we hear [*on laisse entendre*] that 'deconstruction' is destined to remain limited to the 'intellectual criticism' of su-
perstructures. It is as if Marx had already spoken the word [*on fait
comme si Marx l'avait déjà dit*]."[43] Who hears this traducing of deconstruction? Has slander been the translator's surreptitious motive?
Can this phrasing be construed solely as the product of malicious intent? If, in this instance, Derrida is clearly overreacting, is it merely a
coincidence that such behavior occurs in the vicinity of Marx's name?
    In noting this conjunction of a compulsion to repeat with the opera-
tion of a persistent rhetoric of defense, we seem to find ourselves
reading not an interview between Derrida and his critics but *Beyond
the Pleasure Principle*, a text whose insights into the nature of the ego's
precarious boundaries will bear ultimately on the relationship be-

tween deconstruction and Marxism. Freud characterizes the ego in this work as a "boundary creature" [*Grenzwesen*] eluding all classification in terms of simple, binary categories; mediating between the world and the id, the ego seeks to defend itself from "internal" threats by treating them as though they came from without. This ability of the ego to interchange insides with outsides has been identified by Margaret Ferguson as the distinctive feature of the "textual defenses" produced by such authors as Sidney and Shelley (among others):

> [*Beyond the Pleasure Principle*] provides a useful way of thinking about textual defenses—including Freud's own—as "productions of the ego." Defenses generally occur as responses to threats which may be seen as coming from an "external world," and they also characteristically employ a "rhetoric of motives" to express wishes and fears that may be said to come from within the authorial psyche. The distinction between "internal" and "external" in the realm of textual defense is, however, no less complex than Freud suggests it to be in the realm of psychic survival.[44]

If the interview from *Positions* may qualify as such a "textual defense," it is because it calls into question—like the ego described in *Beyond the Pleasure Principle*—the stability of the border between "inside" and "outside." Not only are the questions addressed to Derrida phrased in terms of which discourse is *outside* of (that is, more *comprehensive* than) the other, but even the very form of this interview poses and reposes a problem of borders: when does the interview end—with the termination of the recorded dialogue or with the final exchange of letters? Where are its boundaries between writing and speech, between the spontaneity of its conversation and its supplementary process of editorial revision? If, in addition to a compulsion to repeat, a defensive rhetoric indeed inheres in the structure of this interview, these then are tropes whose topographies "do not yield to the norms of formal logic: they relate to no object or collection of objects nor in any strict sense do they have either extension or inclusiveness [*compréhension*]."[45]

This topographical indeterminacy is responsible, as well, for our inability to identify simply *whose* is the ego producing this "textual defense," *whose* is the ego that forms both "the stake and the agent" of such defensive maneuverings.[46] Rather than attributing this ego-function either to Derrida or to his interviewers (for the phenomena under consideration cannot be reduced to the interplay between individual psyches), perhaps we can suggest that what is at stake is the ego of deconstruction as such. In doing so, we might discover that the connection between this general effacement of limits and Derrida's defensiveness on the question of Marx is something that, in Derrida's words, "belongs to a different labyrinth and a different crypt."[47]

A different crypt? According to Derrida's essay "Fors," a crypt is a defense mechanism taken to extremes (or, if such a word existed, to *in*tremes). As Nicholas Abraham and Maria Torok developed this notion, a crypt is an uncanny ruse of the ego which mimics the operations of the unconscious. While space does not permit a detailed elaboration of this process, what will be stressed here is the crypt's ability to incorporate a foreign body within the self, thereby exceeding any possibility of distinguishing between the inside and the outside:

> The cryptic enclave, between "the dynamic unconscious" and the "self of introjection," forms, inside the general space of the self, a kind of pocket of resistance, the hard cyst of an "artificial unconscious." The interior is partitioned off from the interior. . . . The inner safe (the self) has placed itself outside the crypt, or, if one prefers, has constituted "within itself" the crypt as an outer safe. One might go on indefinitely switching the place names around in this dizzying topology (the inside as the outside of the outside, or of the inside; the outside as the inside of the inside, or of the outside).[48]

The existence of a crypt may be detected through *cryptonyms* which both "protect against a mortal repetition of an excruciating pleasure and provide a displaced expression of a desire which would otherwise have to remain irrevocably silent."[49] Cryptonyms work *anasemically*, establishing correspondences between words not on a semantic basis but through "lexical contiguity" or "formal consonance"; the cryptonym is then treated as a synonym of the initial (interdicted) word of which it functions as a translation. (Derrida's play in *Glas* on the homonymity between the way *Hegel* is pronounced in French and the word *aigle* ["eagle"] might be understood as an illustration of these cryptonymic procedures.) Since such an operation can occur both within languages and between languages, the potential for cryptonymic substitution appears unlimited.

Keeping in mind this pocket sketch of the workings of the crypt, we can take up once more our long-deferred question of Marx's absence from Derrida's text, and conclude that we have simply been searching in the wrong place. For when Derrida writes that "there is no paradigmatic text: only relations of a cryptic haunting from *mark* to *mark*"— or when he argues that translation bears on the concept of economy in its "relationship with time, space, counting words, signs, *marks*"— we indeed have discovered "a certain foreign body . . . working over our household words." Just as Derrida locates a proper name in the sounds of the Freudian text, so we too can recognize such an (improper) presence in the texts of deconstruction.[50] The cryptonym in question is, of course, that of mark(s)/*marque(s)*/Marx. As the inside of the inside of deconstruction's outside, or the outside of the outside of deconstruction's inside, Marx thus inhabits within the confines of deconstruction a very precarious place. It is no wonder that the *Positions* interview bears this same abyssal structure, for when the name of Marx is the subject in question, the deconstructive ego is apt to be highly defensive. Marx, in short, is not "absent" from Derrida's texts as so often is claimed; encrypted in the crypt of its ego, deconstruction has Marx in its protective custody.

The Displacement of Politics

While the discussion above has been somewhat less—or more— than serious, it should serve at least to emphasize that there is something drastically amiss in the oppositional and hierarchical rhetorics typically employed by both Marxists and deconstructionists. For if Marx indeed is encrypted within deconstruction's ego, then the possibility of binary opposition begins to dissolve: "sides" cannot be drawn between these discourses since the one incorporates the other in such a way that *neither* can claim any longer a discrete, self-identical status. Where Marxists have argued that their theory encompasses deconstruction, our "psychoanalytic" reading reveals instead a paradoxical situation in which the supposed container is enveloped by what it contains—a situation that resists any hierarchical ordering in its unstable boundaries between "inside" and "outside." Marxism and deconstruction thus do not simply remain opposed: *interimpli-*

cated in each other's borders, both theories are (as Shoshana Felman says of philosophy and madness) "eccentric to the very framework of their opposition, rebellious to the very structure of their alternative."[51]

If, however, Marxism and deconstruction are not to be seen as antithetical practices—if, indeed, the one forms the other's difference from itself—then neither may they be construed as simple analogues of one another. The latter is a position maintained by Michael Ryan in his recent *Marxism and Deconstruction*, a work which argues at length that Marx and Derrida (despite their many differences) are best viewed as complementary figures. Yet if, as Ryan admits, "there are points of direct contact" but "no strict homology" between his two theories, then the relationship between them must be structured in a very curious way. Ryan is the first to identify this structure as one of supplementarity: "Deconstruction lacks a social theory" but this lack "can be supplemented by German critical theory. . . . Critical theory itself requires the kind of anti-metaphysical differential analysis that deconstruction offers."[52] Ryan, though, never pursues the radical implications of this discovery, choosing instead to ground his analysis largely on the model of analogy, of complementariness. Yet the dual terms of this model, by virtue of being additions to *as well as* replacements of one another, not only exceed the limits of analogy but also—in so doing—ineluctably *exceed themselves*. If, in other words, the integral identities of both Marxism and deconstruction are compromised reciprocally by this supplementary logic, then it frankly becomes questionable whether Ryan's analogical method can, in principle, succeed—especially when, in proximity to the other, neither discourse can simply remain "itself."

Marxism and deconstruction hence pose themselves in dissimilar, though not strictly antithetical, ways, each answering to distinct disciplinary objects: Marxism criticizes capitalism, ideology, structures of class oppression; deconstruction criticizes *criticism*. Like the conflict between consciousness and the unconscious which, in Freud's words, "cannot be settled promptly because—there is no other way of putting it—they are localized in the subject's mind in such a way that they do not come up against each other," so are Marxism and deconstruction related to one another, the former contained in the latter "as its *otherness-to-itself*, its *unconscious*."[53] As a result of this supplementary relationship, it finally becomes impossible to say which of these discourses "forms the border of the other," for "each includes the other, comprehends the other, which is to say that neither comprehends the other."[54] We thus are confronted with a kind of irreducibly structural lability: Marxists will always be able to "contextualize" deconstruction as a reflection of the chaos of late capitalism; deconstructionists will always be able to reply that context inevitably exceeds all such attempts at semantic saturation; and so on indefinitely.

The effects of this supplementary logic can be glimpsed, for example, in the dissimilar responses of Marxism and deconstruction to the customary attribution to literature of some essential, autonomous property called "literariness." Although both discourses will find this post-Kantian, aestheticizing concept to be fraught with inherent political implications, each will assess these implications in a manner radically distinct from—though not simply opposed to—the other.

While Herbert Marcuse considered "the aesthetic dimension" as a universal reservoir of potentially contestatory values, most contemporary Marxists identify this domain as itself the product of bourgeois culture and hence as an ideological rather than essential construct. Raymond Williams, for example, argues that the "aesthetic" and the "literary" did not attain their present significance until the beginning of the nineteenth century, and thus command only a relative rather than a universal bearing within the confines of post-Romantic culture.[55] Accordingly, it is only in a restricted sense, and not as an ensemble of timeless textual properties, that the term "literature" may appropriately be employed today, now designating, in Tony Bennett's words, "a particular, historically determined form of writing, defined by the major forms of bourgeois society, instead of, as is customarily the case, a set of universal attributes which *all* major forms of writing, from Homer to Kafka, are held to have in common. . . . There is no such 'thing' as *literature*, no body of written texts that self-evidently bear on their surface some immediately perceivable and indisputable literary essence."[56] Nevertheless, critical practice since 1800 has proposed one definition of the essence of literature after another. The origins of this essentializing practice have been traced directly to Kant, whose very attempt to differentiate the properly aesthetic from the moral and the cognitive is now seen as betraying an ultimately ideological desire to deny the historical condition of all experience as such. As Frank Lentricchia summarizes it:

> [Kant's] very intention of isolating the distinctive character of the aesthetic experience was admirable, but his analysis resulted in mere isolation. By barring that experience from the truth of the phenomenal world, while allowing art's fictional world entertainment value, he became the philosophical father of an enervating aestheticism which ultimately subverts what it would celebrate.[57]

Kant's own distinction between the aesthetic and the quotidian thus is vitiated by the fact that the former exists only as a historical function. Condemning as an inherently ideological gesture—as a naturalization of class-specific practices—any such recourse to essentializing categories, these Marxist theorists rely on a notion of an ultimate historical foundation by which to displace the concept of the literary from an aesthetic to a political register.

While for Derrida, too, there is "no such 'thing' as *literature*," it must be acknowledged at once that "literature" plays a role in his writings which, undermining the univocal status of all existing "things" (itself included), is finally irreducible to the Marxist relativization of the term. In *Dissemination*, for example, Derrida concurs with the Marxists' view that there are no ascribable essences which make literature literature; he similarly criticizes any conceptual category that aspires to universality, that "seems to aim toward the filling of a lack (a hole) in a whole that should not itself in its essence be missing (to) itself." If, however, Derrida agrees that the specificity of literature consists only in its lack of any proper self-identity—if the relationship between the literary and the nonliterary thus is compromised from the outset—he is quick to draw the unprecedented conclusion that literature therefore must function as *the exception to everything else as well*: "at once the exception in the whole, the want-of-wholeness in the whole, and the exception to everything, that which exists by itself, alone, with nothing else, in exception to all." If, in other words, literature voids itself continually in its total absence of propriety, in its structural inability to differentiate itself *as* a discrete entity, then everything that defines itself in opposition to the literary (which, in the Kantian system, *is* "everything") necessarily will become infected by contact with this radical lack of selfsameness. Retaining the name "literature" (always used in quotation marks) as that which "breaks away from [the essentialist concept of] literature—away from what has always been conceived and signified under that name," Derrida would demonstrate that Kant's founding distinction inevitably must undo itself—not, as the Marxists claim, in its failure to comprehend the historicity of the categories involved, but as a consequence of the subversive impact of "literature" on the integrity of these categories themselves.[58] If, then, it is Marxism's goal to displace the literary from an essentialist into a political dimension, it is Derrida's to indicate that the assumed stability of this very notion of the political (as a historically determined, univocal "final instance") is itself susceptible to displacement through the disseminative powers of "literature."

The double genitive in "displacement of politics" thus can be identified as a supplement in its two mutually exclusive though necessary readings: displacement names both the operation performed by politics and the object of this operation as such. This heading, as a result, can stand emblematically for the relationship between Marxism and deconstruction, for while "literariness" indeed is confronted by each, the terms of this encounter are neither purely antithetical nor complementary but rather supplementary. If the logic of the supplement exceeds the parameters of consciousness on which the notion of choice is dependent, then one cannot *simply* choose between the two theories—for, as Derrida notes in a different context:

> I do not believe that today there is any question of *choosing*—in the first place because here we are in a region (let us say, provisionally, in a region of historicity) where the category of choice seems particularly trivial; and, in the second, because we must first try to conceive of the common ground and the *différance* of this irreducible difference.[59]

Having come, now, to some understanding of the common ground and the *différance* both between and within our two theories, we might try to utilize these insights in a detailed rereading of the Marxist canon—a rereading that would not merely seek to criticize the various institutionalized versions of Marxism in the name of some "original" Marx supposedly untouched by all subsequent vulgarizations, but one that would begin to acknowledge the uncanniness of Marx's writings, the differences between these writings and themselves. The goal, in short, would be to recall Marxism to itself—not in order to contain "scientifically" its own lack of selfsameness, but to indicate how Marxism is *most* itself when that self accedes to the very conflicts it describes. We would recognize, perhaps, that *Marxism* is located in the space "between dialectics and deconstruction"; but this, of course, is a task for subsequent re-marx.[60]

Notes

The Role of Theory in the Study of Literature?
by Gregory S. Jay and David L. Miller

1. See our "Suggestions for Further Reading" at the back of this volume.

2. Paul de Man, *Allegories of Reading: Figural Language in Rousseau, Nietzsche, Rilke, and Proust* (New Haven: Yale University Press, 1979), p. 19.

3. Josué V. Harari, "Critical Factions / Critical Fictions," in Harari, ed., *Textual Strategies: Perspectives in Post-Structuralist Criticism* (Ithaca: Cornell University Press, 1979), p. 10. Harari seems to modify this requirement by the end of his essay; see pp. 70–71.

4. Jonathan Culler, *The Pursuit of Signs: Semiotics, Literature, Deconstruction* (Ithaca: Cornell University Press, 1981), p. 12.

5. Jonathan Culler, *On Deconstruction: Theory and Criticism after Structuralism* (Ithaca: Cornell University Press, 1982), pp. 7–11.

6. Christopher Norris, *Deconstruction: Theory and Practice* (London: Methuen, 1982), p. 82.

7. Jacques Derrida, *Positions*, trans. Alan Bass (Chicago: University of Chicago Press, 1981), p. 52.

8. Of course this is an extreme reduction of Derrida's various and complex reading strategies. In general Derrida does not deconstruct literary texts; he produces unlikely graftings—of Plato and Mallarmé, Blanchot and Shelley, Hegel and Genet—which resist reappropriation by the systems of formal or thematic criticism. On this topic see Samuel Weber, "After Eight: Remarking Glyph," *Glyph* 8 (1981): 232–37; and Rodolphe Gasché, "Deconstruction as Criticism," *Glyph* 6 (1979): 177–215. See also Derrida's *Signéponge/Signsponge*, trans. Richard Rand (New York: Columbia University Press, 1984) for a recent instance of deconstruction's strategies in reading literature.

9. Jacques Derrida, "The Parergon," *October* 9 (1979): 18, 20, 24–26. This essay is an excerpt from Derrida's *La Verité en peinture* (Paris: Flammarion, 1978). The quotation from Kant appears in *Critique of Judgment*, "Analytic of the Beautiful," paragraph 14.

10. Derrida, "The Parergon," p. 20.

11. On double writing see Derrida, *Positions*, pp. 39–46; Jacques Derrida, *Dissemination*, trans. Barbara Johnson (Chicago: University of Chicago Press, 1981), pp. 3–6, 173–285; and Vincent Leitch, *Deconstructive Criticism: An Advanced Introduction* (New York: Columbia University Press, 1983), pp. 179–82.

12. Jacques Derrida, *Of Grammatology*, trans. Gayatri Spivak (Baltimore: Johns Hopkins University Press, 1976), p. 158.

13. The most formidable recent attempt at this is Fredric Jameson's *The Political Unconscious: Narrative as a Socially Symbolic Act* (Ithaca: Cornell University Press, 1981). Jameson offers a powerful vision of a "positive" Marxist hermeneutic practice to counter the "negative" thrust of deconstruction. His brief remarks on Heidegger, however, show that Jameson has yet to grasp how Derrida's deconstruction of dialectics entails a reinscription of such terms as "matter" and "technology" in the wake of classical ontology's "destruction." As his recent comments on "The Origin of the Work of Art" show, Jameson assimilates Heidegger to his utopian project without regard for the *différance* Derrida has introduced into the disclosure of *alētheia*, and without considering how the critique of logocentrism is pointedly aimed at the residual idealism of concepts like "reification." See "Interview: Fredric Jameson," *Diacritics* 12, no. 3 (Fall 1982): 83. Heidegger himself insisted on pointing out the ontological questions "reification" mystified. See Lucien Goldmann, *Lukács and Heidegger* (London: Routledge & Kegan Paul, 1977), pp. 27–28.

14. See Derrida, *Positions*, pp. 62–67, 74–79. For an advanced discussion of some of the philosophical questions at stake here, see Rodolphe Gasché, "Joining the Text: From Heidegger to Derrida," in *The Yale Critics: Deconstruction in America*, ed. Jonathan Arac, Wlad Godzich, and Wallace Martin (Minneapolis: University of Minnesota Press, 1983). Gasché argues that while initially "the Derridean word *text* is a translation (without translation) of the Heideggerian word *Being*," in the end "would one not have to acknowledge that though it formally repeats Heidegger's concept of Being, the text as a re-mark of Being may well be an entirely new concept? . . . The word text, the donation of the text, for re-marking the word Being, is precisely what is no longer answerable to the meaning of Being. . . . With the word text, with the elaboration of the law of supplementarity of the re-mark, Derrida unfolds a discourse which, although it repeats the question of Being, inscribes it, and thus remains altogether extraneous to this still philosophical question" (pp. 160, 172–73).

15. For a clarifying background see Andrew Parker, "'Taking Sides' (On History): Derrida Re-Marx," *Diacritics* 11, no. 3 (Fall 1981): 57–73; Michael Ryan, *Marxism and Deconstruction: A Critical Articulation* (Baltimore: Johns Hopkins University Press, 1982); and Gregory S. Jay, "America the Scrivener: Economy and Literary History," *Diacritics* 14, no. 1 (Spring 1984): 36–51.

16. Barbara Johnson, *The Critical Difference: Essays in the Contemporary Rhetoric of Reading* (Baltimore: Johns Hopkins University Press, 1980), p. x.

17. See Samuel Weber, *The Legend of Freud* (Minneapolis: University of Minnesota Press, 1982), pp. 17–31. For Derrida's response to the feminist movement, see the interview in *Diacritics* 12, no. 2 (Summer 1982): 66–76, a special issue entitled "Cherchez la Femme: Feminist Critique/Feminine Text." A lively and comprehensive account of French feminist revisions of Freud may be found in Jane Gallop, *The Daughter's Seduction: Feminism and Psychoanalysis*

(Ithaca: Cornell University Press, 1982). The interchange between feminism and poststructuralism may also be sampled in *New French Feminisms: An Anthology*, ed. Elaine Marks and Isabelle de Courtivron (Amherst: University of Massachusetts Press, 1980); "Versions/Feminisms: A Stance of One's Own," an issue of *Sub-Stance*, no. 32 (1981); and "French Feminist Theory," a special issue of *Signs*, 7, no. 1 (Autumn 1981). Carolyn Burke discusses Derrida, feminism, and phallogocentrism in "Irigaray through the Looking Glass," *Feminist Studies* 7, no. 2 (Summer 1981): 288–306.

18. Annette Kolodny argues for a diversity of feminist approaches in "Some Notes on Defining a 'Feminist Literary Criticism,'" *Critical Inquiry* 2, no. 1 (Autumn 1975): 75–92; and "Dancing through the Minefield: Some Observations on the Theory, Practice, and Politics of a Feminist Literary Criticism," *Feminist Studies* 6, no. 1 (Spring 1980): 1–25. A variety of responses to the latter, and Kolodny's rejoinder, appear in *Feminist Studies* 8, no. 3 (Fall 1982): 629–75. A cogent review of recent approaches to feminist literary theory is Elaine Showalter, "Feminist Criticism in the Wilderness," *Critical Inquiry* 8, no. 2 (Winter 1981): 179–205, now reprinted in *Writing and Sexual Difference*, ed. Elizabeth Abel (Chicago: University of Chicago Press, 1982).

19. A similar contrast is apparent in Kamuf's exchange with Nancy Miller, published in *Diacritics* 12, no. 2 (Fall 1982): 42–53.

20. Derrida, *La Verité en peinture*, pp. 23–24. Translation our own. For a lengthy and lucid discussion of deconstruction in and of the university, see Jacques Derrida, "The Principle of Reason: The University in the Eyes of its Pupils," *Diacritics* 13, no. 3 (Fall 1983): 3–20. Here Derrida also explicates the *ratio reddenda* alluded to by Heidegger in our epigraph.

21. These qualifications should be taken as underscoring rather than dismissing the importance of historiographical theory. The standard work remains Hayden White's *Metahistory: The Historical Imagination in Nineteenth-Century Europe* (Baltimore: Johns Hopkins University Press, 1973). See also Dominick LaCapra, *Rethinking Intellectual History: Texts, Contexts, Language* (Ithaca: Cornell University Press, 1983).

22. Bahti's treatment of allegories of history owes much to Paul de Man, whose career featured a sustained critique—by way of the instance of "romanticism"—of the premises of literary history. "The possibility arises," wrote de Man, "that temporal articulations, such as narratives or histories, are a correlative of rhetoric and not the reverse. One would then have to conceive of a rhetoric of history prior to attempting a history of rhetoric or of literature or of literary criticism." See "The Epistemology of Metaphor," in *On Metaphor*, ed. Sheldon Sacks (Chicago: University of Chicago Press, 1979), p. 28. For a strong challenge to de Man's positions see Suzanne Gearhart, "Philosophy *Before* Literature: Deconstruction, Historicity, and the Work of Paul de Man," *Diacritics* 13, no. 4 (Winter 1983): 63–81.

23. Michel Foucault, *Power/Knowledge: Selected Interviews and Other Writings 1972–1977*, ed. Colin Gordon (New York: Pantheon, 1980), p. 93.

24. This last point is the gist of Derrida's critique of the early Foucault, who

is portrayed as insufficiently aware of how the problematics of representation thwart his discourse on discourse. See "Cogito and the History of Madness," in *Writing and Difference*, trans. Alan Bass (Chicago: University of Chicago Press, 1978), pp. 31–63. The objections of John Brenkman to deconstruction and his advocacy of the analysis of a social text may be relevant as a response to J. Hillis Miller or to parts of de Man's program, but they misread the protocols of Derrida's positions. Like Jameson, Brenkman mistakes deconstruction for a denial of reference and history; he doesn't appreciate the supplement to Marx Derrida finds in Heidegger. The latent positivism of such returns to reference testifies to the recurrent necessity of challenging classical ontology. See Brenkman, "Deconstruction and the Social Text," *Social Text* 1 (1979): 186–88.

25. Greenblatt offers a parallel argument in "Invisible Bullets: Renaissance Authority and Its Subversion," *Glyph* 8 (1981): 40–61.

26. T. S. Eliot, "Tradition and the Individual Talent," *Selected Essays*, new ed. (New York: Harcourt, 1950), p. 4.

27. Dryden's essay continues an investigation he began in "The Entangled Text: Melville's *Pierre* and the Problem of Reading," *Boundary 2* 7, no. 3 (Spring 1979): 145–73.

28. Geoffrey Hartman, *Saving the Text: Literature/Derrida/Philosophy* (Baltimore: Johns Hopkins University Press, 1981), p. xxi. For an account of Hartman's theoretical position, see Gregory S. Jay, "Going after New Critics: Literature, History, Deconstruction," *New Orleans Review* 8, no. 3 (Fall 1981): 251–64.

29. Hartman, *Saving the Text*, pp. 129, 103.

30. Ibid., pp. 131, 9, 79. Hartman is playing against the memorable Freudian proclamation, "Where the id was, there the ego shall be. It is a work of culture—not unlike the draining of the Zuider Zee" (*New Introductory Lectures on Psychoanalysis*, trans. James Strachey [New York: Norton, 1965], p. 80). But he is also playing off Lacan's notorious subversion of this dictum; see *Écrits: A Selection*, trans. Alan Sheridan (New York: Norton, 1977), pp. 128–29, 171, 299–300, and 329.

31. Hartman, *Saving the Text*, pp. 118–57; Jacques Derrida, "White Mythology: Metaphor in the Text of Philosophy," in *Margins of Philosophy*, trans. Alan Bass (Chicago: University of Chicago Press, 1982), pp. 207–71.

32. Geoffrey Hartman, *Criticism in the Wilderness: The Study of Literature Today* (New Haven: Yale University Press, 1980), p. 199.

Tea and Totality: The Demand of Theory on Critical Style by Geoffrey H. Hartman

1. Stuart P. Sherman, *Americans* (Port Washington, N.Y.: Kennikut Press, 1922), pp. 4–5.

2. "'Where shall we *fressen*?' says Mr. Mencken. 'At the Loyal Independent

Order of the United Hiberno-German-Anti-English-Americans,' says Mr. Hackett. 'All the New Critics will be there.'"

3. Yet C. J. Rawson shows how precarious the "friendship style" was. Swift, he says, "repudiates that intimacy between author and reader which Sterne and Richardson celebrate," even as he calls for "a Parity and strict correspondence of Idea's between Reader and the Author." He fears that familiarity may breed contempt or lead to garrulous self-revelations. "Swift, as much as Sterne, is reaching out to the reader, and the alienation I spoke of does not in fact eliminate intimacy, though it destroys 'friendship.' There is something in Swift's relation with his reader that can be described approximately in terms of the edgy intimacy of a personal quarrel that does not quite come out in the open. . . . It is attacking play." See *Gulliver and the Gentle Reader: Studies in Swift and Our Time* (London: Routledge & Kegan Paul, 1973), chap. 1.

4. I am told by Wallace Martin, who has excerpted Orage's remarks on style in *Orage as Critic* (London: Routledge & Kegan Paul, 1974), that when this comment was made *The New Age* was in financial trouble and Orage needed chatty reportage from Read to increase the popular appeal of a weekly devoted to serious literary and political discussion. Orage's remarks, therefore, are more symptomatic of English taste than of Orage. Yet though Orage dreamed of a "fearless English prose," "written in the vernacular with all its strength and directness," he always qualified that, "but with grace added unto it." His statement, similarly, that in a "pure style," the writer's "idiosyncracies, his class, his education, his reading should all be kept out of sight" also betrays the decorum of the *honnête homme* (see below). Yet compared to what was going on in the *Times Literary Supplement*—"the deadliest mouse in the world of journalism," according to Orage—he was indeed a lively presence. When the *TLS* opined, "The English Plato is still to be," Orage countered with: "I shall withdraw Plato from the position of model, in which I put him. Plato, it is evident, is likely to be abused; without intending it, his mood, translated into English, appears to be compatible only with luxurious ease; he is read by modern Epicureans. And I shall put in Plato's place Demosthenes, the model of Swift, the greatest English writer the world has yet seen" (*Orage as Critic*, pp. 194–96).

5. In a Victorian reaction against the German study of language, which had placed Sanscrit alongside Greek and Latin, and suggested their Indo-European origin, one English scholar declared: "Englishmen are too practical to study a language very philosophically." Quoted by Linda Dowling, "Victorian Oxford and the Science of Language," *PMLA* 97 (1982): 165.

6. If Ricoeur is right, we would have to rethink the emancipation of the university from seminary and divinity school. "To preach," he has written, "is not to capitulate before the believable and the unbelievable of modern man, but to struggle with the presuppositions of his culture, in order to restore this *interval of interrogation* in which the question can have meaning." And, "All that reestablishes the question of humanity taken as a whole, as a totality, has

a value of preunderstanding for preaching." Marxism and religion (and, to a degree, psychoanalysis) are for Ricoeur, as they were for Benjamin, the giant forms to be confronted; not in order to reconcile them but to discover "a reading of the great forces which regulate our economic life, our political life, and our cultural life" ("The Language of Faith," 1973, in *The Philosophy of Paul Ricoeur*, ed. Charles E. Reagan and David Stewart [Boston: Beacon Press, 1978]). On the issue of totality see also my "The New Wilderness: Critics as Connoisseurs of Chaos" in *Innovation/Renovation*, ed. Ihab Hassan and Sally Hassan (Madison: University of Wisconsin Press, 1983).

7. "It is two thousand and hundreds of years since, that the theory was proposed that thought is conversation with oneself," Eliot writes similarly in his essay of 1931 on Charles Whibley, which contains important reflections on the conversational style (and of Eliot himself Blackmur remarked that "his method has been conversational, for he begs off both the talent and the bent for abstract thought"). Henry Fielding's "Essay on Conversation," like Swift's "Hints towards an Essay on Conversation," summarizes toward the midpoint of the eighteenth century the blend of moral, social, and aesthetic motives which go into this ideal. Fielding writes that "the pleasure of conversation must arise from the discourse being on subjects levelled to the capacity of the whole company; from being on such in which every person is equally interested; from everyone's being admitted to his share in the discourse; and lastly, from carefully avoiding all noise, violence, and impetuosity." Erich Auerbach illustrates vividly the rise of this ideal in seventeenth-century France (though there are, of course, adumbrations in Italian circles of the sixteenth century) through an examination of the phrases "le public" and "la cour et la ville" (*Vier Untersuchungen zur Geschichte der französischen Bildung*, Bern: Francke, 1951). Hume remarks in "Of Civil Liberty" that "in common life, [the French] have, in a great measure, perfected that art, the most useful and agreeable of any, *l'Art de Vivre*, the art of society and conversation." In the same essay Swift is identified as the first British writer of "polite prose."

8. The conversational style never took in America, at least not as fixed by eighteenth-century English usage (epistolary rather than spoken, and barely concealing its artfulness). There is, most of the time, a deliberate swerving from elegance, producing the effect of an undertow of colloquialism, or of some kind of slang (real or imaginary). See the form of Blackmur's comment on Eliot, in n. 7, or the assimilative and proverbial style of Kenneth Burke.

9. De Man is thinking of Hellenism as interpreted by the Winckelmann-Schiller-Hegel tradition, which still reaches into Pater's thought (see the essay on Winckelmann in *Studies in the Renaissance*). He does not oppose Hebraism to Hellenism but suggests, with Hölderlin and Heidegger, a more radical "Greek" attitude, which he refuses to confine within a historicist or periodizing frame. Yet the religious shadows cast by this sort of inquiry cannot be avoided. American criticism, on the whole, is "incarnationist," as de Man recognizes; and it often associates this bias with Christian doctrine. Similarly, then, contemporary anti- or nonincarnationist views would move toward the

pole of Hebraism, whether or not influenced by canonical texts from that sphere. Consult, e.g., Maurice Blanchot's "Etre Juif" in *L'Entretien infini* (Paris: Gallimard, 1969) or "L'Interruption" in *L'Amitié* (Paris: Gallimard, 1971); and generally Edmond Jabès, who can aver: "Writing is a revolutionary act, a scrupulously Jewish act, for it consists in taking up the pen in that place where God withdrew Himself from his words; it consists indefinitely in pursuing a utopian work in the manner of God who was the Totality of the Text of which nothing subsists." The withdrawal alluded to is a kabbalistic notion also important for Harold Bloom. Traherne, the English poet, opposes "An easy Stile drawn from a native vein" to "*Zamzummin* words."

10. The etymology is well known. See F. L. Lucas's fine book, *Style* (London: Cassell, 1955), pp. 15–16, which quotes the *OED*.

From the Piazza to the Enchanted Isles: Melville's Textual Rovings
by Edgar A. Dryden

1. Walter Benjamin, *Illuminations*, trans. Harry Zohn, edited and with an introduction by Hannah Arendt (New York: Schocken, 1969), p. 38.

2. Herman Melville, *Pierre; or, The Ambiguities*, ed. Harrison Hayford, Hershel Parker, and G. Thomas Tanselle (Evanston: Northwestern University Press, 1971), p. 339. All subsequent references to *Pierre* will be to the Northwestern edition.

3. For a full discussion of earlier readings of the relation between "The Piazza" and "The Old Manse" see William B. Dillingham, *Melville's Short Fiction 1853–1856* (Athens: University of Georgia Press, 1977), pp. 319–40.

4. Herman Melville, "The Piazza," in *Piazza Tales*, ed. Egbert S. Oliver (New York: Hendricks House, 1962), p. 3. All subsequent references to "The Piazza" will be to the Hendricks House edition.

5. I am indebted here to Harold Bloom's definition of trope in *A Map of Misreading* (New York: Oxford University Press, 1975), p. 93.

6. William Makepeace Thackeray, *Rebecca and Rowena*, in *Works* (London: Macmillan, 1911), 3:95.

7. Nathaniel Hawthorne, "The Old Manse," in *Mosses from an Old Manse*, ed. William Charvat, Roy Harvey Pearce, and Claude M. Simpson (Columbus: Ohio State University Press, 1974), pp. 34, 35. All subsequent references to "The Old Manse" will be to the Ohio State edition.

8. Herman Melville, "Hawthorne and His Mosses," in *Moby-Dick*, ed. Harrison Hayford and Hershel Parker (New York: Norton, 1967), p. 537. All subsequent references to "Hawthorne and His Mosses" will be to the Norton edition.

9. John Bunyan, *The Pilgrim's Progress*, ed. Roger Sharrock (New York: Penguin, 1965), pp. 358, 355.

10. William Wordsworth, "Essays upon Epitaphs," in *Wordsworth's Literary Criticism*, ed. W. J. B. Owen (London: Routledge & Kegan Paul, 1974), p. 123.

11. Nathaniel Hawthorne, *The Scarlet Letter*, ed. William Charvat, Roy Harvey Pearce, and Claude M. Simpson (Columbus: Ohio State University Press, 1962), p. 36.

12. See for example Marvin Fisher's discussion of the sketches in *Going Under: Melville's Short Fiction and the American 1850's* (Baton Rouge: Louisiana State University Press, 1977), pp. 28–50.

13. Herman Melville, "The Encantadas or Enchanted Isles," in *Piazza Tales*, p. 171. All subsequent references to "The Encantadas" will be to this edition.

14. Herman Melville, *Redburn: His First Voyage*, ed. Harrison Hayford, Hershel Parker, and G. Thomas Tanselle (Evanston: Northwestern University Press, 1969), p. 275.

15. Herman Melville, *The Confidence Man: His Masquerade*, ed. Hershel Parker (New York: Norton, 1971), p. 1. All subsequent references to *The Confidence Man* will be to the Norton edition.

Hawthorne's Genres: The Letter of the Law Appliquée by Peggy Kamuf

1. E. D. Hirsch, *The Aims of Interpretation* (Chicago: University of Chicago Press, 1976), p. 157.

2. Jacques Derrida, "The Law of Genre," translation Avital Ronell, *Glyph 7* (Spring 1980). Rpt. in *Critical Inquiry* 7, no. 1 (Autumn 1980): 55–81.

3. Judith Fetterley, *The Resisting Reader: A Feminist Approach to American Fiction* (Bloomington: Indiana University Press, 1978).

4. Judith Fetterley, "Gender and Judgment in Nineteenth-Century American Fiction," unpublished.

5. John Irwin, *American Hieroglyphics: The Symbol of the Egyptian Hieroglyphics in the American Renaissance* (New Haven: Yale University Press, 1980), pp. 278 ff.

6. Nathaniel Hawthorne, *The Scarlet Letter*, 2d ed. (New York: W. W. Norton and Company, 1978), p. 5. All further references in the text are to the Norton Critical Edition.

7. That is, in current usage the distinction novel/romance reverses, to a large extent, the nineteenth-century connotations.

8. Henry James, *Hawthorne* (New York: Harper, 1879), pp. 110, 115.

9. Ibid., p. 114.

10. Irwin, *American Hieroglyphics*, p. 271.

Sexual Politics and Critical Judgment by Elizabeth A. Meese

1. Lillian Smith, "Extracts from Three Letters," *The Winner Names the Age: A Collection of Writings by Lillian Smith*, ed. Michelle Cliff (New York: W. W. Norton and Company, 1978), pp. 217–18.

2. A number of contemporary feminist critics and writers have discussed the politics of literary criticism. See, for example, Fraya Katz-Stoker, "The Other Criticism: Feminism vs. Formalism," in *Images of Women in Fiction: Feminist Perspectives*, ed. Susan Koppelman Cornillon (Bowling Green: Bowling Green University Popular Press, 1972), pp. 315–27; Tillie Olsen, "One Out of Twelve: Writers Who Are Women in Our Century," *Silences* (New York: Seymour Lawrence, 1978), pp. 22–46; Mary Ellmann, *Thinking about Women* (New York: Harcourt Brace Jovanovich, 1968); Cynthia Ozick, "Women and Creativity: The Demise of the Dancing Dog," in *Woman in Sexist Society*, ed. Vivian Gornick and Barbara Morgan (New York: Signet New American Library, 1972), pp. 431–51; Elaine Showalter, "Women Writers and the Double Standard," in *Woman in Sexist Society*, pp. 452–79.

3. Leslie Fiedler, "Literature as an Institution: The View from 1980," in *English Institute: Opening up the Canon*, Selected Papers from the English Institute, 1979, ed. Leslie Fiedler and Houston A. Baker, Jr. (Baltimore: Johns Hopkins University Press, 1981), pp. 73–74.

4. Olsen, "One Out of Twelve," p. 223. Marxist critics, like Fredric Jameson in *The Political Unconscious* (Ithaca, N.Y.: Cornell University Press, 1981), often exclude sex and race as features which also mark a text's exclusion from the literary canon. Most often Marxists consider class the fundamental term in the nexus of sex, race, and class. See, for example, Angela Davis's *Women, Race and Class* (New York: Random House, 1981), in which women's complicity in race and class oppression is considered at the complete expense of knowledge concerning women as an oppressed group.

In *Sex, Class and Culture* (Bloomington: Indiana University Press, 1978), Lillian S. Robinson makes a useful point concerning the politics of exclusion: "Within the limits of literature, at least, women's exclusion is clearly shared by all non-white and workingclass men" (p. 4). As a Marxist feminist, Robinson is careful not to set exclusionary terms in a hierarchy. As a result, she focuses more attention on women, inclusive of race and class concerns, and calls for a literature reflective of the whole culture.

5. Louis Kampf and Paul Lauter present an excellent summary of the changes in the critic's role in their introduction to *The Politics of Experience: Dissenting Essays on the Teaching of English* (New York: Pantheon Books, 1972), pp. 15–18. They correctly note the influence publishing houses exert on shaping literary taste by virtue of their ability to control the range of choice (pp. 45–46), in addition to the control they exercise over the constituting of the text itself. Richard Kostelanetz in *The End of Intelligent Writing: Literary Politics in America* (New York: Sheed and Ward, 1974) elaborates upon other important dimensions of the problem, including the organization of the literary marketplace and the power of advertising.

6. George Stade, "Fat-Cheeks Hefted a Snake: On the Origins and Institutionalization of Literature," *English Literature: Opening up the Canon*, pp. 140–41. In this collection, Fiedler demonstrates how canonized writers like Emerson and Tolstoy also attacked the institution of culture (p. 86).

7. Stanley Fish, *Is There a Text in This Class? The Authority of Interpretive Com-*

munities (Cambridge: Harvard University Press, 1980), pp. 10–11. Further references to this work are in the text.

8. For a discussion of Bloom's work, see Annette Kolodny, "A Map for Rereading: or, Gender and the Interpretation of Literary Texts," *New Literary History* 11, no. 3 (1980): 451–67.

9. M. H. Abrams, "How to Do Things with Texts," *Partisan Review* 46, no. 4 (1979): 587.

10. Olsen, "One Out of Twelve," p. 244.

11. Virginia Woolf, *Three Guineas* (New York: Harcourt, Brace and World, 1938), p. 61.

12. Ibid., p. 86.

13. Annette Kolodny, "Dancing through the Minefield: Some Observations on the Theory, Practice and Politics of a Feminist Criticism," *Feminist Studies* 6, no. 1 (Spring 1980): 4.

14. Norman Mailer, "Evaluations—Quick and Expensive Comments on the Talent in the Room," *Advertisements for Myself* (New York: Putnam, 1959), pp. 434–35.

15. Virginia Woolf, *A Room of One's Own* (New York: Harcourt, Brace and World, 1929), p. 4.

16. Albert Camus, *The Rebel: An Essay on Man in Revolt*, trans. Anthony Bower (New York: Vintage Books, 1956), p. 3.

17. Quoted by Kostelanetz, *End of Intelligent Writing*, p. 243.

18. Woolf, *Three Guineas*, p. 62.

19. Michel Foucault, *Power/Knowledge: Selected Interviews and Other Writings, 1972–1977*, ed. Colin Gordon, trans. Colin Gordon et al. (New York: Pantheon Books, 1980), p. 133.

20. Lillian Smith, "Autobiography as a Dialogue between King and Corpse," *The Winner Names the Age*, p. 191. Rich's essay was published in *On Lies, Secrets, and Silence: Selected Prose, 1966–1978* (New York: W. W. Norton and Company, 1979), pp. 275–310.

21. Camus, *The Rebel*, p. 20.

22. Quoted by Olsen, "One Out of Twelve," p. 229.

23. Kolodny, "Dancing through the Minefield," p. 5.

24. Woolf, *A Room of One's Own*, p. 77.

25. Woolf, *Three Guineas*, p. 90.

26. Diana Hume George, "Stumbling on Melons: Sexual Dialectics and Discrimination in English Departments," *English Literature: Opening up the Canon*, p. 109.

27. Introduction, *Writing and Sexual Difference*, ed. Elizabeth Abel (Chicago: University of Chicago Press, 1982), pp. 1–2. Most of these essays first appeared in *Critical Inquiry* 8, no. 2 (Winter 1981).

28. Fiedler, "Literature as an Institution," p. 91.

29. Hayden White, "Conventional Conflicts," *New Literary History* 13, no. 1 (Autumn 1981): 155.

30. Ibid., p. 154.

31. Foucault, *Power/Knowledge*, p. 133.

32. Ibid.

33. Luce Irigaray, "When Our Lips Speak Together," trans. Carolyn Burke, *Signs* 6, no. 1 (Winter 1980): 69.

Shakespeare and the Exorcists
by Stephen Greenblatt

1. Samuel Harsnett, *A Declaration of Egregious Popish Impostures* (London: J. Roberts, 1603). Horace Howard Furness (*New Variorum Lear*) assigns the discovery of Harsnett's influence to Lewis Theobald, whose edition of Shakespeare was first published in 1733.

2. For extended arguments for and against theory, see Walter Michaels and Steven Knapp, "Against Theory," in *Critical Inquiry* 8 (1982): 723–42, and the ensuing controversy in *Critical Inquiry* 9 (1983): 725–800.

3. I am indebted to an important critique of Marxist and deconstructive literary theory by D. A. Miller: "Discipline in Different Voices: Bureaucracy, Policy, Family and *Bleak House*," in *Representations* 1 (1983): 59–89.

4. *John Wesley*, ed. Albert C. Outler (New York: Oxford University Press, 1964), p. 82.

5. An exception, with conclusions different from my own, is William Elton, *King Lear and the Gods* (San Marino, Cal.: Huntington Library, 1966). For useful accounts of Harsnett's relation to Lear, see Geoffrey Bullough, ed., *Narrative and Dramatic Sources of Shakespeare*, 8 vols. (London: Routledge and Kegan Paul, 1975), 7:299–302; Kenneth Muir, "Samuel Harsnett and *King Lear*," *RES* 2 (1951): 11–21; Kenneth Muir, *Arden Lear* (Cambridge: Harvard University Press, 1952), pp. 253–56.

Since this essay went to press, I have learned that a new book will explore in rich detail the relationship between Harsnett and Shakespeare: see, forthcoming from the Ohio University Press, *Darkness and Devils: Exorcism and "King Lear"* by John L. Murphy.

6. Michel de Montaigne, "Apology for Raymond Sebond," in *Complete Essays*, trans. Donald Frame (Stanford: Stanford University Press, 1948), p. 331.

7. Edward Shils, *Center and Periphery: Essays in Macrosociology* (Chicago: University of Chicago Press, 1975), p. 3.

8. Peter Brown, *The Cult of the Saints: Its Rise and Function in Latin Christianity* (Chicago: University of Chicago Press, 1981), p. 107.

9. Samuel Harsnett, *A Discovery of the Fraudulent Practices of John Darrel* (London, 1599).

10. Carlo Ginzburg, *I benandanti: Recherche sulla stregoneria e sui culti agrari tra Cinquecento e Seicento* (Turin: Einaudi, 1966). This text has recently been translated as *The Night Battles: Witchcraft and Agrarian Cults in the Sixteenth and Seventeenth Centuries*, trans. John and Anne Tedeschi (Baltimore: Johns Hopkins University Press, 1983).

11. For Harsnett's comments on witchcraft, see *Declaration*, pp. 135–36. The relation between demonic possession and witchcraft is extremely complex. There is a helpful discussion, along with an important account of Harsnett and Darrel, in Keith Thomas, *Religion and the Decline of Magic* (London: Weidenfeld and Nicolson, 1971).

12. Brown, *Cult of the Saints*, pp. 109–11.

13. Thomas, *Religion*, p. 485.

14. S. M. Shirokogorov, *The Psycho-Mental Complex of the Tungus* (London: Routledge & Kegan Paul, 1935), p. 265.

15. Brown, *Cult of the Saints*, p. 110.

16. Michael MacDonald, *Mystical Bedlam* (Cambridge: Cambridge University Press, 1981).

17. See Edmund Jorden, *A briefe discourse of a disease Called the Suffocation of the Mother* (London, 1603).

18. Michel Leiris, *La Possession et ses aspects théâtraux chex les Ethiopiens de Gondar* (Paris: Plon, 1958).

19. On attacks on the Catholic church as a theater, see Jonas Barish, *The Antitheatrical Prejudice* (Berkeley and Los Angeles: University of California Press, 1981), pp. 66–131 and passim.

20. Harsnett, *Discovery*, p. A3[r].

21. On the significance of the public theater's physical marginality, its location in the "Liberties" of London, I am indebted to work in progress by Steven Mullaney of MIT.

22. For a brief account of the whole tangled history of Darrel, see D. P. Walker, *Unclean Spirits: Possession and Exorcism in France and England in the Late Sixteenth and Early Seventeenth Centuries* (Philadelphia: University of Pennsylvania Press, 1981).

23. John Bunyan, *Grace Abounding to the Chief of Sinners*, ed. Roger Sharrock (London and New York: Oxford University Press, 1966), p. 15.

24. Edgar's later explanation—that he feared for his father's ability to sustain the shock of an encounter—is, like so many explanations in *King Lear*, too little, too late.

25. Words, signs, gestures that claim to be in touch with superreality, with absolute goodness and absolute evil, are exposed as vacant—illusions manipulated by the clever and imposed upon the gullible.

26. This is, in effect, Edmund Jorden's prescription for cases such as Lear's.

27. In willing this disenchantment against the evidence of our senses, we pay tribute to the theater. Harsnett has been twisted around to make this tribute possible.

28. O. B. Hardison, Jr., *Christian Rite and Christian Drama in the Middle Ages: Essays in the Origin and Early History of Modern Drama* (Baltimore: Johns Hopkins University Press, 1965), esp. pp. 220–52.

29. C. L. Barber, "The Family in Shakespeare's Development: Tragedy and Sacredness," in *Representing Shakespeare: New Psychoanalytic Essays*, ed. Murray M. Schwartz and Coppélia Kahn (Baltimore: Johns Hopkins University Press, 1980), p. 196.

30. Roland Barthes, *Mythologies*, trans. Annette Lavers (New York: Hill and Wang, 1972), p. 135.

Auerbach's Mimesis: *Figural Structure and Historical Narrative* by Timothy Bahti

1. Frank Lentricchia, *After the New Criticism* (Chicago: University of Chicago Press, 1980).
2. Gerald Graff, *Literature against Itself: Literary Ideas in Modern Society* (Chicago: University of Chicago Press, 1979).
3. Robert Langbaum, "Mysteries and Meaning," *The New York Times Book Review*, 4 April 1982, p. 15.
4. Frederick Crews, "Criticism without Constraint," *Commentary* 73, no. 1 (January 1982): 69.
5. Paul de Man, *Allegories of Reading: Figural Language in Rousseau, Nietzsche, Rilke, and Proust* (New Haven: Yale University Press, 1979), p. ix.
6. René Wellek, "The Fall of Literary History," in *Geschichte: Ereignis und Erzählung*, ed. R. Koselleck and W.-D. Stempel (Munich: W. Fink, 1973), pp. 427–40.
7. In this, Auerbach's method is (his own differentiations notwithstanding) essentially the same as Leo Spitzer's, who likewise, in "Linguistics and Literary History," claimed to demonstrate the methodological continuity that obtains between the analysis of a particular word or stylistic feature of an author, and the study of the author's psychology, his place among his people and their time, and ultimately, his place in the life of his language; cf. *Linguistics and Literary History: Essays in Stylistics* (Princeton: Princeton University Press, 1948), pp. 10ff.
8. Timothy Bahti, "Vico, Auerbach and Literary History," *Philological Quarterly* 60 (1981): 239–55.
9. For the most trenchant critical reading of the sublation of the negative in Hegel's philosophic system, see Theodor W. Adorno, "Skoteinos oder Wie zu lesen sei," *Drei Studien zu Hegel, Gesammelte Schriften* 5, ed. Gretel Adorno and Rolf Tiedemann (Frankfurt: Suhrkamp, 1971), esp. pp. 374, 375.
10. Erich Auerbach, "Figura," *Neue Dantestudien, Istanbuler Schriften* 5 (1944): 11–71; trans. Ralph Manheim in Auerbach, *Scenes from the Drama of European Literature* (New York: Meridian, 1959), pp. 11–76. Henceforth cited in the text with the abbreviation F followed by a page number.
11. The technical term is *implere*, but the language of revealing, realizing, consummating, etc., also appears.
12. Erich Auerbach, *Mimesis: Dargestellte Wirklichkeit in der abendländischen Literatur* (Bern: A. Francke, 1946), p. 516; trans. Willard R. Trask as *Mimesis: The Representation of Reality in Western Literature* (Princeton: Princeton University Press, 1953), p. 555. Henceforth cited parenthetically in the text by page number only.

13. Erich Auerbach, *Dante als Dichter der irdischen Welt* (Berlin: W. de Gruyter, 1929); trans. Ralph Manheim as *Dante, Poet of the Secular World* (Chicago: University of Chicago Press, 1961).

Between Dialectics and Deconstruction: Derrida and the Reading of Marx
by Andrew Parker

1. Samuel Weber, *The Legend of Freud* (Minneapolis: University of Minnesota Press, 1982), p. xvi.

2. Karl Kautsky, *Das Erfurter Programm*, cited in Alex Callinicos, *Althusser's Marxism* (London: Pluto Press, 1976), p. 14. On the crisis of Marxism, see Michael Albert and Robin Hahnel, *UnOrthodox Marxism* (Boston: South End Press, 1979); Louis Althusser, "The Crisis of Marxism," in *Power and Opposition in Post-Revolutionary Societies*, trans. Patrick Camiller et al. (London: Ink Links, 1979), pp. 225–37; Stanley Aronowitz, *The Crisis in Historical Materialism* (New York: Praeger, 1981); Isaac D. Balbus, *Marxism and Domination* (Princeton: Princeton University Press, 1983); Murray Bookchin, "Beyond Neo-Marxism," *Telos* 36 (Summer 1978): 5–28; Fernando Claudin, "Some Reflections on the Crisis of Marxism," *Socialist Review* 45 (May–June 1979): 137–43; Lucio Colletti, "A Political and Philosophical Interview," *New Left Review* 86 (July–August 1974): 3–28; Oskar Negt, "Reflections on France's *Nouveaux Philosophes* and the Crisis of Marxism," *Sub-Stance* 37/38 (1983): 56–67; Paul M. Sweezy, "A Crisis in Marxist Theory," *Monthly Review* 31, no. 2 (June 1979): 20–24; and Göran Therborn, *Science, Class, and Society* (London: New Left Books, 1976).

3. Georg Lukács, *History and Class Consciousness*, trans. Rodney Livingstone (Cambridge: MIT Press, 1971), p. 199.

4. Aronowitz, *Crisis in Historical Materialism*, pp. 6, 20. In Aronowitz's conception, "the entire paradigm of historical change offered by Marxism collapses" if it fails in its task of specifying the precise conditions under which revolutionary struggle will occur (p. 7).

5. Alex Callinicos, *Is There a Future for Marxism?* (Atlantic Highlands, N.J.: Humanities Press, 1982), p. 2. For a superb exposition and analysis of Marxism's investment in economic determinism, see Alvin W. Gouldner, *The Two Marxisms* (New York: Oxford University Press, 1982), especially the section entitled "The Dialectic of the Final Instance."

6. In general terms, orthodox Marxism has responded to these movements simply by asserting the priority of class over gender and race. For an analysis of the implicit weakness of this response, and for descriptions of the various neo-Marxist attempts to outline a synthetic approach to these questions, see Aronowitz, *Crisis in Historical Materialism*, pp. 73–121.

7. Balbus, *Marxism and Domination*, p. 3. The need to reformulate the base/superstructure relationship links the otherwise dissimilar projects of Antonio

Gramsci and Louis Althusser. See especially Gramsci's *Selections from the Prison Notebooks*, trans. Quentin Hoare and Geoffrey Nowell Smith (New York: International Publishers, 1971); and Althusser's *For Marx*, trans. Ben Brewster (London: New Left Books, 1977). For the critique of Marxist economism, see Jean Baudrillard, *The Mirror of Production*, trans. Mark Poster (St. Louis: Telos Press, 1975); and Marshall Sahlins, *Culture and Practical Reason* (Chicago: University of Chicago Press, 1976).

8. George Lichtheim, *Marxism: An Historical and Critical Study*, 2nd edition (New York: Praeger, 1965), p. 192. See also Aronowitz, *Crisis in Historical Materialism*, pp. 142–44; Russell Jacoby, "The Politics of the Crisis Theory," *Telos* 23 (Spring 1975): 3–52; and Trent Schroyer, "Marx's Theory of the Crisis," *Telos* 14 (Winter 1972): 106–25.

9. Karl Marx, *Capital*, vol. 1, ed. Frederick Engels (New York: International Publishers, 1967), p. 113.

10. Karl Marx, *Capital*, vol. 3, ed. Frederick Engels (New York: International Publishers, 1976), p. 249.

11. Philosophy's inability to acknowledge the irreducibility of the figural constitutes, of course, one of deconstruction's most insistent thematics. See, for example, Jacques Derrida, "White Mythology: Metaphor in the Text of Philosophy," in *Margins of Philosophy*, trans. Alan Bass (Chicago: University of Chicago Press, 1982), pp. 207–71, and Paul de Man, "The Epistemology of Metaphor," *Critical Inquiry* 5, no. 1 (Autumn 1978): 13–30. See also Derrida's "Économies de la crise," *La Quinzaine littéraire* 399 (August 1983): 4–5, and de Man's "Criticism and Crisis," in *Blindness and Insight* (New York: Oxford University Press, 1971), pp. 3–19, for somewhat analogous treatments of the rhetoric of crisis.

12. As Fredric Jameson admits, "any doctrine of figurality must necessarily be ambiguous"; see *The Political Unconscious* (Ithaca: Cornell University Press, 1981), p. 70. This lesson, of course, will be lost on those who—like John McMurty—would attempt to rescue Marx from "the charge of pervasive ambiguity": "We undertake to distill from the enormous and perplexing range of [Marx's] corpus a clear and integrating structure, which is both propositionally lucid and faithful to his texts. We undertake, in short, philosophy's classic task of underlaborer." See *The Structure of Marx's World-View* (Princeton: Princeton University Press, 1978), pp. 3, 18. To the extent that Marx's readers continue in this way to reduce his writings to a simple inventory of his themes, we may conclude that Marxism—contrary to the famous assertion in the eleventh thesis on Feuerbach—still remains implicated in the philosophical project it would reject. By virtue of its capacity for critical self-engagement, *The Eighteenth Brumaire* has attracted a number of interesting readings in recent years. See, for example, Gouldner, *Two Marxisms*, pp. 299–304; Dominick LaCapra, *Rethinking Intellectual History* (Ithaca: Cornell University Press, 1983), pp. 268–90; Jeffrey Mehlman, *Revolution and Repetition* (Berkeley and Los Angeles: University of California Press, 1977); John Paul Riquelme, "The Eighteenth Brumaire of Karl Marx as Symbolic Action," *History and Theory* 19, no. 1 (1980): 58–72; Edward Said, "On Repetition," in

The World, the Text, and the Critic (Cambridge: Harvard University Press, 1983), pp. 111–25; and Hayden White, "The Problem of Style in Realistic Representation," in *The Concept of Style*, ed. Berel Lang (Philadelphia: University of Pennsylvania Press, 1979), pp. 213–29.

13. In certain respects, this view is consistent with the positions of Baudrillard (*Mirror of Production*) and Sahlins (*Culture and Practical Reason*). I do not wish, however, to endorse their conclusion that the category of production has therefore outlived its usefulness. For when Derrida writes that "production is necessarily a text" (*Of Grammatology*, trans. Gayatri C. Spivak [Baltimore: Johns Hopkins University Press, 1976], p. 164), he acknowledges that production (like representation) is an indispensable, limiting term that cannot simply be surmounted. For a very different reading of this passage from the *Grammatology*, see Wlad Godzich, "The Domestication of Derrida," in *The Yale Critics*, ed. Jonathan Arac, Wlad Godzich, and Wallace Martin (Minneapolis: University of Minnesota Press, 1983), pp. 20–40.

14. Aronowitz, *Crisis in Historical Materialism*, p. 36.

15. David Forgacs, "Marxist Literary Theories," in *Modern Literary Theory*, ed. Ann Jefferson and David Robey (Totowa, N.J.: Barnes and Noble, 1982), p. 160. These formulations are inspired by the classic work on the subject of a Marxist semiotics, V. N. Volosinov's *Marxism and the Philosophy of Language*, trans. Ladislav Matejka and I. R. Titunik (New York: Seminar Press, 1973).

16. Roland Barthes, "Réponses," cited in Jonathan Culler, *Roland Barthes* (New York: Oxford University Press, 1983), p. 51.

17. Fredric Jameson, *Marxism and Form* (Princeton: Princeton University Press, 1971), p. 62.

18. Derrida, *Of Grammatology*, p. 6.

19. See *The Linguistic Turn*, ed. Richard Rorty (Chicago: University of Chicago Press, 1967). One sign of this epistemic change is the fact that even Stalin could not restrain himself from offering his comments on language; see J. V. Stalin, *Marxism and the Problems of Linguistics* (Peking: Foreign Languages Press, 1972). For the ensuing debate among Soviet linguists, see *The Soviet Linguistic Controversy*, trans. John V. Murra et al. (New York: King's Crown Press, 1951).

20. Albrecht Wellmer, "Communication and Emancipation," in *On Critical Theory*, ed. John O'Neill (New York: Seabury, 1976), p. 247.

21. Julia Kristeva, "Pratique signifiante et mode de production," *Tel Quel* 60 (Winter 1974): 26. On Lukács and language see Rosalind Coward and John Ellis, *Language and Materialism* (London: Routledge & Kegan Paul, 1977), pp. 34–36.

22. Raymond Williams, "Marxism, Structuralism, and Literary Analysis," *New Left Review* 129 (September–October 1981): 65. See also the chapter entitled "Language" in his *Marxism and Literature* (Oxford: Oxford University Press, 1977), pp. 21–44.

23. Fredric Jameson, *Fables of Aggression* (Berkeley and Los Angeles: University of California Press, 1979), p. 6.

24. Ferruccio Rossi-Landi, "Sign Systems and Social Reproduction," *Ideology & Consciousness* 3 (Spring 1978): 58. See also his *Linguistics and Economics* (The Hague: Mouton, 1975), and *Language as Work and Trade* (So. Hadley, Mass.: Bergin and Garvey, 1983).

25. For what is, perhaps, the fullest exposition of the Tel Quel project, see Julia Kristeva, *La Révolution du langage poétique* (Paris: Seuil, 1974).

26. See Jean-Louis Houdebine, *Langage et marxisme* (Paris: Klincksieck, 1977), pp. 117–73. Among the many recent studies that attempt to combine Marxism with linguistics, the following are of special interest: Jean-Louis Baudry, "Linguistique et production textuelle" and "Le Sens de l'argent," in *Tel Quel: Théorie d'ensemble* (Paris: Seuil, 1968), pp. 351–64 and 406–11, respectively; Catherine Belsey, *Critical Practice* (London: Methuen, 1980); Jean-Pierre Faye, *La Critique du langage et son économie* (Paris: Galilée, 1973); Jean-Joseph Goux, *Économie et symbolique* (Paris: Seuil, 1973); Bennison Gray, "Is Language a Superstructure?" *Semiotica* 25, no. 3/4 (1974): 319–33; Stephen Heath, "Language, Literature, Materialism," *Sub-Stance* 17 (1977): 67–74; Dean MacCannell and Juliet Flower MacCannell, *The Time of the Sign* (Bloomington: Indiana University Press, 1982); Peter Madsen, "Semiotics and Dialectics," *Poetics* 7 (1972): 29–49; Michel Pêcheux, *Language, Semantics, and Ideology* (New York: St. Martin's Press, 1982); John Rajchman, "Semiotics, Epistemology, and Materialism," *Semiotext(e)* 1, no. 1 (February 1974): 11–27; David Silverman and Brian Torode, *The Material Word* (London: Routledge & Kegan Paul, 1980); Genevieve Vaughn, "Communication and Exchange," *Semiotica* 29, no. 1/2 (1980): 113–43; Judith Williamson, *Decoding Advertisements* (London: Marion Boyars, 1978); and Peter V. Zima, ed., *Semiotics and Dialectics: Ideology and the Text* (Amsterdam: John Benjamins, 1981).

27. Marx, *Capital*, 1:74.

28. For the passage quoted, see Vincent Descombes, *Modern French Philosophy*, trans. L. Scott-Fox and J. M. Harding (Cambridge: Cambridge University Press, 1980), p. 145. See also Jonathan Culler, *On Deconstruction* (Ithaca: Cornell University Press, 1982), pp. 86–89, and Paul de Man, *Allegories of Reading* (New Haven: Yale University Press, 1979), pp. 107–10. The inversion of priority between base and superstructure would not simply install the superstructure in the position formerly occupied by the base, thereby creating a new "final instance"; rather, it will allow us to posit a "generalized superstructure" as the condition of possibility for any subsequent differentiation between base and superstructure (understood here in their customary senses).

29. Barbara Johnson, translator's introduction to Jacques Derrida, *Dissemination* (Chicago: University of Chicago Press, 1981), p. ix. One might reread the famous exchanges between Adorno and Benjamin in light of the conclusion drawn above. Adorno criticized Benjamin's "metaphorical" understanding of the relationship between base and superstructure, contending that attention must be directed to the problem of mediation. Benjamin, however, seems to be arguing for the irreducible figurality of the base/superstructure

model, and thus can be acknowledged as an early critic of the concept of mediation itself. See Ernst Bloch et al., *Aesthetics and Politics* (London: New Left Books, 1977), pp. 100–41.

30. See Michael Ryan, "Self-Evidence," *Diacritics* 10, no. 2 (Spring 1980): 2–16; and idem, *Marxism and Deconstruction* (Baltimore: Johns Hopkins University Press, 1982).

31. Paul Ricoeur, "The Critique of Religion," in *The Philosophy of Paul Ricoeur*, ed. Charles E. Reagan and David Stewart (Boston: Beacon Press, 1978), p. 214.

32. Marx, *Capital*, 3:791 (my emphasis).

33. Jacques Derrida, "Ja, ou le faux-bond," *Digraphe* 11 (1977): 118–20. See also Derrida, *Dissemination*, p. 43. In *Positions*, trans. Alan Bass (Chicago: University of Chicago Press, 1981), p. 63, Derrida similarly argues that Marxist texts "are not to be read according to a hermeneutical or exegetical method which would seek out a finished signified beneath a textual surface." For Derrida on fetishism see *Glas* (Paris: Galilée, 1974), pp. 232–53. Adorno's statement that "at the outset there is fetishism and the hunt for the outset remains always subject to it" (*Negative Dialectics*, trans. E. B. Ashton [New York: Seabury Press, 1979], p. 111) thus can be read as one measure of his distance from the main currents of Western Marxism.

34. Fredric Jameson, "Reflections in Conclusion," in Ernst Bloch et al., *Aesthetics and Politics*, p. 212.

35. Derrida, *Positions*, p. 57; idem, *Writing and Difference*, trans. Alan Bass (Chicago: University of Chicago Press, 1978), p. 211.

36. J. Hillis Miller, "Theory and Practice: Response to Vincent Leitch," *Critical Inquiry* 6, no. 4 (Summer 1980): 612; Terry Eagleton, *Walter Benjamin; or, Towards a Revolutionary Criticism* (London: Verso, 1981), p. 137; Jacob Rogozinski, "Déconstruire la révolution," in *Les Fins de l'homme*, ed. Philippe Lacoue-Labarthe and Jean-Luc Nancy (Paris: Galilée, 1981), p. 520; Andreas Huyssen, "Critical Theory and Modernity," *New German Critique* 26 (Spring/Summer 1982): 6.

37. Derrida, *Positions*, p. 62 (translation modified). Jean-Luc Nancy recently has suggested that the time has come to supply a reading of Marx in the space of these lacunae. See, for the beginnings of this project, *Rejouer le politique*, ed. Jean-Luc Nancy and Philippe Lacoue-Labarthe (Paris: Galilée, 1981).

38. James Kearns and Ken Newton, "An Interview with Jacques Derrida," *The Literary Review* (Edinburgh) 14 (18 April – 1 May 1980): 22; and *Les Fins de l'homme*, p. 527.

39. Ryan, "Self-Evidence," p. 2 (my emphasis). For similar arguments, see John Brenkman, "Deconstruction and the Social Text," *Social Text* 1 (Winter 1979): 186–88; Robert Holub, "Leftist Recreation: The Politicizing of Deconstruction," *Enclitic* 7, no. 1 (Spring 1983): 62–65; Frank Lentricchia, "Derrida, History, and Intellectuals," *Salmagundi* 50–51 (Fall 1980 – Winter 1981): 284–301; and Richard Terdiman, "Deconstruction/Mediation: A Dialectical Critique of 'Derrideanism,'" *Minnesota Review* 19, n.s. (Fall 1982): 103–11.

40. Derrida, *Positions*, p. 92.

41. J. Laplanche and J. B. Pontalis, *The Language of Psychoanalysis*, trans. Donald Nicholson-Smith (New York: W. W. Norton and Company, 1973), p. 78; Jacques Lacan, *The Four Fundamental Concepts of Psychoanalysis*, trans. Alan Sheridan (New York: W. W. Norton and Company, 1978), p. 51.

42. Derrida, *Positions*, p. 62 (my emphasis).

43. Jacques Derrida, *La Carte postale: De Socrate à Freud et au-delà* (Paris: Aubier-Flammarion, 1980), p. 285 (my emphasis).

44. Margaret W. Ferguson, "Border Territories of Defense: Freud and Defenses of Poetry," in *The Literary Freud*, Psychiatry and the Humanities, vol. 4, ed. Joseph H. Smith (New Haven: Yale University Press, 1980), pp. 150, 155.

45. Nicholas Abraham, "The Shell and the Kernel," trans. Nicholas Rand, *Diacritics* 9, no. 1 (Spring 1979): 28.

46. Laplanche and Pontalis, *Language of Psychoanalysis*, p. 104. See also pp. 130–43.

47. Derrida, *La Carte postale*, p. 349.

48. Jacques Derrida, "Fors," trans. Barbara Johnson, *Georgia Review* 31, no. 1 (Spring 1977): 74–75.

49. Peggy Kamuf, "Abraham's Wake," *Diacritics* 9, no. 1 (Spring 1979): 37.

50. Jacques Derrida, "Living On/Border Lines," in Harold Bloom et al., *Deconstruction and Criticism* (New York: Seabury, 1979), pp. 137, 169–70; idem, *La Carte postale*, p. 333, and "Fors," p. 83.

51. Shoshana Felman, "Madness and Philosophy; or, Literature's Reason," *Yale French Studies* 52 (1975): 226.

52. Ryan, *Marxism and Deconstruction*, pp. 56, 35, 116. On supplementarity see Derrida, *Of Grammatology*, pp. 141–64.

53. Sigmund Freud, *Totem and Taboo*, trans. James Strachey (New York: W. W. Norton and Company, 1950), p. 29; and Shoshana Felman, "To Open the Question," *Yale French Studies* 55/56 (1977): 10.

54. Derrida, "Living On/Border Lines," p. 99; Derrida is commenting here not, of course, on Marxism but on a text by Blanchot.

55. Williams, *Marxism and Literature*, pp. 45–54.

56. Tony Bennett, *Formalism and Marxism* (London: Methuen, 1979), pp. 14–15, 9.

57. Frank Lentricchia, *After the New Criticism* (Chicago: University of Chicago Press, 1980), p. 41.

58. Derrida, *Dissemination*, pp. 56, 3.

59. Derrida, *Writing and Difference*, p. 293.

60. Portions of this essay appeared previously, in a slightly different form, as "Of Politics and Limits: Derrida Re-Marx," *SCE Reports* 8 (Fall 1980): 83–104; as "Literariness—The Politics of Displacement," in *Displacement: Derrida and After*, ed. Mark Krupnick (Bloomington: Indiana University Press, 1983), pp. 133–38; and as a review of Michael Ryan's *Marxism and Deconstruction* in *MLN* 97, no. 5 (December 1982): 1217–21.

Suggestions for
Further Reading

A number of excellent bibliographies in critical theory have recently appeared (see the volumes by Culler, Eagleton, Harari, and Norris cited below). Since the field changes so quickly, however, and its boundaries remain so indeterminate, even the best bibliographies quickly become dated. New books appear constantly, as do important essays in such journals as *Critical Inquiry*, *Diacritics*, and *New Literary History*—indeed, most of the established as well as more recent academic journals now feature articles focusing on issues of interest to critical theorists. Thus what follows is a highly selective and necessarily personal list of books we have found useful as guides into the maze.

Modern Literary Theory: A Comparative Introduction, edited by Ann Jefferson and David Robey, offers expert chapters by various hands on most of the major schools of interpretive practice. Terry Eagleton's *Literary Theory: An Introduction* is a handy overview and a good place for the beginner to get a sense of the territory. Eagleton's Marxist perspective leads to summaries that, if not entirely accurate, are often witty and provocative. Frank Lentricchia's *After the New Criticism* is both a history of American criticism since Northrop Frye and a polemic against that criticism's tendencies toward aestheticism and formalism. *Structuralism and Since*, edited by John Sturrock, presents a series of cogent essays on the careers of Claude Lévi-Strauss, Roland Barthes, Michel Foucault, Jacques Derrida, and Jacques Lacan. *Language and Materialism: Developments in Semiology and the Theory of the Subject*, by Rosalind Coward and John Ellis, offers a sophisticated account of recent theoretical innovations and their importance for a general critique of ideology. A helpful volume on the cultural roots of current debates is Vincent Descombes's *Modern French Philosophy*. *Textual Strategies*, edited by Josué Harari, is an anthology of poststructuralist criticism heavily weighted toward Continental examples. For British and American samples in this vein, see *Untying the Text*, edited by Robert Young. Two other notable collections are *The Structuralist Controversy*, edited by Richard Macksey and Eugenio Donato, and *Velocities of Change*, edited by Richard Macksey.

None of the above-mentioned books includes a chapter on feminist criticism or theory. *Feminist Literary Criticism*, edited by Josephine Donovan, may serve as a useful start, as will *Women Writing and Writing about Women*, edited by Mary Jacobus. Other interesting collections include *Women and Language in Literature and Society*, edited by Sally McConnell Ginet et al., and *Writing and Sexual Difference*, edited by Elizabeth Abel. Two journals in particular, *Signs* and *Feminist Studies*, regularly publish important articles and bibliographies in feminist theory and practice.

Of the handbooks to deconstruction, Christopher Norris's *Deconstruction: Theory and Practice* gives the briefest and liveliest survey of Derrida's philosophy, its roots in modern thought and its impact on American criticism. Jonathan Culler's *On Deconstruction* presents the most lucid and thorough explanation of Derrida's work, though it skirts philosophy and concentrates on deconstruction as a theory of reading. Vincent Leitch's *Deconstructive Criticism* is the widest in scope of the three, containing chapters on a variety of European and American poststructuralist writers. *The Yale Critics: Deconstruction in America*, edited by Jonathan Arac et al., brings together different perspectives evaluating the American domestication of Derrida in the work of Harold Bloom, Geoffrey Hartman, Paul de Man, and J. Hillis Miller. *Displacement: Derrida and After*, ed. Mark Krupnick, is a fine collection of essays that both illuminate Derrida's contribution and demonstrate its impact on the reading of various texts and cultural problems.

Contributors

Timothy Bahti teaches German and comparative literature at Northwestern University. He has published essays on Petrarch, Romantic poetry, and modern criticism, as well as the English translation of Hans Robert Jauss's *Toward an Aesthetic of Reception*. He is completing a book entitled *Allegories of History: Literary Historiography after Hegel*, of which the present contribution is a part.

Edgar Dryden, Professor of English and Head of the Department at the University of Arizona, is the author of *Melville's Thematics of Form* and *Nathaniel Hawthorne: The Poetics of Enchantment*, as well as many articles on the interpretation of American literature. He is currently writing a book on the genre of romance in American fiction.

Stephen Greenblatt has written numerous essays and books on literature, society, and culture in Renaissance England. His most recent volume, *Renaissance Self-Fashioning: From More to Shakespeare*, received the British Council Prize in the Humanities. He is completing a study of Shakespeare and the poetics of culture. Currently Professor of English at the University of California at Berkeley, he is also a cofounder and editor of the journal *Representations*.

Geoffrey Hartman's work over the last three decades has had a profound impact on the study of Romanticism and the practice of literary criticism. His distinguished career as a scholar and theorist includes *Wordsworth's Poetry 1787–1814* (winner of the Christian Gauss Award), *Beyond Formalism, The Fate of Reading, Criticism in the Wilderness*, and *Saving the Text: Literature/Derrida/Philosophy*. He is Karl Young Professor of English and Comparative Literature at Yale University and Director of The School of Criticism and Theory.

GREGORY S. JAY is the author of *T. S. Eliot and the Poetics of Literary History* and of essays on Poe, genre, the Yale critics, and the dispute between Marxism and deconstruction. He teaches critical theory and American literature at the University of South Carolina.

PEGGY KAMUF teaches in the Department of French and Italian at Miami University of Ohio. She is the author of *Fictions of Feminine Desire* and has published on literary and feminist theory in *Diacritics*.

ELIZABETH MEESE has written on Djuna Barnes, Eudora Welty, American Transcendentalism, and various problems in the study and teaching of women's literature. Her contribution to the present volume forms part of a book-length manuscript, *Crossing the Double-Cross: Feminism and Critical Theory*. She is Assistant Dean of the College of Arts and Sciences at The University of Alabama, where she teaches women's studies, feminist theory, and American literature.

DAVID L. MILLER's essays on Spenser have appeared in *ELH, Modern Language Quarterly*, and the *New Orleans Review*. He currently teaches English literature and critical theory at The University of Alabama, and is at work on a study of Spenser's poetics.

ANDREW PARKER has written on Foucault and Derrida in *Diacritics* and on the economy of Ezra Pound's anti-Semitism in *Boundary 2*. His essay here is part of a book in progress on deconstruction and the reading of Marx. He teaches literature and critical theory at Amherst College.

Index

Abel, Elizabeth, 97
Abraham, Nicholas, 162
Abrams, M. H., 88–89, 127
Addison, Joseph, 33, 37
Adorno, Theodor, 33, 185 (n. 29)
Althusser, Louis, 31, 122, 153
Arendt, Hannah, 47
Arnold, Matthew, 33
Aronowitz, Stanley, 148
Atwood, Margaret, 95
Auerbach, Erich, 44; "Figura," 130–35;
   *Mimesis: The Representation of Reality in
   Western Literature*, 19, 28, 127–45
Authority: and originality, 47–68; and
   textual editing, 73–74; and the institu-
   tions of criticism, 88–100

Bahti, Timothy, 19, 28
Bakhtin, M. M., 38
Barber, C. L., 121
Barthes, Roland, 40, 123, 152
Beauvoir, Simone de, 85
Benjamin, Walter, 33, 47, 129, 145, 152–
   53, 185–86 (n. 29)
Bennett, Tony, 165
Blackmur, R. P., 39
Bloom, Harold, 24, 88, 89
Booth, Wayne, 2n–3n
Brecht, Bertolt, 122, 152
Brenkman, John, 172 (n. 24)
Brown, Peter, 104, 106, 107
Bunyan, John, 48, 56, 60, 62, 113–14
Burke, Kenneth, 39, 174 (n. 8)
Byron, George Gordon, Lord, 34

Camus, Albert, 93, 94
Cavell, Stanley, 43
Chatterton, Thomas, 65

Collins, William, 65
Crews, Frederick, 124–25
Criticism: as framing, 1–10; and deconstruction, 6–10; genealogy of, 11;
   problem of style in, 24–25; and politics, 33–34; and philosophy, 41–45. *See
   also* Deconstruction, Feminist criticism, Literary history, Marxism
Culler, Jonathan, 5
Curtius, Ernst Robert, 129

Dante (Alighieri), 47, 127; "Inferno,"
   133–44
Darrel, John, 104, 107, 112
Darwin, Charles, 60
Deconstruction: and criticism, 6–10, 14;
   and Marxism, 11–14, 28, 147, 155–68;
   and feminism, 13–17, 70–72, 96–100;
   and style, 41. *See also* Derrida, Jacques
De Man, Paul, 4, 21, 39–40, 127, 171
   (n. 22), 174 (n. 9)
Derrida, Jacques: and literary criticism,
   5–10, 18–21, 25, 31–32, 39–41, 44,
   166–67, 169 (n. 8); and Marxism, 11–
   14, 147, 156–68; *Dissemination*, 166;
   "Fors," 162; *Glas*, 26, 40–41, 162; "La
   Loi du genre" ("The Law of Genre"),
   70; "The Parergon," 8–10; *Positions*,
   159–63; *La Verité en peinture*, 17; "White
   Mythology: Metaphor in the Text of
   Philosophy," 26
Dewey, John, 41
Dilthey, Wilhelm, 33, 34
Donoghue, Denis, 31, 35
Dryden, Edgar, 23–24, 27

Eagleton, Terry, 157
Edmunds, Father (William Weston), 101,
   105–107, 113, 114, 117

Eliot, T. S., 23–24, 32, 35, 174 (n. 7)
Empson, William, 32, 39, 44

Felman, Shoshana, 164
Feminist criticism: and deconstruction, 13–17, 70–72, 96–100; and Marxism, 16–17, 177 (n. 4); and literary theory, 69–75; and canon formation, 73–74, 86–96
Ferguson, Margaret, 161
Fetterley, Judith, 72–74
Fiedler, Leslie, 86–87, 97
Fielding, Henry, 174 (n. 7)
Fish, Stanley, 15–16, 88–93, 95, 97, 99, 100
Flaubert, Gustave, 133–34, 138–44
Foucault, Michel, 20, 31, 94, 98–99
Freud, Sigmund, 13, 33, 146–47, 164; *Beyond the Pleasure Principle*, 159–61. *See also* Psychoanalysis
Frye, Northrop, 42

Gadamer, Hans-Georg, 38, 44
Gasché, Rodolphe, 170 (n. 14)
Gascoigne, George, 111
Geertz, Clifford, 21
George, Diana Hume, 96
Ginzburg, Carlo, 105
Goethe, Johann Wolfgang von, 33–35
Graff, Gerald, 125
Greenblatt, Stephen, 21–22, 28
Gross, Seymour, 73

Harsnett, Samuel, 21–22, 101, 103–10, 112–19, 121–23
Hartman, Geoffrey, 24–27
Hawthorne, Nathaniel: and Melville, 24, 47–48, 50, 53–59; "The Custom-House," 50, 73–74; *Mosses from an Old Manse*, 48, 50, 53–57; *The Scarlet Letter*, 14–15, 27, 72–84
Hazlitt, William, 37
Hegel, G. W. F., 8, 18, 19, 34, 40, 129, 130, 132–33, 137, 144
Heidegger, Martin, 5–6, 8, 11–13, 29, 32–33, 39, 41, 44, 129
Hirsch, E. D., 11
History, and literary criticism, 17–22, 101–103, 124–25, 144–45

Houdebine, Jean-Louis, 159
Hume, David, 41, 174 (n. 7)
Husserl, Edmund, 29, 43
Huyssen, Andreas, 157

Interpretation, 75–84
Irigaray, Luce, 100
Irwin, John, 73, 82

James, Henry, 76–77
Jameson, Fredric, 45, 152, 153–54, 170 (n. 13)
Johnson, Barbara, 13
Jones, R. F., 38

Kamuf, Peggy, 14–16, 27–28
Kant, Immanuel, 8–9, 43, 125, 165–67
Kautsky, Karl, 148
Keats, John, 29, 33
Kermode, Frank, 39
Kolodny, Annette, 90, 95
Kristeva, Julia, 31, 153

Lacan, Jacques, 25–26, 31, 74
Langbaum, Robert, 125
La Rochefoucauld, François de, 38
Lawrence, D. H., 33
Leavis, F. R., 32–33
Leiris, Michel, 108–109
Lentricchia, Frank, 125, 166
Lichtheim, George, 149
Literary history: and intertextuality, 23–24; theories of, 19, 125–30, 138, 144–45. *See also* Auerbach, Erich
Lukács, Georg, 33, 34, 129, 153

Macherey, Pierre, 122
Mailer, Norman, 91–92
Marcuse, Herbert, 165
Marx, Karl, 18, 28, 147; and Derrida, 11–14; and feminism, 16–17; on political economy, 149–52; on language, 152–54. *See also* Marxism
Marxism, 33, 40, 44, 148–52; and deconstruction, 11–14, 28, 147, 155–68; and feminism, 16–17, 177 (n. 4); and literary criticism, 102, 122, 150–52, 154, 165–67; and psychoanalysis, 146–47; and language, 152–55

Mather, Cotton, 36, 40
Maugham, Somerset, 35–36
Meese, Elizabeth, 15–16, 28
Melville, Herman, 23–24, 27, 44, 47–68;
and Hawthorne, 24, 47–48, 50, 53–59;
The Confidence Man, 47, 66–68; "The
Encantadas," 47, 59–66; "Hawthorne
and His Mosses," 48, 53–55; "The
Piazza," 47–59; *Pierre*, 47, 52, 62; *Red-
burn*, 59
Mencken, H. L., 30–32
Miller, J. Hillis, 125, 157
Milton, John, 29, 47
Montaigne, Michel de, 103, 127

Napier, Richard, 107
Nietzsche, Friedrich, 31, 69, 129
Norris, Christopher, 5

Oakeshott, Michael, 42
Olsen, Tillie, 87, 89
Orage, A. R., 34, 45
Originality, 47–68

Parker, Andrew, 12, 28
Pater, Walter, 37, 38, 40, 44
Plato, 37, 38, 42
Proust, Marcel, 37
Psychoanalysis: and feminism, 13–14,
71–72; and Marxism, 146–47; and
cryptonyms, 162–63. *See also* Freud,
Sigmund

Rawson, C. J., 35
Read, Herbert, 34
Reed, Ishmael, 93
Rich, Adrienne, 94
Richards, I. A., 32–33, 39
Ricks, Christopher, 44
Ricoeur, Paul, 35, 44, 156, 173–74 (n. 6)
Riddel, Joseph, 11
Robinson, Lillian, 177 (n. 4)
Rogozinski, Jacob, 157
Rorty, Richard, 41–44
Rossi-Landi, Ferruccio, 154
Ruskin, John, 33
Ryan, Michael, 156, 158–59, 164

Sade, Marquis de, 41
Sainte-Beuve, Charles Augustin, 31,
34, 37
Sartre, Jean-Paul, 31, 40, 51
Saussure, Ferdinand de, 11, 26
Scarpetta, Guy, 159
Scott, Sir Walter, 49–50
Selincourt, Basil de, 34
Shakespeare, William, 28, 37, 47, 48, 127;
All's Well That Ends Well, 112; *The Com-
edy of Errors*, 111; *Cymbeline*, 50–51, 65;
Hamlet, 54; *King Lear*, 21–22, 101,
103–104, 113–23; *Macbeth*, 56; *A Mid-
summer Night's Dream*, 56, 112; *Othello*,
65; *Twelfth Night*, 111, 119; *The Winter's
Tale*, 49–50
Shelley, Percy Bysshe, 161
Sherman, Stuart, 30–31
Shils, Edward, 21, 104
Shirokogorov, S. M., 107
Sidney, Sir Philip, 112, 113, 161
Smith, Lillian, 85, 94
Snell, George, 38
Socrates, 37
Spenser, Edmund, 29, 37, 57; *The Faerie
Queene*, 48, 62, 64–65
Spitzer, Leo, 44, 181 (n. 7)
Stade, George, 87
Steele, Richard, 33, 37
Steiner, George, 29, 39
Stendhal (Marie Henri Beyle), 139
Stevens, Wallace, 25
Swift, Jonathan, 35, 173 (n. 3)

Tennyson, Alfred, Lord, 48, 57
Thackeray, William Makepeace, 49–50
Torok, Maria, 162
Trilling, Lionel, 32

Vergil, 29
Vico, Giambattista, 129–30

Weber, Samuel, 146
Wellek, René, 126
Wesley, John, 102
Weston, William. *See* Edmunds, Father
White, Hayden, 98

Williams, Raymond, 153, 165
Williams, William Carlos, 45
Wittgenstein, Ludwig, 29, 41
Woolf, Virginia, 89–90, 92, 94–96, 100
Wordsworth, William, 26, 41

Yeats, William Butler, 44